A Hostile Plea

By A.C. Obika

 New Generation Publishing

About the Author

A.C. Obika is a graduate of London University and South Bank University where he obtained LLB and Msc in Property Law respectively, before attending law school at College of Law, Guildford. He trained with a London firm to qualify as a lawyer. He lives with his family in England.

For Bev and Alvinator....always.

Acknowledgments

First, to my daughter, Beverley Obika, for working so hard on this project especially during the research and editing of this book, and to my son, Alvin Obika, for believing in me through very testing times of this project. I cannot fully express my gratitude to my mum, Mrs Grace Obika and my late dad, Chief Aaron Obika for buying me books when I was young, without which my accomplishments in later life and my love for writing would never have been possible.

My sincere appreciation to Daniel Cooke and his team at New Generation Publishing for their encouragement and professionalism.

And finally, to all the victims of corruption in Africa and around the world who have touched my life and inspired me to undertake this project.

A Hostile Plea
Prologue

"Counsel, I want a jail term and a safe exit to a country of my choice after my imprisonment," he said coldly as I shut the door behind me.

"Pardon!" I jerked to a halt.

"I'll accept 10 years or more, no less."

"Sorry?"

He hesitated then sat up taller, straightening an inch, "I won't be state witness against anyone," he added.

"I don't follow," I said.

"In return, I will plead guilty at the earliest opportunity," he added.

A chair heavily stained from years of constant use stood empty on the other side of the table. One half of the wall was littered with graffiti. The other half displayed a sketchy drawing with two fingers stuck up, and an inscription underneath it that read: "up the judge's ass."

"You lost me," I said flatly resting my briefcase on the table.

"Don't make yourself comfortable just yet." He waved me off the table. "First tell me, will you negotiate these terms with the Crown Prosecution Service on my behalf?"

A hostile plea.

I lifted my briefcase off the table and considered him quietly. His bluntness was staggering. He sat there cross-legged, with a toothpick stuck between his lips. His eyes were calm and piercing like laser beams. He wore a contemptuous grin as though terrorising lawyers were ingrained in character.

Malik Penman was slim, medium height; his thin black hair was neatly cut. He looked in his mid forties. His eyes were big, almost bulging so that when viewed together with a bony pointed nose, they gave an owlish look. His lips were surprisingly meaty.

A poorly ironed shirt hung loosely on him like he had lost half his weight, since he first checked into prison. His expensively tailored grey suit also ill-fitted him, parting at his chest line. He still managed to look respectable, business-like, even without a tie. A shiny black crocodile-skin shoe hung gracefully on the crossed foot; its sole looked as though it had only ever stepped on a marble floor. For a man in a high security prison facing serious counts of criminal conspiracy, this man was too relaxed.

I considered him further.

Malik did not look like a Mr. Big portrayed by the Prosecution who had weaved several inter-continental money laundering schemes which netted more than half a trillion pounds. It was hard to believe he was the head of a global network with links to corrupt African countries intent on stealing their respective country's wealth, with impeccable skills to hide the loots where no one could find them. Inconceivable that he had evaded the watchful eyes of the MI5 and Interpol for two decades and he was now rich enough to sponsor a revolution and the ability to unseat any third world government of his choosing.

As he sat and watched me intently, I struggled with the ethics of his request. It was more a demand. Like a young doctor facing his first mercy killing, I was wary but determined. Malik seemed like a man to whom a negative response would be an affront. I knew then that anything other than yes would send me tumbling out the door. I shifted uneasily.

This case guaranteed to gross our firm more than half a million pounds and the thought of losing it was much like contemplating suicide. Private clients like Malik were highly coveted and besides, my mission statement was explicit: "This client is highly recommended - take care of him." The boss had decreed.

I grimaced.

Then followed by a sense of anxiety at the looming prospect of writing my own requiem at this stage of my career, I mused, should I bend over backwards for this guy?

Finally, I placed my briefcase back on the table, aware of his intent gaze. His face was devoid of all expression; only a defiant grin parted his smooth face creating hollow cheeks like an aftermath of a mild earthquake. His hand locked firmly into the other the whole time as if they were co-joined.

I tried to make sense of his type. On the surface he seemed to be unassuming kind of guy. Then his quiet dispositions made him appear like a silent destroyer, who could slip through a herd of cops unnoticed, and would still pause to ask them for directions before disappearing into a busy street. An intelligent client was a lawyer's worst nightmare. Now, faced with one who was cunning and intelligent in equal measure gave me the shudders.

This was not going according to plan.

"I'll negotiate those terms for you - if that's what you really want. But on one condition."

He raised his eyebrows and his stare was still placid.

I swallowed.

He stretched and laughed, a rather mechanical grating laugh. There was no telling whether there was insult or humour in his laughter. But one thing was certain. This man gave me the creeps.

I sat down to meet him eye to eye.

"I like you," he said reclining on his chair and grinning benignly. His hands folded just above his stomach, displaying a pair of gold cuff links. "You're a stubborn son of a witch."

I scowled at him.

"I suppose it runs with your reputation," he continued, "there's a pit full of brilliant criminal lawyers out there. Any one of them would love to represent me. Let me tell you this. I didn't choose your firm because you're the best in the business. No. My only interest in you is your reputation as a shrewd negotiator. I hear your firm is tough." He leaned forward, his eyes searching. "Now, Counsel, is there any sense in continuing to object to my terms?"

I thought about it and decided the answer was no, especially in a profession where the bottom line was money. But old habits died hard. An innate sense of good practice would not give, at least not that easily.

"Yes," I said finally, "I believe you should at least hear my professional opinion." I broke his gaze momentarily. "You should at least hear it."

He yawned.

"There's only one reason why you want to offer your opinion. To make me change my mind about my proposal, right?" Malik said.

I shook my head. "You're wrong."

He looked at me as if he could see the lie dripping down the corners of my mouth. Then he cupped his ears with both hands. "I'm listening."

"I want to make sure you fully understand the pros and cons of the step you want to take," I said.

"Cons such as?" He said half attentive, almost dismissive.

"First, there's insufficient evidence to support most of these charges."

"I know that," he said calmly, a ring of contempt about it.

What an arrogant bastard, I thought.

"And," I continued, "there's a possible jurisdiction argument, potentially, a problem for the prosecution. The Prosecution is unclear about where the conspiracies were hatched. This could present them with serious problems. We could have most of these charges thrown out."

"Tell me something I don't already know." He lifted his chin and stared knowingly at me.

I stood up and paced the room, hands thrust deep in my pockets. His head didn't turn with my movement. Only his eyeballs darted after me from one corner of the room to the other like a predatory fox crouching on unsuspecting hens. "Besides," I continued, "we know three of the main prosecution witnesses have embraced their own fate," I paused again leaning on the scribbled wall. "One hanged himself, the other dived from a twentieth floor without growing wings first...."

The smugness suddenly left his face, and in its place was a certain curiosity strewn across his forehead.

I sat down and let him brim with suspense for a moment: a mind game which lawyers employed with finesse in a courtroom to gauge a jury's interest and would trigger a barrage of notes to the judge for clarification. I stared back ignoring his questioning eyes.

"You didn't say what happened to the third witness."

"Oh. I thought that was obvious. Of course, he died," I said.

"How?" He said impatiently.

"He swallowed fatal lead pellets which left his brain tissues strewn all over his bedroom wall."

For a moment he looked thinner, his eyes sunk in his head. Perhaps it was anxiety? Fear? Sorrow? I couldn't be sure. But one thing was beyond doubt – he suddenly seemed ill at ease, trying hard to compose his thoughts.

Malik was an enigma; he defied all rationality. He seemed troubled that crucial prosecution witnesses against him had been murdered. Rather than a toasting victory for him, this had instead reduced him to a picture of deep gloom. Why?

"I don't mean to frighten you. I only want you to have all necessary information to reach an informed decision," I said dragging the last two words.

He eyed me momentarily. "I stand by my decision." He was less forceful now. "What you have told me has made me even more determined to stay this course."

"Fair enough," I said struggling to hide my displeasure. "One more thing," I added dryly.

I noticed that Malik was now uncertain - anxious, as children are in the middle of a fairytale. Even his exquisitely tailored suit seemed to have lost its elegance.

"You should at least have a plan B in case the prosecution calls your bluff," I said calmly.

There was a long stony silence. For the second time that afternoon, I noticed about Malik a deep-seated sense of realism behind the facade of indifference. He stood up and shed his jacket. Surprisingly he looked even richer and more intelligent. He fumbled in his suit pocket and removed a small bottle of pills. He swallowed three.

"Can I call for water?"

He waved dismissively towards me without looking at me.

"No. I've not considered a plan B," he finally said, staring blankly into space as if somewhere in the room lay a full-scale fallback plan. "Perhaps we should," he added grimly.

I noted with quiet exaltation his use of 'we'. To finally gain his confidence felt like an accomplishment. With that, we were guaranteed a chunk of his huge wealth. "I certainly think we should," I added.

"What's the Plan B?" he asked.

I shook my head slowly. "I need time to think about it."

He chewed on the stick with steely determination. "I look after my lawyers."

I tried to restrain my delight. There was nothing more satisfying to a lawyer than a vulnerable wealthy client. For a moment I visualised the sharks in our billing department setting upon Malik like a starved lion to a goat.

"Give me a little time to think of a backup position." I said.

His voice sank to a whisper. "How much time?"

"A few days at least."

"That shouldn't hold up the process, should it?"

I shrugged. "Perhaps not. We have time"

"What does that mean?" Malik said.

"We sit back and let them make the first move."

"Hmm…I don't like that," he said.

"I know. But we can't be seen to be courting the Prosecution like a bunch of wallies."

"We can do what we like. We need them more," he said.

"The Prosecution would eat you alive if you did that."

He leaned back in his chair, a picture of a man who didn't get his way. "What now, then?"

"We wait. We play hard to get."

He studied me for a moment. "OK. But I'm not going to wait forever. In any case, get a deal before Pleas and Directions. Don't push it too far, Counsel."

I shifted uneasily as my intrigue in him deepened. "I still can't get my head round the fact that you want to stay in jail for long time."

His face shut down like a screen out of power. Then he chewed the stick some more and spat it on the table. It suddenly dawned on me this was the only wind of his secret he wanted to let out for now.

***

A week later I received papers from the Prosecution regarding the full extent of Malik's sins, and crucially what the intelligence community thought of him. The dossier was huge and uncomplimentary but lacked the witness statements to back up the allegations. It was a familiar trick from the Prosecution, nothing surprising – designed to unnerve the fainthearted into submission. Despite my experience, the revelation was shocking; it wasn't clear whether it was the extent of the alleged crimes that sent shock waves down my spine or the sophistication of the alleged criminal activities. Either way, I was quietly concerned whether I had the stomach to fight with the enemy – the machinery of the state already so fierce and well entrenched in their position.

I went back to prison to see Malik about the papers received from the Prosecution, hoping he would give me proper instructions. He would need to start talking to me and fast too. He had been very discreet about his involvement in these crimes, but the time to be untrusting and coy was over, and it was either total co-operation with me so I could prepare his defence or …Then it suddenly dawned on me that my options were less certain if Malik chose to reveal nothing about his involvement or lack of it. He had hinted he might sack us if necessary, then how could I explain my failure to the one that sent me? Now all my plans were overlaid with renewed and more acute anxiety.

As I sat in the room waiting for Malik, I knew this was my most important legal visit of this case and one I most dreaded. Even before I had unpacked my bag and positioned arch-files on the table I had steeled myself for the ordeal of meeting Malik's cold eyes, eyes that would gaze into mine with sustained suspicion as soon as I began to ask him questions.

When Malik entered the room, he at once gave me an almost imperceptible nod of the head and sat down. He quickly pushed an arch-file towards him and began reading the papers. His face remained expressionless as he leafed through the dossier: it wasn't clear whether he was paying any attention to detail or merely confirming what information the authorities held on him. Even as he got to the end of the dossier, nothing in his demeanour betrayed the depth of his feeling or lack of it. Then he said firmly, 'I take it this is my copy to keep.'

I nodded. 'Now I need to hear your side of the story and make notes,' I said drawing a pen from my inside pocket. 'You will tell me everything beginning from when you were in your mother's womb until now, who you are, the school you attended, the job you ever held and how you got to this this…'

Malik was neither resentful nor aggressive as he reclined to his seat and crossed both hands over his chest. Undeterred by his benign objection, I summarised the crux of the allegations he faced: the Prosecution charged him with 112 counts of money laundering and 96 counts of conspiracy with others to commit fraud. It alleged that Malik had been criminally involved in 96 contracts between several companies he owned and the governments of Nigeria, Democratic Republic of Congo and Sudan. Each contract was executed with the dishonest involvement of senior government officials of the respective country; some concerned the supply of large number of military equipment and helicopters, some concerned the illegal lifting of oil and other mineral resources, some involved underpayment for oil and other mineral resources. The

Prosecution said that Malik had been involved in the inflation of contract prices with the tacit agreement of senior government officials to pay the monies so obtained by way of kick-backs to those connected with the respective regimes. It was alleged that the illegal inflation of the contract prices going back seven years was in the sum of $1.5 trillion. The true purchase price for each item was inflated by up to 1000% and as a consequence Malik charged the respective country the inflated price for an item which was worth considerably less. It further said that the contract monies were received into 40 Swiss accounts opened by sleepers from all over Europe but all the accounts were controlled by Malik. It was alleged that Malik then paid some of these monies in bribes from the sale proceeds to coded and company bank accounts in Switzerland, Western Europe and around the world linked to senior government officials in question. Malik opened these accounts for the senior government officials in fictitious names. The Prosecution further alleged that some of the senior government officials did not access some of these illicit monies totaling $200 billion because they died from natural causes or were killed following political rivalry in their respective countries. Malik concealed and disguised property for those government officials who wanted their proceeds converted into property and he charged huge amounts for this service. It was alleged he made close to $900 billion from the entire criminality. It further alleged that he paid bribes for import licences for oil and other mineral resources, and he made huge profits from his investment by paying low prices for them and evading taxes. On many occasions, he was allowed to illegally lift oil and other mineral resources from these countries and he paid kick-backs to senior government officials in the way already described. Whilst the authorities had traced and frozen some of the accounts linked to the criminality, it was alleged that a total of $1 trillion was still unaccounted for, believed laundered in other jurisdictions linked to rogue states such as Lebanon and Syria.

I paused for his comment, any comment would make my life less miserable, would give the least semblance of normality, but the silence was as striking as the blank expression on his face. He listened as he had done so many times before, I knew this because his eyes were open and he was not deaf. Even I had taken the pain to pronounce every word as succinctly as I could placing emphasis on key words like kick-backs, inflated prices, senior government officials, $1.5 trillion etc...surely he heard every word and if he had chosen not to say a word in rebuttal then it was willful. He was being deliberately mischievous.

'Well,' I said folding my notepad and packing my bag, 'nice meeting you again.' I rose and hurried towards the door.

'What else do you want to know, counsel?" He said without turning to look at me.

"Everything. From your perspective."

"Ok. On one condition."

"Which is?"

"No notes."

Without setting my bag down again, I listened to Malik as he quietly told me about his life. His tale lacked detail at times, at other times he was deliberately evasive. His mother was dead and he had been estranged from his father. He hadn't set out to be on the wrong side of the law but had been forced into it after he lost his job in the city as a broker. He loved his job as a broker but his life at work was less satisfactory. It was a disaster. He had been pushed around and frustrated and for long periods he had confronted the bad times with steely determination and pain. He despised his colleagues, he loathed his superiors and saw them as arrogant and spoilt. When they had bothered to notice his deep hatred of them – that he no longer showed the deference they expected from an inferior, their response had been quick and disproportionate. They had sacked him. He had become desolate and been through hell and wanted to kill himself. Then a friend told him about a consortium involved in international business and offered him to join. He had volunteered his skills and experience as an ex-banker and warmed into the organisation's heart without having to contribute a penny. Then he had grown in stature within the organization and later became head of it. They were involved in international money laundering and fraud and they had government officials on their books paying them not to be hostile to their illicit activities in their jurisdictions. They had thrived. His organization had actively targeted senior government officials and presidents from African countries for three reasons; one was their mineral resources, second was their insatiable appetite for greed, third they were stupid lacking in intelligence. His organization took advantage of it and prospered. Although there were other foreign organisations competing against his organisation in corruption trade in Africa, his position had been secure and entrenched. Then he had acquired so much money that it didn't make him happy any more and he wanted to quit the murky business. Also his conscience had gotten the better of him as he could no longer stand the sight of starving African children on television, he could not help but feel pity for those youths perishing at sea in an attempt to find a better life abroad because their country held no hope for them. Then he knew it was time to stop.

"Did you quit?" I said quietly.

"I tried. My decision split the organization right down the middle," he said reflectively. "Those who wanted to continue began to wage war against me. They see me as a traitor."

"Why so?" I said.

He paused for a moment. "Now the organisation has been hijacked by persons with extreme political and religious agenda. For them it's no longer a quest for personal gain. They are now going to be using gains made from African countries to seek global political and religious domination. These funds are now being used to acquire dangerous military hardware for possible war against the West. I know they have acquired many manpads - shoulder launched anti-aircraft missiles capable of bringing down a civilian aircraft. They also have a lot of SA –7 missiles and chemical warfare bought from suspect governments at huge costs. That's not what I'm about, am opposed to this agenda."

I stared back at him momentarily, struggling to find the right word for the moment. "This…this is why you fear for your life?"

"Life? What life? Am a dead man walking, counsel."

Chapter One

Two weeks later.

It was 9.30am when I arrived at the Old Bailey for Malik's Pleas and Directions hearing. Armed police had cordoned off the vicinity of the court entrance resembling more like a building under siege than a house of justice. Only officials and lawyers filtered through the tight security, even then only with proper identification. The press clustered behind the security line with long-range cameras and microphones angling for a close-up shot of Malik. He was their business now, and the public's fascination with the criminal mind ensured there was no business like tabloid press.

A police helicopter hovered noisily above causing a spectacle, and some passers-by paused to cast a curious eye in the sky before hurrying away. It was as if the neighbourhood had not seen the like of it for a long while.

As I approached the security line, a herd of reporters and TV crew suddenly surged towards me, and in no time, anxious faces mobbed me.

"Mr. Dias, how will your client plead today?" They asked collectively.

"No comment." I said without stopping.

"Mr. Dias, did he do it?" Asked another.

"I can't comment on that."

"Mr. Dias, is it true he's connected to an international gang?"

I quickened my pace and felt relieved when I had passed the Security disappearing into the court building. I checked my watch. There was enough time before the 10 o'clock hearing, and plenty of time to catch up on judicial gossips in the staff cafe.

The large cafe was deserted even for a morning session. A handful of lawyers sat at tables across the room reading the morning broadsheets. Early morning sunrays and the smell of fresh coffee filled the room. I ordered one. Sitting at a table closest to the counter, I started on my paperwork for the Hearing. There was not a great deal to do; no complex legal arguments would be needed. The case was going well but all that remained was for the Prosecution to make that vital move. They too seemed to be playing hard to get and it was now a matter of who wanted it more.

"Excuse me," a male voice interrupted startling me.

I took a deep breath.

He was probably in his late twenties, clutching a pile of papers bound together by a red ribbon and a copy of Archbold. He wore a wig and gown that looked new.

"You must be Dias," he said with no emotion in his voice or on his tone. Only beads of sweat on his forehead betrayed certain uneasiness.

I kept an impassive face and nodded.

He looked directly at me and offered a hand. "I've heard so much about you."

"Nothing horrible, I hope," I said taking his hand.

"Oh no. Your notoriety over the Malik's case is only one reason."

I shrugged. "Unjustly in my view. You're new?"

He nodded. "My first case."

"I can tell. Don't worry. Though you could do with taking off your wig and gown until you're ready for court."

He smiled uneasily and flashed his eyes across the room. "I'm the odd one."

"Just the fresher's initial obsession with egoism, and again it's normal."

He checked his watch. "Nearly time anyway. I might as well keep them on."

"Which courtroom are you?"

"Court 5."

"Same as me. I can tell you this. You won't find this judge a very nice man."

"Ah! That takes me to my next point?" This time his voice had a ring of innocence, perhaps vulnerability about it, although his face still radiated some confidence. "I've heard about this judge, his reputation for intimidating lawyers in his court. I wonder if you would let me sit close to you, and perhaps…"

"I understand," I interrupted, gathering my paperwork. "Every one of us has passed through this moment. Come on. First lesson, Judge Pilate

3

doesn't tolerate latecomers in his court." I rose. "What do I call you?"

"Paul."

"Come on, Paul. We've got to rush."

***

The courtroom was half full, mostly court officials. Surprisingly few reporters occupied the section on the left. The jury box to the right was empty. In the far corner, beside the jury box was a two-row section for the Probation. A grey haired man sat in the first row. He looked the type who had long past his retirement. He wore a thick pair of dark glasses that made him look more like a retired drug baron than a probation officer. He was reading a broadsheet that covered part of his face, unclear if he was focused on the paper or was watching the arena below him.

I slipped into the second row of the Counsel's table. Paul sat in the third, directly behind me. I glanced at the public gallery, which stood above the courtroom to our left and found the rows were packed full. An armed guard stood in the aisle watching the courtroom below.

Cecil Darlington swaggered into court in his black gown, hands tugged away behind his back. His junior clutched bundles of arch-files behind him, her face strained as if she had been begrudging him for making her do all the hard graft. Not that Darlington cared anyway. He changed juniors as often as he switched his

4

underwear. For him, they were no more than tools of the trade and the state owed him an interminable supply.

I leaned backwards and whispered to Paul. "He's the Prosecutor."

Cecil Darlington placed his wig on the first row table and walked over to me. "Good to see you, Phil," he said offering a hand and smiling deviously. His French cuffs glittered in the light.

I regarded him with quiet contempt.

Cecil Darlington exuded an air of confidence about him, the flair of a Prosecutor who loved his work more than anything else, even more than his life. The most remarkable aspects about this man were his striking handsome features. In his late thirties, he was as abrasive as he was a bully: smug, self-righteous and over-zealous. Over the years, he had gained a reputation as a precious jewel within his rank, with immense influence in the judiciary.

I shook his hand.

"I don't suppose this is going to be a long hearing," he said.

I shrugged. "Who knows?"

"Unless of course, there's something up your sleeve," he pressed.

He was fishing. I could see a net cast wide swinging my way.

"Don't worry, Cecil. I won't spring a surprise on you."

"I'm not worried."

"Well then," I said.

"In fact I've never been more confident about a case."

"I wouldn't be too confident if I were you."

He shot me a shifty look. "But of course, my door is open."

"Don't waste your time, Cecil. You don't have anything we want."

A light knock interrupted us and the Learned Clerk announced the judge. Cecil Darlington reluctantly returned to his table, and seemed unhappy I'd had the last say in our war of words.

We all stood.

Judge Pilate shot into Court and cast a fleeting glance across the courtroom before settling into his high chair. A thin pair of round glasses hung loosely at the bottom of his nose blending in with a neat grey moustache.

Judge Thomas Howard was known as Judge Pilate amongst his contemporaries for his harsh sentences. And like his name's sake in the bible, he kept a white basin in his chambers where he washed his hands after sentencing to rid him of guilt. Though generally merciless in his treatment of the socially downtrodden, he was widely respected by his peers.

Judge Pilate also basked in his reputation as the white knight in shining armour that did not hesitate to take the Prosecution's side, a mutual relationship that had earned him as many enemies as powerful friends. His wheeling and dealing with the ruling class had shot him to an untouchable status. Even his colleagues at the Old Bailey trembled at the influence he radiated within the judiciary. One such bitter rival was Judge Forbes, his senior by far. There had been rumours that these two judges clashed over who should hear Malik's case. Assisted by his powerful allies in the Lord Chancellor's Department, Judge Pilate had sidelined his senior colleague to land himself this case so he could shine in the glare of publicity, which the case would generate. This had provoked Judge Forbes into breathing fire and brimstone threatening revenge. A diminutive figure at sixty-eight, Malik's case had been the high profile case that Forbes had hoped would have propelled him to the pomp and glory of the Court of Appeal. But it had begun to dawn on him that with a fast shrinking brain and a sagging body, that part of his dream might now remain unfulfilled, thanks to Judge Pilate.

Judge Pilate was fifty-six, though he could easily pass for his mid-forties. A great scholar, he was renowned for his quick grasp of evidence and razor blade concentration.

I leaned back. "How are you doing back there?"

"Nervous," Paul whispered.

Judge Pilate disliked me with the venom of a viper. In the times I had appeared in his court, the relationship had been stormy. He hated my witty interrogating tactic, something he himself had employed with menacing effect when he was a practising barrister. Was this envy? I could not be sure. But I knew he begrudged the limelight I enjoyed in the centre courts. And perhaps also, my promotion to solicitor-advocate, which had bestowed upon me right of audience in the Crown Courts, had not helped his mood. He had vigorously challenged the move to dismantle the Specialist Bar for no reason other than he thought it threatened his colleagues' livelihood. Our cat and mouse relationship was an open secret.

A few moments later, heads turned towards the rear as an armed guard shuffled into the dock above, followed by Malik, then another armed guard. Malik sat between them, his face expressionless as he stared up at the judge.

Judge Pilate turned to Darlington.

Darlington cleared his throat softly. I could see the reporters sketching furiously. Then he made representations for the record and introduced me. Half rising, I nodded to the judge.

Darlington continued, "His Lordship might want to proceed right away with pleading, unless I can be of further assistance to His Lordship before we commence."

Judge Pilate grinned. "Thank you Mr. Darlington." The judge turned to me. "Yes Mr. Dias."

I quickly rose. "If your lordship please, I would be greatly assisted by a brief consultation with my client. Your lordship will be aware that due to intense security around my client, he was brought straight into court from the helicopter which brought him from Belmarsh prison."

"Yes. I'm fully aware of the unusual circumstances of this case. You may take the time you need." His accent was clipped but his tone dispassionate.

"I'm grateful." I hurried to the rear. The piercing eyes of the armed guards scanned me suspiciously.

Malik leaned forward resting his elbows on the wooden railing, staring down at me.

"Hi," I said quietly.

He ignored me.

"The Prosecution has not approached me yet," I whispered, "I take it we're sticking to the plan. You will enter a not guilty plea?"

"No." His voice was raised.

"Keep your voice down. But we agreed a strategy."

"Remind me Counsel."

I looked over my shoulder momentarily. Judge Pilate had leaned back in his chair; cold impatient eyes stared at me over the rim of his glasses.

"We agreed to wait until the prosecution have made the first move," I said anxiously.

"Yes. But they haven't come to us. Now I'll take it to them. What's so complicated about this, Counsel?" His eyes bulged out even more.

"Can't you see it, you - - -." I restrained the urge to profane and taking a deep breath, continued, "Can't you see it would be an indication of weakness in your case if you pleaded guilty. To wait, and keep them sweating, would enhance your position in any future plea bargaining negotiations."

"No. I'm going to plead guilty now. I have full confidence you can still negotiate the best deal for me afterwards. Good morning, Counsel." He leaned back.

I strolled back to my table amidst staring eyes. "Thank you, my Lord," I managed to say. "We're ready to plead."

Judge Pilate leaned forward. "Defendant, please stand." He gave the Learned Clerk an imperceptible nod. "Yes, Miss Marcia."

Malik and the guards rose, and almost instantly, the Learned Clerk read his personal details which Malik confirmed. Then she read out the charges, pausing momentarily to gather her breath. I could visualise that all eyes had riveted on Malik. Pausing momentarily and looking at Malik, the Clerk added, "To the first count, do you plead guilty or not guilty?"

Chapter Two

Malik pleaded not guilty to all counts. The court stirred and quickly quietened as Judge Pilate flashed a stern stare across the room. But not everyone had heeded the warning shot. He straightened himself listening intently like an antelope sensing danger, and frowned at the subdued voices coming from the press section. The reporters started filing out under his watchful gaze. The charges and his pleas were simply too hot for them.

Darlington rose. "If his Lordship please, the Crown would suggest the end of August for trial."

Judge Pilate quickly browsed through his diary. "That's nearly six months from today."

"Yes, my Lord. That would enable the Crown to tie up loose ends in relation to disclosure."

Judge Pilate turned to me.

I rose. "The defence does not object to this time frame. I urge my learned friend to expedite matters on disclosure of material."

Judge Pilate turned to Darlington. "You will expedite matters, Mr. Darlington, especially with trial set in six months time."

"My Lord, there's some difficulty because much of the undisclosed material comprises intelligence reports, and no decision has been reached on how this can be managed without compromising national security."

"The dilemma you face is understandable, however I'm more concerned about the implications of delays on the ability of the defence to prepare and present their case," the judge said.

"I understand this my lord, but - - -," returned Darlington adjusting his wig.

"Mr. Darlington," Judge Pilate interrupted, "you will ensure the defence can have all relevant material within four weeks. If this deadline is not met, this matter is to be re-listed for mention before me."

Darlington frowned.

Judge Pilate continued, "failing that, I would like to see the sensitive material so court can assist you in deciding their suitability or otherwise for disclosure." He scribbled something in his notebook, and added, "This matter is listed for trial on the twenty-fourth of August."

As I took down details of the ruling, I noticed from the corner of my eye that someone was standing beside me. I looked up and found Paul. His skin seemed paler. The collar of his shirt was soaked. His face creased into a nervous grin.

"You OK?" I said with obvious concern.

"Your client has requested a sheet of paper."

I handed him an A4 paper. "Thanks Paul," I said without looking up.

"The pleasure is all mine."

His footsteps had barely trailed away when a voice shouted, "Hey, stop."

I turned.

It was the grey-haired man sitting in the probation section. I signalled to him that it was all right, but he didn't take any notice of me. His attention was fixed on Paul.

"I need to pass this paper to the defendant," Paul said as he took another step forward.

"Stay where you are. My colleague will take the paper to him," the man said with an urgent edge to his voice.

Paul swung round and took off his wig revealing a silver gun. He levelled the gun and fired at the guard who slumped forward. I froze in disbelief.

A loud gasp erupted, followed by a frenzy as people screamed, diving to the floor. Malik ducked down, so did the second guard.

Then Paul turned swiftly to his right and shot the guard in the public gallery. Blood gushed out of his chest as he slumped forward crashing down on the wooden rail. He made towards the dock. The grey-haired man shouted, "Armed police! Put your gun down and raise your hands above your head."

Paul raised his gun above his beltline when his neck suddenly exploded into a fountain of blood. A second shot rang out hitting the same spot tearing his skin. Paul staggered back, and for a moment stood motionless, then he fell to his knees clutching his gun. Then slowly he slumped to the floor in a pool of blood.

More armed guards burst into the Courtroom. One sneaked behind Paul and secured the gun. He checked his pulse. "Target is down and secure," he spoke into a microphone hanging around his chest, "Yes sir, two officers are down," he added scanning the room. "No other casualties that I can see. How long before the paramedics get here? Thank you, sir."

I glanced round the front. Judge Pilate was behind his swivel chair peering cautiously. He looked traumatised.

Darlington had taken cover in the safety of the witness box. Clenching the wooden railing with his hands, he slowly raised his head. His eyes darted from one end to the other.

I turned to the dock. Several armed guards had gathered around Malik. Apart from a bemused expression he was calm. He stared at me as if wondering how come his lawyer had got mixed up with the deadly gunman.

Chapter Three

Arriving at D&L just after lunchtime, I pulled into the firm's car park at the rear and turned the engine off. The silence that followed was comforting. It was then that the full impact of the tragedy at the Old Bailey had begun to kick in. The thought of it still sent shudders down my spine.

The gunman, Paul, could quite easily have shot me. I stared silently but disdainfully at the multi-storey glass building before me. The building set in the heart of the City of London had become the symbol of D&L's status for several generations. The gnawing thought that it might have been business as usual at D&L had I been killed earlier, left me feeling despondent. There was little doubt as I walked into the building that the security, the self-assurance I'd taken for granted for so long had finally come to an end.

The lift was faintly luminous, lit only by skylights attached to the ceiling that cast soft glows on the gold-plated interior. A red carpet added the splendor of royalty. Everything was designed to impress clients.

The reception area on the fourth floor was unusually quiet for this time of the day. The reception team was the nerve centre of the firm;

they supplied a lifeline to over forty- five lawyers, paralegals and secretaries.

I stepped closer and looked in the backroom of the reception lounge.

One half of the lounge was lavishly furnished with leather chairs and sofas. Buffed up mahogany bookshelves were neatly packed with volumes ranging from philosophy to science. Classical music filtered lightly from invisible speakers, and padded desks with computers and dictaphones formed two rows on the other half of the lounge. A secretary sat behind her desk dabbing her eyes with a tissue, but stopped sniffing the moment she noticed me.

"Where's everybody?"

"In the conference hall," she said tearfully, her voice trailing off to a whisper.

"Conference hall? What's the matter?"

"Sorry." She tried to speak but stopped. Tears welled up in her eyes. Then she sniffed and blew noisily into the tissue. "It's. Phillipa Simpson." Her gaze dropped and she sobbed some more.

"What's wrong with Phillipa?" I gave an encouraging smile.

"She was found dead in her flat this morning."

I felt a sharp stabbing feeling in my stomach.

Phillipa Simpson dead!

Phillipa Simpson had climbed to the height of her career making fewer enemies than Mother Theresa. In her capacity as Practice Manager she'd exuded confidence and intelligence, perhaps sometimes too intelligent for a peaceful coexistence with her male colleagues. Her strict regime earned her the admiration of the big boys in the firm, with that, an increased stature. Now this.

"Hello, Phil. You OK?" Morris Ricci's eyes were all over me as he entered the lounge. His voice had a ring of concern.

Morris Ricci was thirty-two and overweight. Naturally clumsy, he was always quick to admit his deep-seated dislike for the legal profession. It was either this or baby-sitting for him and he ended up being pushed into law.

"I'm fine, thanks," I said absentmindedly.

"You just heard about Phillipa?"

I nodded. "Do we know how she died?" I said.

"She hanged herself."

"Oh shit."

"Anybody know why?"

"No. No suicide note found. That's what the detective said anyway. No one knows why. She remained a complete enigma to the end," Morris said.

"Can't imagine any reason why she might commit suicide." I said.

Morris shrugged again. "The detectives are asking the same question. I don't know. They want anyone with any information to contact them."

"How's the mood generally?"

"Somber. I didn't think she radiated so much admiration amongst staff," he said quickly.

"Don't knock her now. She was both admired and respected."

17

"So I see. But I didn't like her and she didn't like me, so that was fine. We'll now take it to the after life."

"Come off it, Morris."

He threw both hands in the air. Then he considered me for a few moments. "You OK, though?"

"Just tired. It's been a hectic day."

His head leaned to one side. "Listen. We heard what happened at the Old Bailey. It's not that anyone is playing it down – it's pretty shocking, but the news of Phillipa's death kind of forced itself to the fore. Hope you understand."

"Of course I understand," I said.

"At least, you didn't get shot or anything. Good gracious! What's the world coming to? Gun totting in our courts? You could've been killed, damn it."

"That would've done us all a great service," a voice cut in. "Instead, we're having to mourn the one person we were happy with."

"You son of a bitch!" I snarled.

"Hey, take no notice of him," Morris said as I stared stonily at Tobias Sevenson.

Tobias was in his early forties. He was tall, slim with sunken cheeks and a full head of wavy brown hair receding at the crown. He wore sleek gold-rimmed eyeglasses and looked more intelligent than he really was although he was both clever and witty.

Tobias smiled deviously, unmoved by my outburst.

"That's loutish behaviour," Tobias said, "and unbecoming of a partner let alone one who positions himself for the top job in this firm." His tone was mocking.

"Back off now, Tobias," Morris warned. "You're being deliberately provocative and childish. Just back off."

For a few moments, Tobias and I stared at each other with mutual contempt. Though we'd never been close pals, I couldn't put a finger on exactly when my working relationship with Tobias began to deteriorate. Tobias attacked me verbally whenever he got the chance. It was as if he was no longer getting any job satisfaction unless he made my life a misery. And it hadn't helped that both of us were the only serious contenders for the top job at D&L. For Tobias, he had the God given right to head the Firm next, and that was non-negotiable. His only worry was that not everyone agreed, not least the present holder of the post. And it was all down to me, or so he believed.

Breaking his gaze, I stormed out.

***

Whether the staff were still mourning Phillipa's death was less clear. But business soon resumed. It wasn't very long afterwards that lawyers swarmed back over the building with only one objective in mind; bill clients until they drop dead. No lesson on its execution was needed. Everyone simply learned on the hoof.   Perhaps what was most painful was that even those of us with scruples had accepted this practice unashamedly, pursuing it with equal zeal.

My office was lavishly furnished, spacious, and the view was sweeping. Standing near the window, arms folded, and staring out at the grey sky, I heard the phone ringing. I considered the flashing button for a moment before answering it.

"Mr. Dias," a voice called.

"Yes."

"Have a moment?"

"What's this about?"

"A fax just came in for you. I think you better see this."

"Ok. Come in."

A moment later, Dora Penn tapped lightly on the door and entered. Closing the door, she leaned against it, clutching a file to her chest.

Dora Penn was my secretary. At thirty-eight, medium height, with short straight black hair, Dora Penn wasn't exactly attractive but she was street wise and assertive.

I sank into my high swivel chair. "What's the fax about?"

She didn't answer; instead she sat in front of me. I could tell she was dying to say something. She leaned forward, her elbows pressing down on the padded table, pulled a sheet from the file and laid it before me.

I scanned the fax message. Short and incomprehensible, it resembled a carefully crafted command from a coffee drinking Army General facing extinction of his entire battalion. The more I read it, the more each word of the ten-word script evoked different meanings. And underneath each meaning lay a certain terror.

I looked up at her as if she held the decoder for the script; I sank back in the chair with obvious unease.

"Anyone know about this?" My demeanour was calm. The last thing I wanted was to rattle Dora even more.

"No, no-one knows," she said. Her eyes quickly shifted to the fax sheet and back to me with the same intensity of curiosity. "Are we . . . are you in trouble?" She corrected herself, her voice quivering.

"There's nothing to worry about Miss Penn. I'll take care of this."

She was now the very face of anxiety. She rose quietly, pausing half way to the door as if terror itself lurked outside.

"Miss Penn," I called out gently as she reached for the door handle. "This is between us, right?"

She turned and looked at me, her eyes appraising. "Are you going to meet this person?"

I did not answer.

In fact, I'd never considered that, and even long after she shut the door behind her, that question continued to gnaw at me.

Chapter Four

That evening, I drove straight from work to see Dandy Fallon. He lived in Hampstead, an affluent part of London. A quiet neighbourhood; manicured bushes sprawled in front of each house on both sides of the street, a picturesque image that would leave every environmentalist gasping with delight.

An infrared lamp suddenly cast a spell of blinding light as I stepped onto the driveway. Squinting against the brightness, I found the doorbell.

Silence greeted me.

I rang it again, this time holding it down until shuffling noises grew louder behind the door. There was a brief silence. I felt tired eyes peering at me from behind the spy-hole.

"Dandy!" I called out.

Dandy muttered something as he struggled to open the door.

"Come on in," he said opening the door. His words were slurred.

"Sorry I turned up unannounced," I said.

"Don't worry about it. No one drops in here on invitation anyway. It's the cops I mind," he said with a weak smile.

Dandy led the way towards the living room, almost tripping over twice. Every time he waved a hand clumsily in the air to signal he was okay.

The smoke filled living room was exquisitely furnished. A twenty-horse power scanner stood in one corner, trapping codes and profanities from the airwaves. Dandy would record every sound and in his quiet time, plough through it sifting out anything that sounded interesting - sensitive. Buyers of the classified information were never in short supply and his customers came from all walks of life. The only qualification required as a buyer was the ability to pay. And placed next to the scanner was an industrial paper shredder designed to destroy cardboard within seconds leaving only dusts in its wake. A dimly lit mini bar in the far corner provided the only light.

He pulled a leather barstool out from behind his mini bar for me to sit, and as if by magic, he produced a bottle of Dom Perignon.

"What's eating you?" He said, pushing the bottle towards me.

"I've got something to show you." As I went for the fax sheet, the sound of a flushing toilet stopped me on my tracks. Dandy quickly met my stare.

"Didn't know you had company," I said anxiously.

Dandy waved a hand dismissively. "Chief Superintendent."

My forehead furrowed. "Trouble?" My voice dropped to a whisper.

"Naah. Business." He fixed himself vodka. "He's under pressure to solve the Harlesden gang murders. Three generations got wiped out. Killer didn't leave clues."

"I heard it on the news," I said.

"Ghastly," he returned sipping his drink. "I don't normally share intelligence with police on crimes. But when people kill women and children, it stirs my conscience."

"Mr. Fallon, what's bugging me about this investigation is..." Chief Superintendent stopped in mid-sentence when he saw me.

"Sup, he's cool. Phil's like a son," Dandy said as he lit a cigar. He drew hard on it and coughed softly.

The Chief Superintendent gave me a wary nod and said nothing. Probably in his mid-fifties, he wore a dark suit, and smelled strongly of aftershave. He walked over to the settee, looked at me again and grinned.

"Something the matter, Sup?" Dandy said.

"I'm fine, Mr. Fallon, I don't mean to be rude, but I can't stay." He took a few quick strides towards the door.

'Your call, Sup." Dandy said.

The Chief Superintendent hesitated for a few seconds, eyes darting from Dandy to me and back again.

"I'll wait outside." I offered.

"No, Phil. You sit right there," Dandy said

"Can I have a quick word outside," The Chief Superintendent said.

"No, Sup. Don't question my judgement. I see no need continuing our conversation," Dandy said.

"Sorry!"

"Get the hell out of here. Go pester someone else."

The Chief Superintendent quickly buttoned his jacket and slammed the door behind him.

A brief silence followed.

"That was harsh," I said finally.

"I won't lose sleep over him. He needs me. He will come back." He poured himself more drink and emptied the glass in one gulp. "Well, then. I will ask you one more time. What's eating you?"

I found the fax and unfolded it.

His eyes swept through the script. He seemed unfazed. Then he scanned it a second time and straightened up. He drew hard on his cigar. For someone who moments earlier had struggled to walk a straight line, his focus now startled me. Any wonder he was sought-after by nearly everyone?

"The syntax is Eastern, or at least from someone with an Eastern connection," he said, smoke curling out of his mouth and nostrils.

I swallowed rapidly. Though I wasn't exactly sure what this meant, the phrase 'Eastern Connection' left a sour taste in my mouth. Was the connection not a synonym for an organised criminal gang? The Mafia? My instant gut feeling was that something was very wrong.

Dandy was now a face of deep contemplation and to my best guess, an expression that confirmed my worst fear.

"That bad?" I muttered.

He grinned benignly as if to hide the seriousness of it all, and then he said, "I think you've got something they want badly. I'll say it's a Russian Connection."

Chapter Five

Russian Connections!

Something they want badly! I recalled as I made the journey home. As much as I wanted to stop thinking about it, I couldn't blank it out of my mind. Over-reaction?   Perhaps. But the rattled expression on Dandy's face after reading the script left no doubt about its seriousness.

What might that something be?

Malik?

Ridiculous! Surely if it was about him, would it not be easier for them, the so called Russian Connections to organise his escape from prison?

Tobias Sevenson? There was no doubt he strongly believed I was the major stumbling block in his ambition to head our firm, but he didn't have the influence or power to propagate this kind of thing, I thought. He couldn't be behind this.

In the anxiety that pervaded me came something I thought I recognized - the fear that could result from trying hard to figure it out but not getting your head round it. There was no greater danger than the fear of the unknown.

I turned off the motorway into a two way lane; less than half an hour later, I turned into a dead end road lined with trees close together that led to my

27

house. I drove through the steel gates and up the gravel driveway. Neatly hemmed plants formed a fence round the thirteen-acre grounds on which our mansion stood in the outskirts of Surrey. I pulled up behind my wife's Porsche and switched the engine off.

It was immediately obvious that something was wrong. My wife wasn't standing in the doorway waiting to embrace me, something that had since become a ritual greeting for both of us.

Oh shit! I suddenly gasped. I got it.

I had some explaining to do. It was that special day of the month when she was most fertile, that rare moment when she could give up anything for a romantic evening with me; she expected similar commitment from me in her tireless search for a child. Lorna was a lawyer, and she had forged a successful career and name for herself but had given all that up to focus on the business of making a family. Yet that ambition remained unfulfilled, she was determined to succeed in this as much as she had done in her career – she had risen to become one of the best criminal and family lawyers the city ever knew. At thirty-six, and proud of her new role as a full-time housewife, she sometimes gave speeches to raise money for charity.

Lorna blamed our childless marriage on work; returning home late, eating late, too tired to make love after heavy work schedules. The evils that the profession bred, to her mind, seemed endless, and well out of proportions to the creamy lifestyle it provided. It was now easy for Lorna to make such judgement having escaped the cruel hands of poverty for the remainder of her life.

I headed through the hallway and up the stairs to the master bedroom. I fumbled my way to the bed in the dark and switched on the light dimming it. Kneeling beside the bed, I stroked her hair.

"I'm so sorry," I whispered. "I can explain."

"Get your hands off me," she said.

"I'm sorry, hon."

"I need to be left alone right now."

"OK. I love you, and I'm sorry." I said and quietly left.

Halfway down the hallway, I heard her sobbing. I continued down the corridor to the spare bedroom. It wasn't a good idea hanging around when she was mad, never a bad idea moving away from harm's way. I stripped down to my boxer shorts, and lay in bed wondering if this was the right time to come clean with Lorna. Perhaps the truth would set us all free and eliminate unrealistic expectations.

Should I tell her?

I remembered the fruitless visits to the doctor's, all the dietary recommendations she'd followed to the letter hoping the answer lay in proper eating, all the time we had made love, her eyes fixated on the ceiling in dire and silent prayer that it might just be the one. The guilt I bore knowing that all the effort would eventually come to nothing had become too much over the years. The lie, I was living was bringing untold consequences and misery onto the woman I loved. There was that excruciating moment when her menstruation would appear as surely as day follows night. Her frustration, her hate for life, her anger at the cruel fate that refused to make a full woman she yearned for, usually carried on for some time until the dust settled and she re-energised herself for another try. No, I mused. This couldn't go on much longer, I decided. She had the right to know I could not father a child. I should have told her long time ago, but was afraid I would loose her. Today was early. Tomorrow might be too late. The truth would hurt, would tear her apart, but at least would set her free. Then we might consider adoption. There were options after-all, so I should tell her at the first opportunity. On reflection, I grimaced at what lay ahead if I told her the truth. It might be the deceit that would seal my fate...

The bedroom light suddenly flicked on.

Lorna was standing in the doorway. She looked beautiful as ever. She would've made a great model had she not settled for a more hazardous career as housewife. The only thing missing as she stood there staring down at me in her see-through nightgown was a seductive smile. Instead, tears had left vertical lines on her cheeks. The sadness brought about by fate was only too visible in her expression.

"What's the excuse this time?" She said behind clenched teeth.

I half sat up and ran a hand through my hair. "It's not what you're thinking. It was not work." I could see fire brewing in her eyes. "Something came up and I had to see Dandy about it."

Her breathing shot up with frightening intensity. "There's always something taking priority over me, now it's this scum," her voice rose sharply. There was a way she'd dragged the last word as if she'd done so for lack of a better one. Lorna disliked Dandy. In her eyes, Dandy was shady and worse.

"Honey."

"Don't honey me." She snapped. "You're there for everybody but me."

"Calm down."

"Don't tell me to calm down." She shouted, "You promised you'd be back early. You promised,"

"I know. And I was..."

"The one day in a month I have the greatest chance of having your baby, and you couldn't even be here for me," she paused for breath and sobbed.

"Lorna..."

"You can't even make an effort to give me the one thing I want most from you. You don't care. You disgust me," she added sobbing some more.

"I'm sorry. But something . . ."

"I don't want to hear your silly excuses," she snarled. "You're taking me for a fool. I'm nobody. I'm nothing to you because I can't have your baby. That's why, isn't it? Then you're going to leave for another woman who can bear you a child, huh. I'm worth nothing to you, admit it." She screamed, staring into my eyes as if she were searching for the truth behind my eyeballs. "Go on, admit it. That's the truth, isn't it?

"Lorna!"

"Don't you Lorna me either, go on and admit it. You don't love me anymore?" She cried, launching forward, she clawed at me, fists flying.

I grabbed her hands and held them. It was either this measure or a bloody nose; I was determined to avoid the latter. She struggled to set her hands free, cursing and screaming. I maintained a firm grip until she was tired and suddenly stopped. She started sobbing, her face buried in my chest.

"It's OK, hon," I said stroking her hair. She sobbed uncontrollably.

"I'm sorry, babe. I don't mean to be this horrible," she said, her face pressed against my chest, my t-shirt was soaked with tears.

"Don't be sorry, hon.," I said kissing her eyes, rolling her onto the bed. Her teary eyes stared up at me; even then there was no longer any trace of pain, only love now shone in her eyes as her mouth parted invitingly. I took the bait as we kissed passionately.

"I'm sorry," I groaned, as we rolled between sheets and made love.

Chapter Six

Next morning, a pale autumn sun had already set in the east, casting orange rays across the sky.

"Breakfast's ready," Lorna called.

"Coming."

I drifted down the stairs to find Lorna in the dining area, pouring coffee. Standing behind her, I held her from behind and kissed her cheek.

"How's my babe, this morning?"

"Better." She said smiling.

I kissed her again. "I love you."

'Love you too, handsome. Come on, your food's getting cold. And you don't want to be late for work, do you?"

I glanced at my watch before settling at our large oak dining table.

She poured herself orange juice and sat down. Handing me the Times, she flipped the pages of the Daily Telegraph until she latched on to its fashion column.

"Coming home early, tonight?" She said without looking up.

"I shouldn't be too late."

"I guess that means no, don't wait up." She wasn't angry.

In the familiar pause that followed, I watched her. Her head was buried in the newspaper she was reading, completely at ease with herself, complicating things even more. Much as I hated to shatter her peace, I couldn't find an easier way of doing this. She had to know and she had to know now. Delaying it further wasn't an attractive option and could even be disastrous. First, I would have to get her attention. There was no limit to Lorna's fascination with law reports and fashion columns, especially the latter, and she didn't tolerate distractions. It was her indulgence.

"Anything interesting in there today?" I said.

She looked up and down again. "One second. Sorry you're feeling left out." Then she read some more and finally looked up. "I don't agree with her views."

"Lorna, you say that all the time."

"I mean it."

"Yet you've never missed her column in ten years."

"Uh-huh. Perhaps the buzz is in the disagreement. I don't know," she shrugged with a smile.

"Yeah right. I'm sure that's why she commands a wide readership."

"I don't mean to say she isn't good. Sometimes, she's irritatingly brilliant. I suppose I'm jealous."

I cocked my head to one side. "Listen up, hon., there's no need to be jealous of her. You built up a successful career too, and just like her, you were brilliant at it," I paused. "Your career will always be there if you want to return to it."

"That's really sweet, but I'll stick to the plan, maybe I might return after my first child is born, who knows. Depends on how bored I am," she said with a giggle.

I forced a grin.

"Hon," I added quietly, "there's something I've got to tell you."

She bristled suddenly and shut the newspaper. "Oh okay."

"Please don't take this the wrong way . . ." I said unsure if this was the right time and occasion to have this conversation. There was no going back now, the die had been cast and judging by her curiosity, her anxiety, it would be disastrous not to go ahead with saying what I had to say.

"Tell me," she encouraged with a wary smile. "Just say it and don't worry about how I might take it. I'm strong." Her voice raised a fraction. "Are you having an affair?" She said quietly.

"Oh no, don't be silly. I'm happily married and I'm not going to throw that away."

She heaved a sigh. The shade on her face quickly lifted and she leaned back in the chair.

"Well?" She said.

"I tried to tell you last night but of course you were too upset," I said quietly. "I received a mysterious fax yesterday. Dandy thinks it's pretty dark, there's something they want from me."

"They?"

"Who?"

35

"None of this is clear." I said.

"Some people are after you for something?

I nodded.

"Who are they?"

"I don't know. Dandy thinks it's probably a Russian connection."

She was coping better than I'd feared. Apart from a puzzled expression, there was no other obvious emotion. This was Lorna showing her other side - the lawyer side. It wasn't entirely surprising that she'd retained her nerves of steel after all this time; it was now ingrained in character by training.

"What are you going to do? Ignore them?" She said.

"Dandy doesn't think that's a good idea."

"What then? What exactly does Dandy think you should do?" She said impatiently.

"I need to find out who's behind this and what they want."

"How do you intend to do that?"

"They demanded a meeting tonight."

Lorna thought for a moment. "I don't think it's a good idea," she said, shaking her head. "I think you should involve the police."

"Not before I know who they are and what they want."

"I don't feel good about any of this," she said with concern.

"There's no need to worry. Just so you know, don't leave windows and doors open."

"Now you're going to have me worrying all day. Why not involve the police if you think there's something sinister about this?"

"Trust me, hon. I know what I'm doing. Dandy knows about these things better than we do. He certainly thinks it's a bad idea involving the police before we get to know who they are and what they want. Don't worry, okay?"

She shrugged and started clearing the table. I walked over to her and wrapped my arms around her.

"Hey, don't worry, okay, this is probably nothing," I reassured her.

She nodded unconvincingly. "You'd better run along or you'll be late. Phil, please be careful," she pleaded.

***

Half-hour later, as I weaved the SLK 500 convertible through traffic across central London, my mobile phone rang. I scanned the number but didn't recognise it.

"Hello."

"Phil?"

"Oh, hi, Dandy?"

"You in comfortable surroundings?"

"Sure. Driving and I'm alone."

"You thought any more about this?"

"All night."

"What're you going to do? I need to know."

"I'll give it a shot."

"You don't sound so sure about this."

"I suppose I'm still in two minds."

"You've been talking to Lorna?"

"Yeah. She thinks I should contact the police."

There was a brief pause.

"It's your call pal. But I'd say keep the cops out for now," Dandy said firmly.

"I agree. I guess I'm a little apprehensive about this meeting."

"You trust your secretary to keep a seal on this?"

"No more than you can trust a dog with a bone. Why?"

"This is serious stuff. You need to play this as close to chest as possible, and unless your secretary can be trusted to keep this to herself, you're in deep shit."

"I'll see what I can do."

"You make sure of that. I'll be in touch." The line went dead.

***

I arrived at D&L just after nine and caught the lift. Resting my briefcase between my legs, hands tucked away in pockets, with my head drooped, I waited for the door to slide closed. As the doors were sliding towards the centre, a woman slipped through. She almost crashed into me, stopping only by a hair's breath. Not that I would've issued a writ for trespassing, but equally relieved to be in one piece.

"Morning." She said energetically.

"Morning." I returned, grinning.

She looked in her late twenties, brunette. A white blouse was tucked into a black skirt, long tanned legs stretched into beautiful medium heeled shoes. The fragrance of her perfume permeated gently into the thin air leaving me gasping insatiably with delight.

"Which floor are you headed?" I volunteered with the grace of a vicar wrestling with his vows.

"I'm not sure," she said, with a slight giggle, and then she struggled with a fleeting glance at a piece of paper cramped in her palm. "Oh, reception," she added quickly.

"Same floor as me," I said.

She smiled at me as if I were the next best thing since the invention of the silicone breast implant.

As the lift made the short flight, I wondered which one of our several matrimonial lawyers she was going to see. Not that it mattered much which one; they were all trained butchers masquerading as officers of the law. She was the sort of client they thrived on. Our matrimonial department alone had netted twenty five million pounds in the three quarters of the past year. The management responded swiftly as petals to light, by recruiting six more top lawyers at D&L. Even then the increased workforce had done little to meet spiralling demand for the services.

The ding-dong sounded, and the lift swung open.

"Reception is down there," I said, stepping off the lift.

She smiled thinly.

"You're very kind," she said. Turning from me with the elegance of a model, she headed towards the reception.

I entered my office and slung the briefcase onto the table. Ah! First things first, I rubbed my face thoughtfully and slumped into the chair. Dandy was right. Dora needed reminding in the strongest terms possible of her duty of confidentiality. It was not hard to imagine what risk she posed knowing as much as she knew. I dialled her extension. It rang several times but Dora didn't pick up.

Then I rang Morris Ricci's extension.

"Hello, Mr. Ricci's office, Morris speaking."

"Sorry to bother you, Morris. It's me, Phil."

"Oh, hi, Phil."

"Have you seen Dora around?" I asked.

"Not this morning, no. I could look in the staff cafe if you want."

"Would you mind?"

"Of course not. It's a welcome distraction. I'll let you know," he said.

"Thanks." I hung up.

I stared into space with certain uneasiness. It was totally out of character for Dora to be skiving.

Then the phone rang.

"Yes?"

"It's me."

"Thanks for ringing me back, Morris. Any luck?"

"Dora hasn't turned up this morning."
Silence.
"Are you there, Phil?" He said.
"Yeah, yes, thanks."

Chapter Seven

I momentarily shut my eyes, and felt the sheer weight of what was unfolding. Though it was anyone's guess as to why Dora hadn't turned up for work this morning, there seemed only one logical conclusion for her absence; she might have panicked. I wondered if I had left it too late. Perhaps, I could have done more to reassure her?

The phone rang.

"Yes."

"Pop over for a minute," the caller said and hung up.

When Michael Levine had cause to chase after his lawyers, it was either for a good reason or an urgent one, or both. At sixty-eight, he was crude and self-righteous, and bore a striking resemblance to Danny DeVito. A brilliant property lawyer, he had the knack of blending hot cash into real estate, leaving no trace, only to resurrect it months afterwards in a Swiss or offshore accounts. Levine had been head of D&L for the past twenty years steering it to great heights.

I made my way to his office wondering what this could be about.

Levine was sitting behind a large oak desk. Leaning back in a high swivel chair, he spun slowly in an arc. His head tilted back against the headrest, eyeing me warily.

He waved me to a chair across from him.

Levine favoured me to succeed him as head. He had never explained his choice to anyone, not even me. Everyone simply made his or her own assumptions. He measured friendship in terms of its commercial value, and he had never spoken at least not openly, about what I was worth by his estimation.

"I spoke to Dora," Levine finally broke the wall of silence.

I looked at him curiously.

Levine continued, "She phoned in sick this morning. I did ask if she'd informed you and she said yes." Levine maintained a steady stare as if he was expecting a response.

I was wide-eyed like a drunk in denial, and for a brief moment, lost for words.

"Well. Yeah," I lied with a shrug.

"Never mind. I'm aware that a replacement from Icon recruitment agency is on her way. We don't know how long Dora will be away."

I nodded uneasily.

"Ah. Just one more thing." He walked over to me and stood in front of me, his forehead reflecting the light that shone brightly above him. "I hope . . . I hope you understand that you have my deepest sympathies on your near tragic experience at court yesterday."

"Sure. You already expressed that yesterday."

"You know you can always approach me if you need help."

"Sure."

He dimmed his eyes.

"How's Malik's case going?"

"OK. It's pretty involving. But it's fine."

"You look like you could do with a break. But there's no one I'd rather have on this case. I need you to stay focused on this one and let me know on a regular basis how it's shaping."

I nodded in agreement.

His intercom buzzed, he stretched across the table and grabbed the receiver. He listened for a moment.

"Beautiful," he said. "Send her through." He replaced the receiver and turned to me. "Dora's replacement is waiting in the reception."

Levine returned behind his desk.

A moment later, there was a tap on the door. Entering the suite and walking gracefully towards Levine's desk was the brunette I had met in the lift. A seductive smile hung at one corner of her mouth as she announced, "I'm Tania Jones, from Icon recruitment agency," extending a hand to Levine.

Chapter Eight

"There's Mr. Darlington on line one. He says it's urgent. Would you like to take the call?" Tania's voice resonated softly out of the speaker.

"Put him through." I said.

The speaker crackled into life. "I hope this isn't a bad time," Cecil Darlington said.

"Never a good time, fire away."

"I see your hands are full."

"You're the one hounding them with the mercy of the devil. So they run to me."

"I make no apologies for that. When I get every one of them, I'll lock them away and throw away the keys."

"Hmm. A hint of sadism there?"

"Always a great pleasure when a criminal goes down."

"That's not in your job description."

"Grow up."

"I'm serious. Last I heard a prosecutor's duty is to dispassionately apply the law firmly and fairly."

"Get real, Phil. My duty is to track down those smart criminals who hire top lawyers like you to get them off the hook."

There was a short pause.

"Now, back to business. Talk to me, Phil," he added.

"About what? Spit it out Cecil."

A shot of air rattled the speaker. He was laughing, a quite sadistic type of laughter.

"You know," he said, "there's a strong perception around here that you've been earmarked for high offices within the judiciary."

There was another pause.

"You still with me?" He continued.

"My patience is running thin."

"Too bad. I'm bending over backwards to see that everyone gets a little of what they want."

"Cut out this bullshit. What exactly do you want?"

"Intelligence uncovers your client's criminal enterprise spanning across Western Europe and Africa. We believe he has something in the region of half a trillion pounds in bank accounts in Switzerland alone," he paused as if to allow me time to evaluate the magnitude of Malik's sins.

"To date," he continued, "as you know, two prosecution witnesses have been murdered. Though no evidence has so far linked these murders to your client, you will no doubt accept this will be a significant factor when measuring the gravity of offences he is facing."

Darlington allowed another short recess for effect.

"Do you follow me so far, pal?" he said.

"I followed your rehearsal for an opening speech for the jury. But it's total bullshit; show me the evidence for that." I said.

"No, no, no. You misunderstand me, pal," he said angrily. "This isn't the platform for testing the substance of our case against your client. I come to you as comrade to comrade."

"Our comradeship counts for very little where my client's interests are at stake. Our loyalty to our clients is total."

"So is your duty to the state."

"I don't need a lecture on my duty as an officer of the court and . . ."

"Pal," he interrupted. "You're in denial. I tell you this. Your duty requires you to do everything within your power to achieve benefits for the larger society."

There was a momentary pause. I rose and walked across the room to the window.

"All I ask for is a little co-operation,' his voice was gentle, his approach, terse. "We know about his cohorts in the financial world who'd played crucial roles in laundering huge sums of money for themselves and for corrupt African leaders." he said.

He allowed a longer pause.

"We are aware your client is complicit in corruption in Nigeria and other places, helping top government officials and ex-presidents to fleece nearly $500 billion dollars in oil theft from those countries," he continued.

"I'm not aware my client has been charged with theft of oil from Nigeria?" I said.

"Not directly he hasn't."

"Then why is it an issue in the case?" I said.

"Because we can't prove his direct involvement in the oil theft from that country, it doesn't mean he is innocent. Look pal, without the connivance of sophisticated foreign criminal gangs that you defend, these Africans cannot loot their sovereign purse. You and I know this. These corrupt leaders have such low IQs and cannot pull this off without smart guys like your clients."

"What makes you think they have low IQs?" I said.

"It doesn't need rocket science to figure that out pal. It's a no brainer stealing from your country and then letting their conniving foreign counterparts keep seventy percent of the loot. That's not clever, and that's why we want to hunt down criminals like your client and make them pay."

"So my client is the cause of Nigeria's ills, right?"

"He is part of it. If he doesn't provide the technical know-how and wherewithal to illegally lift oil from that country and launder the proceeds in secret bank accounts for these corrupt leaders then this illicit trade would stop. Then we would put a stop to the death of millions of poor innocent children and women from hunger and starvation, from poor hygiene, from lack of affordable healthcare," he paused. "Only then can we avert

48

the environmental consequences to our standard of living arising from excessive African migration."

"Environmental consequences?" I said.

"Yes pal. Uncontrollable migration onto our shores is our share of the mess. Off the record. You can't blame people escaping from man-made deprivation and misery brought about by these corrupt leaders, with assistance from your client and others."

"Mmm…but we're lawyers not politicians, Cecil. We can't get involved in such matters."

"Of course we can. Nobody admits but we help shape social policies. We are social crusaders who happen to know the law. Pal, we need your client to cooperate with us to expose the full extent of the largest scandal coming from Africa since the slave trade. It's the big players we want to root out. Plus, we want full co-operation from him in recovering the entire funds. These poor African kids and women need every penny they can get back. In return, we will look favourably upon any reasonable request you may make."

A pause.

"One, my client will not rat on others. Two, he wants a safe exit to a country of his choice rather than being returned to Lebanon. Would you agree to these terms in return for his co-operation?" I said.

"We're not that stupid. Bringing down the network is the most important part of our mission. We could arrange his safe passage to any country of his choice but he has to rat on the network," he said.

"Not much of a carrot for him then, is it?"

"And it won't be held out indefinitely," he said, coldly.

"Sorry Cecil, I have no authority to offer you more."

"Hmm. In summary?" He said.

"Fund recovery is out of the question, I can confirm my instructions on that. He would offer his head to you on a silver platter; he's relaxed on sentence. He won't snitch." I said.

"Bullshit. Fund recovery and providing A class assistance against the network are key for us." There was a hint of irritation in his voice, followed by a quiet almost pleading tone. "Can you not see we're in deep shit unless we can sort this out?"

"Sort what out?"

"Corruption in Africa. Illicit financial outflows from that continent."

"How's that my problem to sort out?"

"Because corruption in Africa is inextricably linked to global instability. You cannot feel safe walking down the city of London with so much money being banded around by shady characters like your client."

"Darlington, you're being alarmist…."

"Actually am not pal. Off the record…I have read intelligence reports not readily available to you and I know what am talking about. Instability in the West is an issue. Not to mention the other ills – the devastation this causes to millions of

African children and youths, the devastating impact corruption and other illicit financial outflows are having on economic development and poverty alleviation on that continent, the impact on their healthcare, education and infrastructure, the brain drain on the continent as a result of mass migration to greener economies, the lost generation syndrome etc. Pal, do you not owe the world a duty to protect it from those intent on harming it?"

There was a short pause. "Am not sure I can," I returned quietly. "I couldn't protect the world even if I tried. Am a lawyer trying to do my best for my client. Am not a politician. Let the Prime Ministers of this world sort it out...the Presidents, the UN, the G8, the G20..."

"Oh give us a break pal. They are wimps. Again, off the record, people pay lip service to this. If they are serious about eradicating this problem it would take them a flick of the finger, but they don't want to do it, at least not yet."

"But they are already making plans to introduce a universal system on transparency, fair taxation, lifting the veil of secrecy behind which many shady companies thrive, publicly naming beneficiaries of shell companies..."

"What would that do? It would simply drive criminals like your clients underground. Rather than washing illicit funds through shady companies with bank accounts in Switzerland, Britain and USA, these criminals would buy property and gold and then turn them into cash.

You see, they are simply paying lip service to this problem."

"It can't be mere lip service if they have repatriated stolen money in the past. Switzerland, Jersey, Britain and USA are tracking and freezing these illicit funds held by corrupt government officials and their cronies, I know this."

"Yes, they are. But they are not repatriating proceeds from investments made using these funds. These illicit funds are lent to Funds managers in exchange for handsome returns; the lending bank would take their share; the state would take its share through tax payable on the returns, these revenues are used by the state to support their welfare system. Now pal, knowing this, would you expect the West to sort Africa's problems quick enough?"

"Hmm…"

"Well pal, just do your part, don't leave it others."

There was a long pause. Though Darlington had made a convincing case for my loyalty, yet this was the wrong time to be showing weakness.

"I have told you what my client wants out of any deal," I said finally, "you take it or leave it, Cecil."

"That's a load of bull, pal,' he thundered. "You're not offering us much. Make no mistake about this. Funds recovery and giving us his cohorts are central. Without these, no deal. No safe passage to a country of his choice. You let him know that."

"Not my call, Cecil. I take instructions, not give them."

"About time you started giving them. I'll sit by the phone until Thursday afternoon. Good day, pal." He hung up.

Staring blankly into space, I smiled. It wasn't a bad bout for me. The stage had been set for a second round of plea-bargaining and there was certainly enough room for flexibility. Would Malik be prepared to be flexible too? They wanted him to pull the plug on the entire network, something he didn't want to do. But why was Cecil Darlington desperate to push for a deal?

Then the intercom buzzed.

"Yes." I answered.

"I've been trying to reach you, Mr. Dias," Tania's voice came on, "Mr. Levine wants you in the conference room straight away. An emergency management meeting."

I made my way to the conference room.

The room was packed; everyone was sitting at the table. There were no smiling faces, only anxious tired ones. There was nothing unusual about that. Happy times were rare at D&L. Morris Ricci gave me an almost imperceptible nod as I sat next to him.

"What's this about?" I whispered.

"Don't know," Morris returned. "Who's that sitting next to Levine?"

"Never seen him before. My guess is he's either a taxman or an undertaker."

Levine finally cleared his throat cutting conversations in mid-sentence.

"Thank you ladies and gentlemen," he paused. "I'm afraid a situation has arisen and it's with sadness that I announce another death in the firm. The second one in a few days."

Suppressed murmurs erupted.

"Please, ladies and gentlemen," Levine interrupted, half-raising a hand in the air. "Mr. Palmer here is the detective investigating the death."

The detective cleared his throat as he rose to address his captive audience. "A body was discovered late this morning by a cleaner. The circumstances of her death are not clear. So we're keeping an open mind about it. Please, I'd be grateful for your co-operation with the investigation team in the coming days. Any information, however insignificant would be gratefully received,"

There was a complete silence.

Someone blurted out, "Can you at least reveal the identity of the deceased?"

Palmer hesitated momentarily and finally said, "Miss Penn. Dora Penn."

My heart skipped a beat.

Chapter Nine

The meeting ended in the same way it began, somber and uncertain, the partners filed out of the conference room not saying a lot. It was unclear if they knew more or were pretending to know; either way everyone else was in the dark anyway and it didn't matter in the end. What was evident on the faces of all those who had attended the meeting was a pervading feeling of insecurity. It was largely unspoken, but it was on everyone's lips. I sat back in quiet contemplation, staring blankly, overwhelmed by it all. The news of Dora's death was a total shock.

I noticed that Morris Ricci had also remained in his chair. He seemed genuinely shocked; it was unlike him to betray deep emotions.

I looked up and there was Tobias.

"I'm very impressed by your class act," Tobias said.

I ignored him.

"But you don't fool me. Perhaps you care to explain why you drove Dora to her death." Tobias insisted.

"What are you on about?" I shouted.

"You heard me. You killed her, didn't you, Phil?"

My breathing shot up.

"You bastard," I snarled and lunged wildly at him. I hoisted him up an inch and pinned him to the wall "Repeat that once more and I'll break your neck, you scum."

"Phil, let him go," shouted Morris forcing himself between Tobias and I.

Tobias looked stunned. He had not expected the outburst, not least within earshot of the two most powerful men in the firm. He shook himself free and straightened his suit.

"Gentlemen, in my office. NOW," Levine said gravely and shot out of the room, followed by Dennis Dobbs.

Levine was not impressed. The height of contempt, he ranted. Then he paused and looked at me, a judgemental stare.

"Tobias provoked this incident," I protested.

"Did he?" Said Levine behind clenched teeth.

"He accused me of killing Dora. That's gross." I said.

He turned to Tobias. "Did you?"

"I did. I have grounds for making it." He said defiantly.

Levine looked at Dennis Dobbs.

Dennis was a cunning man - a diplomat by nature without the razor sharp intelligence. He didn't make it as a criminal lawyer, resorting instead to civil litigation. Though his income was enormous, close to two million pounds before tax, only second to Levine in the Firm, he disliked the notion of tax and didn't miss any loophole to avoid paying it. In the past eighteen months, he had spent a tenth of his annual income visiting a shrink. Diagnosis? Sleeplessness. He now spent much of each night fending off his wife's ghost because she was nagging him, he claimed, sometimes aggressively insisting on her death wish being honoured. Prognosis? She wanted a decent burial with tombstone in a very exclusive and expensive part of Chelsea. But this would never be realized because not only that Dennis Dobbs had not buried her remains and erected a tombstone in Chelsea, her ashes had drifted down the river Thames on a transatlantic voyage. Dobbs would now continue to dread the nights - up all night and whinging all day.

Dobbs loved Tobias like he was his own son - his obvious choice for Levine's successor. There was his unflinching support for Tobias, his tireless campaign to ensure that Tobias, not me, would succeed Levine, his almost arrogant ambition to scupper my chances within the firm. Levine on the other hand had risked all when he threw his weight behind me as his preferred choice for the position, and since then, Dobbs had been waving a sword.

Levine regarded Dobbs quietly.

"What's this about Mr. Dias killing Dora?"

"Well," said Dobbs, "some information came to light. I know what you're thinking, why I didn't tell you. Well, there wasn't any time to tell you before the meeting."

"What might this highly classified information be?" There was derision in Levine's tone.

Dobbs rubbed his jaw thoughtfully.

"A secretary told Tobias that Dora had confided in her about her insecurity with Phil. She was afraid, almost shaken."

"So?" Levine said.

Dobbs shrugged. "Well, the suggestion that Dora had been insecure less than twenty four hours before she died and, that Phil had caused that insecurity would appear to a reasonable person a poignant factor." His voice had risen sharply.

"And you conclude on the basis of this . . . that Phil killed his secretary?" Levine said with puzzled expression.

Dobbs pursed his lips reflectively for a moment.

"Well, whilst I don't wish to judge Phil hastily, I believe Tobias is entitled to reach his own conclusion based on what he'd been told," Dobbs said defensively.

"That's ridiculous." Levine sank back in his chair.

Dennis Dobbs did not respond, he was taken aback and stared into space.

"Dennis,' Levine continued with a more subdued tone, "I am disappointed you allow sentimentality to cloud your judgement. You must stop fuelling the feuding between these two."

Chapter Ten

Wang Lu, a Chinese restaurant in the south of Soho, was packed when I got there a little after 9 pm.

Heading towards the reception desk, I noticed a fat Chinese man standing in a corner, hands crossed over his large belly. His eyes steered searchingly in my direction without moving his head. Then he turned his head slowly like a robot running out of batteries and fixed me with a silent stare.

"Hi. I've got an appointment to meet someone here."

"You are, sir?"

"Phil Dias."

He considered me briefly, a censorious look.

"Wait here sir."

He scrambled behind the counter, picked up the phone and spoke without dialling, turning twice to look at me as if he were assessing how much of a threat I posed. Finally he dropped the phone, grinning broadly, he waved me on.

His strides were short but quick for a man labouring under a massive lump of fat. I followed closely through a dark corridor. An ancient lantern, fastened to the wall cast an orange glow leaving patches of shade just enough to keep the fat figure within view. I stumbled into him a few times. If he'd felt the collision he did not show it.

"Please wait," he said, pointing to a leather chair and left without another word.

I sat and wondered again why I hadn't heeded Lorna's advice to involve the police. Here was another hint that something was wrong or shady at best. No lawful business was conducted in the dark I mused. Perhaps Dandy had got it wrong this time. This was no way to live, stuck in these undignified surroundings not knowing what to expect or who would walk through the door next. On the other hand this needed sorting out once and for all. With my patience waning and reassured by a greater desire to go to the police as soon as this meeting was over, I waited, giddy with anxiety.

Suddenly, a light cold breeze filtered through the room and I knew I had company. I listened intently in the dark.

Moments later, I noticed that a shadowy figure was standing over the table. My heart hammered against my chest as if a wave of electricity had passed through it. I strained to get a better view relying on the weak glow from a fish tank in the corner, but everything beyond the table surface was out of my view.

He sat across from me, thickset judging by the size of his stomach. His black silky suit faintly reflected in the weak light, leather gloves covered both hands. Beyond that I could make out nothing else.

I sniffed uneasily, beads of sweat formed on my forehead like a fever patient. Was this the man behind all this?

"Please accept my apology for this unusual setting," the man said at last. It was instantly obvious it was not his natural voice; he was wearing some kind of voice scrambler. "You're probably thinking this arrangement defies all standards of respectable behaviour, something resembling civilization of ancient Babylon. However, I'm assured, reluctantly I might add, that this is a necessary precaution to ensure the security of our itinerary."

"What's all this about?" I blurted impatiently. "A lecture in behavioural science? Why don't you . . .?"

"Please! Please!" He interrupted. "I hear you're a man for whom time is money. Of course, you're going to be rewarded beyond anything you can ever imagine. So, please allow me the latitude to indulge your time."

There was a brief awkward silence.

"Drink?"

I said yes. I needed calm nerves.

"Any particular preference?"

"Cognac." I said.

He slipped his hand inside his jacket pocket and removed a mobile phone. A brief conversation in a foreign language ensued and moments later a pair of hands shielded from view by grey leather gloves delivered a silver tray containing drinks before disappearing as effortlessly as they had come.

"Please help yourself," he said.

I mixed a strong drink of brandy and lime knocking it back in one gulp. I could almost sense my nerves sapping the spirits with the greed of a child to sweets.

"Counsel, please listen to me very carefully." His voice was firm.

I mixed another drink, aware my head was buzzing lightly.

"You may call me Shadow," he said.

My eyebrows narrowed.

"My client, for whom I undertake this mission wishes to hire you, for a fee of half a million pounds."

I swallowed hard. "I can't take another case on, my diary is full for the rest of the year," I said.

"Oh, I know you can."

I shrugged. "That's brazen arrogance."

"We're not looking for anyone else to do this work," he said.

"Why me? Surely, with so much to spend you can get the best around," I said.

"Absolutely."

"So why me?"

He hesitated for a moment. My frustration was mounting.

"Because," he said finally, "you're best placed to deliver what we want."

"To deliver what?" I said.

"Malik." He spat the name as though he was ridding himself of an inconvenient fish bone.

My immediate reaction was one of disbelief, followed by a stab of fear.

"You're crazy," I managed to say through clenched teeth.

"In a sense, yes," he returned flatly. "I'm still in business because reason doesn't form part of what I do."

"Listen up, whoever you are," I said impatiently, with a hint of anger, "I can't help you."

"Mr. Dias," he said gravelly, "we know you can deliver him to us."

"Hey, you're not listening to me. I won't get involved . . ."

"Mr. Dias..." He interrupted sharply.

"No," I interrupted back.

In the silence that followed, he slipped his hand inside his jacket and removed a manila envelope. He emptied the contents on the table displaying a pile of photographs. Then he waved me towards the photographs.

"They are for your viewing pleasure," he said casually. "Please."

Reluctantly, I shot a fleeting glance at the pile and the cover photo immediately caught my attention. Then I looked more closely, my eyebrows narrowed in astonishment. My breathing was suddenly fast and shallow.

Staring back at me under the glare of the naked lamp was one of several photographs of Judge Pilate having sex with what looked like an under-aged boy.

Chapter Eleven

The photographs had stirred my consciousness; the child was bending over a bed, his face creased in pain, and seemingly too weak to offer resistance to Judge Pilate as he pushed against his rear. Then there was that last photo. The child's face was a picture of fear, tears trickling down his cheeks, head slightly bowed.

I dropped the photographs back on the table and staring stonily at them. Quietly in my head, I fitted the last piece of the jigsaw. Shadow wanted Judge Pilate blackmailed into releasing Malik, and for my proposed role, a fee of half a million pounds. There was no doubt the photographs had made out a compelling case for lynching Judge Pilate, even then this was not enough to participate in a conspiracy to blackmail him? I thought. One thing was crystal clear. These photographs, to some extent, had further demonstrated Shadow's power, influence and perhaps determination. There was more. Something else was strange about Shadow. It was not exactly his piercing coldness or his intelligence that was all pervasive, there was a stifling suspicion he was appraising me the whole time. The silence seemed to grow more and more judgmental by the second. His control over me was total: he could see me, watch me, assess my every thought and demeanour but I could not see him. All I had was my imagination and it was not nearly enough.

Finally, I broke the dense silence. "I still won't get involved."

He did not seem fazed; no stamping of feet in frustration, nor did he bang the table. Instead the silence that followed bore the hallmark of a man at ease with his destiny.

"Counsel," he said at last, "these photographs only tell half the story. I'm going to tell you the other half."

I sipped my drink and said nothing.

"The child in the photographs is Langley. He was only twelve when these photographs were taken. As he grew older, his parents forced him to study law despite his protestations. Poor chap. He only wanted to become a fireman, a modest ambition, you might think. But that did not fit in with his father's aspirations. Firemen of course, do not go on to become judges, prime ministers - the power peddlers."

He allowed a brief pause.

"Wanting to please his father, Langley was relentless in his quest for success. In his frantic search for identity, recognition, perhaps peace of mind, he learned early that no price was too great for a status as a barrister - if only as a means to his father's heart," he paused.

Shadow picked up the photographs, sifted through them until he revealed one of Judge Pilate grinning broadly, partly clothed. He flung it on the table.

"Langley was thrown at the mercy of this man," he said pointing at the lone photograph, "now Judge Pilate, then a senior counsel, who was entrusted with mentoring the fragile young mind to the height of the legal profession. At least so Langley's father thought."

I scanned the photograph. Judge Pilate was barely recognisable without his now customary grey moustache.

"Instead of instructing the child in the path of good knowledge and sound practice as hoped, Judge Pilate did the opposite," Shadow continued, "over many years, he subjected Langley to the worst forms of sexual abuse promising him heaven and earth. One such promise was to pave a way for him to a tightly controlled profession. Determined to make success of himself, albeit, for his father's sake, Langley endured years of sexual exploits from an insatiable vile man," he paused.

I swallowed uneasily, my mind flagged up Cecil Darlington and I wondered whether he had gone through a similar experience to get where he was. There was no doubt he wielded so much influence amongst the judges, and there had been rumours.

"After all that," he continued, "Langley, now thirty, is still a struggling barrister with an unfulfilled ambition. No confidence. Cannot hold down a relationship. Confused about his sexual orientation. And he still believes Judge Pilate holds his key to a lucrative career at the bar. Maybe he does," he paused briefly. "But with this strong hold on him, the Judge continues to indulge his sexual fantasies with him."

I sensed angry eyes all over me.

"This is absolutely disgusting, very unfair," I said quietly.

"But however distasteful you may find this," he added gently, "we're not concerned about the moral questions relating to what he has done. We leave judgement for his maker. We're only interested in this as a means of securing Malik's release. I trust we're clear on this, Mr. Dias?"

"I don't want to be part of it, this is crazy." I said flatly.

"No, no, there's nothing crazy about this." He interrupted with a raised voice. "You misjudge me."

His breathing was heavier.

"Mr. Dias," he said sharply, "undertaking an assignment of this magnitude - for world peace, is hardly within the capability of a crazy mind." He was breathing faster, his fist clenched. Suddenly he withdrew his fist from view and let out a mechanical laugh.

"Your sense of humour amuses me," he said. "Your criticism of me was insulting at best."

"It's just that what you propose is insane," I said defiantly.

"Objection counsel!" His voice was sharp. "Again you misjudge me. I've an unrivalled reputation for good judgement as you'll soon find out yourself."

"Don't count on my cooperation; I won't be around long enough to find out. I want to leave now."

"You see," he said ignoring me, "you're being offered the enviable chance to help stabilise world peace. Sacrificing your personal or professional integrity is a small price to pay for a place in the roll of honour of global significance."

"Masterminding the escape from justice of your partner in crime has nothing to do with world peace," I returned quickly.

"Nonsense. Malik is not my partner in crime." His voice was terse.

"So why are you paying half a million to assist his escape from justice?" I said.

He allowed a long pause, as if he wasn't sure how much he should tell. Suddenly, the question I had intended as no more than a passing shot quickly assumed some significance. If this wasn't about helping a criminal associate escape the firm clutches of the law, why was he going through so much trouble?

Finally, Shadow broke the silence.

"Mr. Dias," he said quietly, "this operation is of utmost confidentiality to my client. I'm not at liberty to divulge any part of it to you. Perhaps, just as well. You're safer remaining in the dark about the details of this."

I stirred, swallowing hard.

Then he continued, "My client is reluctant to blackmail a senior judge. But they're keen to honour their commitment to their allies globally. Currently, only one man is standing in the way. Malik. He threatens the entire Western and Eastern civilisation. I wish I could tell you more."

I had no idea what he was saying. My client. Their commitment. Their allies globally. Who could this client be? How was Malik a threat to the whole Western and Eastern civilisation?

"Who are you?" I said coldly.

There was a momentary silence.

"Not so much who I am as what I do, "he ventured calmly. "I undertake near impossible tasks around the world, for which I'm richly rewarded," he paused. "I do all I can to avoid casualties in my work, but on few occasions people have died, I must admit. In all those cases however, choices were given to the victims and wrong choices made in each case. Now, Mr. Dias, I offer you a similar choice."

"I won't be bullied," I said firmly.

"Then you leave me no choice." His voice was steely cold. "I'd hoped for a better working relationship. Perhaps you want to think this through."

"No. You're wasting your time," I said.

"Very well," he said calmly. "You will be shown out."

The lamp suddenly went off plunging the room into darkness. Then I felt hands underneath my arms, as two shadowy figures guided me out of the room towards the corridor. Half way down the dark corridor they released their grips leaving me to find my own way out.

***

The motorway was virtually deserted at that time of night as I made my way home. It took only an hour to get home, and despite the elation and relief from rebuffing Shadow's advance, I was still in a low mood. What was bugging me even more than his threat was Dora's needless death. If only she had trusted me. But there was a snipping guilt that I had driven him to her death. Perhaps I hadn't done enough to help her overcome the fear in her eyes the day she received the fax message; the anxiety was etched all over her face. How could I not have foreseen the danger she had faced?

In spite of the self-criticism, I knew it was Shadow who was ultimately responsible for her death. How could one individual wield so much power and influence on others? Then my thoughts centred on the dossier on Judge Pilate going back many years. How many other judges had he got dossiers on? There was no doubt about what I needed to do at first light. But on quiet reflection, even the police powers seemed antiquated against Shadow's sophistication. Perhaps going to the MI5 was a safer thing to do, I decided as I pulled into the garage.

I switched the engine off, and steadied nerves. I could hardly wait to see Lorna's delight at seeing me home earlier than she hoped. And that would only mean more quality time. A knowing smile creased my face and suddenly all my troubles melted away.

"Babe, I'm home," I called out fondly as I rushed through the double doors.

I knew Lorna's game. My pulse rate quickly shot up in anticipation of pleasure. She was feigning sleep, like daring the prince to sweep her off her feet to a wonderland and make love to her until dawn. I smiled.

I threw my briefcase to the floor and quickly shed my jacket trampling on it as I crept into the living room. But Lorna was not sprawling sensuously on the sofa, ready for me. A slight irritation hit me as the expectation of a sofa session quickly disappeared. We had had our best moment on the sofas.

I climbed the stairs. She was not in the master bedroom; the bed was undisturbed. I checked the next room and the one after that and yet Lorna was nowhere to be found. This time, the frenzy of love had gone and panic had set in.

The visitor's suite downstairs, I thought.

"Hon?" I called. My voice echoed in the house. I returned to the living room searching frantically for a note or something to explain her absence. Had something come up and she had to rush out? My breathing had become faster.

Then the telephone rang startling me. Babe, your explanation had better be good, I mused under my breath as I scrambled for the hands-free set and pressing it firmly to my ear, "Honey where the hell . .."

"Listen very carefully."

I held my breath for what seemed like a long time slumping back onto the sofa, wide-eyed, and protested, "No, no, if you hurt her . . . if you lay one hand on her, I swear, I'll kill you. You bastard!"

There was a short pause.

"Unless you do as I say, your beautiful wife will be returned to you bit by bit." He paused. "Wait for my next instruction and don't go to the police."

Chapter Twelve

Next morning, I arrived in the office tired and dishevelled.

It had been a long night. For a considerable length of time during that night, Lorna's abduction had been a frightening shock. Gradually anxiety had taken over and my mind soon twirled with every rescue plan imaginable, each one carefully analysed for safe execution. I had hunched on the settee as the night progressed, my heart had thumped furiously with every thought, my head dizzy and gathering pain, not entirely convinced by any of the options I had considered. In the end I had closed my eyes for what felt like a brief sleep. Next, daylight had come and there was no way of knowing if I had slept at all.

Now sitting in the office, contemplating my next move, I was suddenly aware of the phone bleeping. I finally depressed a button and Tania came on.

"Reschedule all my appointments for today," I said before Tania could say a word.

"Too late, Mr. Dias. Your 10 o'clock appointment is waiting in the reception." She said.

"Well, don't keep him much longer. Tell him to go. I can't see anybody."

"Mr. Dias, he's flown in from Ireland to keep this appointment. Apparently, he's a very important witness in one of the cases you have conduct of."

"I know about Jack O'Rea's importance in the case. But…"

"Perhaps - - -."

"Tania," I snapped.

There was a short pause.

"Tania," I repeated gently, "offer Mr. O'Rea my apologies, and arrange for all his expenses to be reimbursed." I hung up and quickly dialled a number.

Dandy picked up after two rings.

"Hey Phil. Been expecting your call. Can you talk?"

"Yes. I'm in the office, alone."

"You don't sound good."

"They've got Lorna."

"Shit."

I took a deep breath and leaned back in the chair.

"When?"

"Last night."

"What do they want?"

"Malik."

There was a short pause.

"Dandy? Are you there?" I said.

"You told them no?"

"I said I couldn't do it."

"Wrong choice of word," Dandy said with a deep sigh. "In a kidnap situation, there are two words you don't use. Can't and won't. You get that? If you want to see your wife again, you better learn to say the right words," he paused.

"I don't like any of this. This man is dangerous."

"What does he look like?"

"Couldn't see a thing. The place was pitch black and he used a voice scrambler."

"Hmm. Did he say why he wants Malik?"

"He was evasive about that. He thinks Malik is a threat to Western civilisation and should be stopped."

Dandy exhaled noisily.

"Next contact?"

"I'm expecting him to contact me soon."

"OK. Meanwhile keep things nice and easy. No big ideas. No cops. You hear me. Your wife's life depends on it. I'll stay in touch." He hung up.

I walked over to the window and stood there staring thoughtfully at nothing in particular. The sky was grey, weak sunlight bounced off glass windows and birds swooped past. The streets were quiet. People walked past speaking on phones, texting, gesturing. Some animated, others less so. Some headed west, others south. It was as if the world was unconcerned about the evil that went on around them. It suddenly dawned on me that no one really cared about me, about Lorna; we were just an insignificant part of the big picture. We were no more important than an ant crushed under the heels of an unsuspecting stranger.

Then the phone rang bringing me back to life. Activating the speakerphone, I said, "Yes."

"Delivery for you at the reception. He insists you have to take personal delivery," the receptionist said.

"OK. Be there in a sec."

The courier, wearing a leather suit and a helmet was pacing the floor when I entered the reception. He stopped suddenly and peered at me from behind a black visa. I discreetly held up two fingers, something Shadow had demanded in his instructions. The courier gave me an imperceptible nod, handed me a parcel and quickly disappeared down the staircase.

Back in my office, I ripped the parcel open and the same photographs Shadow had shown me the previous night formed a pile on the table. A neatly folded typewritten note lay in the middle. My face distorted into a frustrated frown as I read the note. Forty-eight hours to deliver Malik!

Leaning back in the chair, frustration and fear set in as I analysed my predicament. Judge Pilate was an obstinate man. What if he refused to play ball?

A scuffle outside the door distracted me.

The door threw open.

"I'm, sorry, Mr. Dias. I tried to stop him," Tania said eyeing a man who had now leaned sloppily against the doorframe, and was grinning mischievously. Only decency had stopped Tania from shoving him back out the door.

"I'm sorry," the man said still grinning. "I don't mean to make a fuss."

Suppressing my annoyance, I analysed him some more.

"And you are?" I said firmly.

He glanced at Tania, then back to me.

I reflected quietly. Though it wasn't clear what this man wanted, but with Lorna's life at stake, everything was significant.

I nodded at Tania. Her disgust was apparent as she brushed past him almost knocking him over.

He looked in his early thirties, with a certain boyish vitality about him. Medium height, slim, he had a handsome face and did not seem to take himself seriously. His sky blue shirt clashed with his pink tie, and black trousers hung over his worn heels. He wrapped his jacket around his left hand as if he disliked the idea of a suit in the first place.

"Yes," I said straight faced, as he shut the door gently walking towards the table. His hand fumbled clumsily inside his jacket, he finally pulled a badge and flashed it at me.

"Des Riley. Detective Inspector, City of London police," he paused briefly. "I'm investigating the murders of Phillipa Brown and Dora Simpson," he added engaging my stare.

Murders.

Dora and Phillipa murdered? I gasped quietly.

Chapter Thirteen

"Tell me; don't you think the law is such an ass?" Des Riley said dropping in the chair across from me like a spoilt child.

"I'm sorry, I don't get you?" I said absentmindedly.

Who could've murdered Dora and Phillipa? I wondered.

Mr. Riley threw both hands in the air like a child caught stealing chocolate.

"Politically incorrect analogy, I know," he said flashing an apologetic smile. "But on a serious note," he continued, "The law is such an ass, you agree?"

I did not answer. Swinging the swivel chair slightly to the left, I crossed one leg over the other. Head tilted to one side, I looked at him warily. He stared back with quiet determination. Silently, I wondered whether this was stupidity, or tactic but you could not help noticing he was having fun at my expense.

"Well," he shrugged, "at least, that's what I think about the law," he added crossing his legs too. He allowed a short pause. "I know what you're thinking. What a poor opinion of the law from a guy charged with enforcing it, yeah?"

My patience was running thin.

He shrugged again. "Maybe, you don't think that, but an average person would. There again, you're in a different class to the rest of us."

I swung the chair back so I faced him, "Mr. Riley..."

"No," he interrupted, "Call me Des. Just Des.'

'How may I help, Mr. Riley?"

"I know you're pressed for time," he said in a pious tone, smiling. "This is only routine practice. Times like this, I think the law is such an ass you know. You must be thinking my visit here today makes a mockery of our system."

"Why do you think that?' I said.

Trying to sound less impatient, I added, "The beauty of our system is that no-one is above or under it. Imperfect as it may seem, it works beautifully."

He shook his head slowly, a wry smile spread across his face.

"You know, I'm happy where I'm at. I could never have made it as a lawyer," he paused staring expectantly at me and when I made no attempt to join in, he added, "I could never answer questions like you do, giving answers that can be interpreted either way. I swear, you leave me in the end not knowing whether you think the law is an ass or not. Yet I feel content with your answer. Perfect. What can I say?"

I shifted impatiently in my chair.

"I'll be straight with you," he said, leaning back in his chair. "I didn't want to come here fishing around." He paused. "You're after-all the custodians of the law. I'm here to understand the victims a bit more." He looked at me longingly like a singer expecting a supporting chorus for his vocal repertoire.

"You do what you've got to do," I said.

"Personally, I don't think the clues to the murders lie anywhere around here. I hope I'm right, because the very fabric of our society depends on the integrity of its custodians."

There was a brief silence.

"Inspector . . ."

"No. Please call me Des."

"Of course. I'm sorry."

"It's OK. But please cut out the officialdom. Not Inspector, not Mr. Riley. I'm most at ease with just Des."

"Mr. . . . I mean Des," I raised a hand apologetically. "I take it you're here to ask me questions about the murders, right?"

He nodded thoughtfully.

"Well?"

"This is of course routine."

"I understand. Please feel free. We've been expecting you guys since Mr. Palmer broke the news yesterday."

"Mr. Palmer is no longer on this case," he said quickly. "This will make you laugh. Though an experienced officer with a track record of more solved cases than unsolved ones, he's thought to have a striking resemblance to a bull," he said laughing. Then punctuating the rest of his words with laughter, he added, "Our boss feared he would be a public relations disaster if he stayed on."

I checked my watch.

"Sorry I've taken too much of your time already." He reached into his jacket pocket and pulled out a notebook. "You know, what kept me awake at night are the striking similarities of the murders, especially the effort to make them look like a suicide."

I regarded him with a stony contempt.

"Can you think of any reason at all why anyone might wish to harm Dora?" For the first time he was less than pleasant.

"No." Somehow I thought my voice quavered a little. Anyone would buckle under his piercing stare. Des was nobody's fool. All that boyish mannerisms had suddenly gone, leaving an accomplished detective and he was appraising me closely.

"And do you know anyone who might wish to kill her?"

"No."

"Did you notice anything unusual about her the days before her death?" He said writing furiously in his notebook.

"No." My voice was emphatic.

He flipped through his notebook quickly and then looked up. "I take it you hadn't noticed she was . . . um, detached, unhappy and frightened."

Though he had uttered the words with less enthusiasm, I nonetheless, understood that each word was significant. The directness of his inquiry was causing me unease.

"I hadn't noticed anything."

"Okay," he said grinning. Somehow I felt he was less than sincere.

Des rose and offered his hand and I quickly took it with some relief.

"I understand this is a difficult time for you and your colleagues," he said, "I hope we can wrap this up with minimum disruptions to your busy schedules." He walked towards the door and suddenly stopped, turning slowly, his face reflective, he added, "Can you remember the last time you spoke with Dora?" His gaze dropped to the parcel on the table.

"Yesterday."

"That would be in the morning of her death?"

"Correct. If she died that morning," I said struggling to be less nervous.

"Which number did she call you on?" Des said.

"Um . . . on my mobile phone . . . the number is.. ."

He waved a hand dismissively. "We've already obtained that information from Levine - nice man. He spoke highly of you."

I pursed my lips.

"How long did that conversation last?"

I shrugged.

"Approximately," he added quietly.

"Sixty seconds - give or take," I said.

"Why did she call?"

"She said she was too ill to come in. And I said fine. Take the time you need. That's that." I grinned cautiously.

Des was straight faced.

"You know, if she were alive today, I would ask her why she had telephoned Mr. Levine and yourself just to give the same information," he paused reflectively. "I get the feeling the answer to this puzzle may ultimately determine the direction this investigation will take." A devious smile weaved across his face as he turned, clutching the door handle; he gently pulled the door and swaggered off with the contentment of a decorated war hero.

Long after the door had clicked shut, I continued staring blankly at it; it suddenly struck me with the sting of a thunderbolt how quickly my world was collapsing at every turn.

Chapter Fourteen

The lunchtime traffic was less hectic as I drove to the Old Bailey. For the umpteenth time, I wondered if Lorna was all right. Where was she being held? How was she being treated? Was she alive?

Slowly a sense of anger began to descend on me. Gentle at first, but it quickly intensified until it was almost crushing. Then there was the task ahead. How could Shadow be so naive to think he could pull this off? How would Judge Pilate react? Though there was nothing to suggest he was going to be a walk over, but then no right thinking man high in the echelon of his profession would decline a deal to save him from public humiliation and, from imprisonment. Clearly, responsibility for Lorna's safety had been placed in my hands, although it was Judge Pilate who might ultimately decide her fate.

With a picture forming in my mind of a subdued Judge Pilate - keen to cooperate in return for the photographs, my frustration soon crystallised into a momentary flash of hope. I took a deep breath and continued down the corridor towards the judge's chambers.

Marcia Blackwood's office was spacious; a large padded desk occupied the far corner facing the entrance. A small photo frame of her in warm embrace with a handsome looking man stood prominently on the desk. Except for a computer, a telephone and a pile of files neatly tucked away to one corner, the desk was clear. A grey steel cabinet stood alone opposite the desk, on top of which stood a bunch of flowers.

Marcia was bending over the cabinet humming quietly.

"I'm sorry. The door was open,' I said loudly.

She spun round with a startled look on her face.

Gathering herself, she leaned against the cabinet to steady herself. She returned to her desk, swept her glasses off the table and put them on.

"How may I help you, Mr. Dias?" Her voice was dead serious, her spikes drawn and threatening. She was like a woman uneasy at being caught out early in the morning without her make-up on.

"I need to see Judge Pilate, oops sorry, Judge Howard. It's important," I said.

"Is he expecting you?"

"No. But . . ."

"Mr. Dias," she interrupted, her voice defiant. "You know the judge doesn't entertain members of the public. In any case, he can't see anyone at a short notice."

"I know that. But this is urgent." I insisted.

"Everyone says that. If the judge should attend every lame matter, he'd find no time to carry out his ..."

"Miss Blackwood, this is of utmost importance. I don't have time for this." She studied me and suddenly her face became less fierce.

"I'll ask the judge if he wants to see you. Wait here," she said and hurried off.

It was like an age-long wait, and all I could think about was Lorna. Finally I heard the door shut quietly in the corridor, then Marcia's echoing footsteps - quick and firm, grew louder and closer. She entered the room.

"He won't see you. Too busy," she said returning behind her desk.

"Oh well, we'll see about that," I turned and headed down the corridor towards judge Pilate's chamber.

"Mr. Dias. Mr. Dias!" She called after me.

I ignored her and kept going, searching for a door with Judge Howard's name inscribed on it. Marcia gave chase. I finally found a door with a gold-plated sign that read Judge Howard set in black letters. I turned the doorknob and stepped in. And at the same moment, Marcia swept past spreading her hands before me.

"You'd better leave now." She growled between clenched teeth.

Judge Pilate sat erect, looking like a rattled cobra ready to spring.

Marcia turned to the judge. "I'm sorry, my lord. I tried to stop him."

"Obviously, you didn't try hard enough. Call security," the judge said.

"I wouldn't do that if I were you." I told the judge.

Marcia turned to me, her face strained. "You must leave immediately."

"I need only a few minutes. Alone." I said to Judge Pilate.

"No," Judge Pilate said. "So you're clear about this, I shall report this incident for the special attention of the President of Law Society himself," he paused, looking at Marcia. "Don't stand there, Miss Blackwood, call security," the judge added.

"OK," I said finally, hands in the air like a terrorist under fire. "I'll leave now, but you might want to discuss this." I dropped a manila envelope on to a leather chair.

Judge Pilate's eyes dropped to the envelope, his brows narrowed. With Marcia now breathing down my face, I left the judge's chamber followed closely behind, by Marcia.

I stopped outside her office.

"You can't hang around mine either. Leave the building now or I'll call security."

"OK. Ok." I said deliberately moving slowly.

"Keep moving, Mr. Dias," Marcia prompted, "I'm going to escort you out of the building."

Then her telephone rang. She hesitated for a moment as if unsure what was more urgent, getting rid of me or answering her phone. In the end she chose the latter.

"I've had enough of your nonsense," she said heading for the telephone.

My heart was pounding.

She lifted the handset. She looked at me, her stare disapproving. I could tell she was listening with rapt attention. Suddenly she broke her gaze before adding quietly. "Yes, my lord."

She dropped the handset in its cradle, and with a flat, almost inaudible voice, said, "the Judge will see you now."

Chapter Fifteen

Judge Pilate seemed unperturbed by the revelation. At least there was little about him to betray his emotion. Instead, he stood by the window staring out like an army general under siege. His hands held together behind his back, he looked like a man considering his next move knowing there were few options.

He looked small without his wig and gown. His grey half-jacket fitted neatly with a striped white shirt, linen cuffs and silver links. His conservatively tailored trousers gave the impression of poor taste, no style. But the quality of the material stood out, the pure wool looked like it had been extracted from a special breed of sheep.

"Sit down." He said without turning, his voice steely.

I shut the door and took a few strides towards a large mahogany desk. A glossy shelf stretched across one wall, lined with books. In the far corner stood a silver basin where Judge Pilate ritualistically washed his hands after sentencing, to rid him of guilt. He had earned a reputation for his harsh sentences on those he called the scum of the society. He hated criminals and they loathed him with equal venom.

"I was right about you all along. You don't belong here. You never have and never will be," he paused. "Instead, you have consistently fought this establishment ever since you gained a foot in the door." He paused again, turning slowly to me. His face was like a deflated balloon.

Then he quickly broke his gaze and sat behind his desk, the very countenance of a man struggling to keep his feet firmly on the ground. His eyes were dull, his general disposition cool as though in quiet contemplation.

I drew a chair away from the desk and sat down.

"May be you're right," I said. "I don't belong to an establishment which systematically abuses trust society has placed in it."

He gently tugged on the sleeves of his shirt and rested his elbows on the table, hands held together.

"None of us is infallible." His tone was defensive.

"Indeed, we're all fallible," I said, rising and pacing the floor in slow deliberate strides, "but human fallibility is one mitigation you have scorned and rejected time and again in your court."

"That's different," he said quickly and looked away.

"Why do you think that?" I said.

"They're criminals."

"And so are you," I said firmly. "The only difference between you and those criminals is you've not been caught and convicted."

"Nonsense." He barked.

"Is it?" I snapped.

His head tilted slightly to one side. I stood behind the chair opposite him, hands on the headrest and met his defiant gaze.

"Let's examine the facts, shall we? Having sex with a child is a criminal offence, yes His lordship?" I said.

He shifted uneasily frowning his face.

"He's not a child." His face was dry.

"No, he's not anymore," I paused. "But he was when you first abused him."

"He was mature for his age. I'm not listening to this argument," the judge said.

Leaning forward and staring intently into his eyes, I said, "He might have been mature for his age but he was still a child."

He dropped his eyes and began to flip through the photographs.

"I didn't know he was under age. I was deceived." His voice quavered. I sat back down with a devious smile on my face. He reminded me of a trapped, desperate mouse encircled by hungry cats. He watched my every movement with a sense of hopelessness.

Finally, I said, "His lordship, that defence will not wash. Something you have often scuffed at in your courtroom when raised by defendants. These photographs only tell half the story."

He gave me a distant look. And like a cornered mouse, Judge Pilate was growing increasingly anxious, trying to figure his next escape route.

"Well?" He said.

"Perhaps I should call his father to take the stand. Am sure he would be happy to remind His lordship of the boy's age when he first entrusted him into your care."

There was silence. Judge Pilate did not offer further resistance. It wasn't just the photos that formed the evidence against him; there was also a story behind it. I had both and together they had formed a compelling case against him. Instead, his thin lips curled and a distrustful grin slowly began to seam across his face as he gazed thoughtfully into space. He was no different to anybody else. Now caught in the act, he began to weigh his options. Though there was no way of knowing what he was thinking, but one thing was clear. Whatever plan he was hatching in his mind was being assessed with ruthless zeal. Judging by his stern expression, all options would seem to be on the table including feeding me to the sharks. At last, Judge Pilate leaned back in his chair, his veined hands interlocked.

"How much do you want?" He said quietly.

I slowly walked around the back of his chair.

"Malik." I whispered in his ear.

"What about him?"

"You will release him on bail."

"I will not." He was emphatic.

"Sssh, His lordship. You hand over Malik to me, I give you my silence. Guaranteed. Plus, all photographs would be handed to you at no extra charge."

"The answer is still no." His face was ashen as if the last drop of blood had been drained from it.

"You're on the road to imprisonment and public humiliation," I said, trying to remain calm.

"Guarding the integrity of the judiciary is one ideal for which I'm prepared to die." His eyes were now as cold as steel.

I dropped my card on his table. "His Lordship has no later than 9pm tomorrow night to cooperate. Keep the photos, there's plenty more where they came from."

I began walking towards the door.

"Mr. Dias," he said softly.

I paused at the door and turned.

"What you ask is impossible. If this is the only objective you seek to achieve from this, I'd rather not endure this blackmail much longer," he said with the determination of a man about to swallow a cup full of acid.

Chapter Sixteen

I left the court building with an overwhelming sense of dread. Judge Pilate had shown little interest in playing along. His refusal to betray his office and let Malik go was a bundle of contradiction in his character. In one sense he was a dogged defender of the law and in another sense he was at ease with breaking it. His remarks echoed in my mind like the whisperings of death.

Guarding the integrity of the judiciary is an ideal for which I'm prepared to die! I'd rather not endure this blackmail much longer!

I pondered his utterances some more, every time the effect was as chilling as the one before.

Momentarily, the compulsion to force his hand grew ever more intense, the reason more urgent and compelling. Was I walking away from Lorna's last chance?

Then on deeper reflection, I managed to shrug off any suggestion to use force. The last thing I wanted was to draw unhealthy attention onto me. That might complicate things even more. Attempting to force the hands of a man with little too loose was dangerous, much like flogging a dead horse. That might only worsen the situation and how would that secure Lorna's freedom?

I picked up the phone and called Morris Ricci's number and his secretary picked up after two rings.

"Mr. Ricci, please."

"I'm afraid he's unavailable. May I know . . ."

"Put him on the line. It's Phil Dias."

"Oh! I'll put you through, Mr. Dias."

A moment later, Morris Ricci came on the line.

"Hi Phil."

"Listen up. I've got a legal argument at Guildhall Crown Court at 3pm. Can you go and get an adjournment for me?"

"Oh Phil, that's kind of hard."

"This is really important to me. Something's come up."

"How about I send a junior to do it?"

"No, Morris. I need an experienced person on this one. There's no telling how the judge might react."

There was a brief silence.

"Which judge is it?" He said finally.

"Judge Cullenham."

"Oh no, not him, I don't want to go in front of him."

"He doesn't bite, he only barks."

"That's not my idea of fun this afternoon."

"I'll buy you a drink."

"That's under-estimating the enormity of the task."

"Then I'm grateful."

"You're welcome," he paused. "Look Phil, I know this is not my business but there are rumours about."

"What rumours?"

"You know, about you behaving strangely since Dora's death, there's a talk about you taking personal delivery of a parcel today, another one about you cancelling all scheduled appointments. Like I said, it's not my business, but you'd better watch it. You know you can always count on me."

"I appreciate that, Morris. Listen, it's a long story but you know me, I couldn't hurt a soul, let alone kill someone."

"Sure, sure. All I'm saying is you're drawing adverse attention to yourself."

"Thanks, Morris. Got to run." I hung up.

***

Later that evening, the drive home was filled with concern for Lorna. Her absence had unearthed emptiness, guilt and a sense of helplessness that I had never felt before. Then a momentary surge of irritation hit me. It had taken such an unpleasant circumstance to realise how much she meant to me, how much I'd taken for granted her love that was so pure and simple.

Pulling into the garage, I turned the engine off and met a deafening silence. Suddenly, I heard a thudding sound and held my breath. Listening intently for a moment, I heard nothing. Was it my imagination? Then the car stirred. There was no mistake about it... my perception was good. I slowly got out of the car and grabbed a hammer from a pile in the corner. I crouched low, heading towards the car-rear, the hammer raised and ready to swing into action. Apprehensive, I took short cautious steps until I reached the rear of the car and looked around. There was nothing. Just then, the car stirred again. It was obvious it was coming from the boot. I cautiously unlocked it and in the dim glow of the bulb, a body lay in a foetus position.

I dropped the hammer, quickly lifted the lifeless body over my shoulder and staggered towards the corridor, hands dangling limply behind me. I put the body on the bed, removed his jacket and took a closer look at him. His skin colour was pale and he looked strangely peaceful, like an embalmed corpse. I wondered if Shadow had done this to Dandy.

Chapter Seventeen

Dandy lay still, sweating profusely and moistening his clothes. His breathing was irregular and he looked pale. There was a fresh bruise on the side of his face. The only real evidence that he had been roughed up.

Dandy was no stranger to combat situations; in fact it gave him a buzz to be chased after by police and the bad boys alike. He often boasted about his knowledge of a hundred ways to escape from danger. And it didn't matter how dangerous it was, he had a survival kit ready for any eventuality.

That fact that Dandy had been cut out cold this time was only testament to the dexterity of his assailants whoever they might be.

He stirred sputtering and rubbing at his temples, and with some obvious relief I helped him up until he sat up. He rubbed at his bloodshot eyes as he tried to make sense of it all.

Dandy had been unconscious for the best of thirty minutes. It had been anxious moments for me as I sat there agonising over what would happen if he died. How could I have convinced anyone that I had nothing to do with it? With Des O 'Reiley still prodding me in the back over Dora's murder, another suspicious death around me would have sealed my fate.

Dandy's eyes quickly darted around the room, then he forced a smile, as he realised he was in good hands. He sat up some more and put a pillow behind, scanning his surroundings. He looked at his jacket. Instinctively, I knew what he wanted; smoking was a second nature to him.

I fetched the cigar and a gold-plated lighter from his jacket pocket, suppressing a slight irritation. I wanted to hear it all but Dandy betrayed no urgency and seemed totally impervious to my anxiety.

Then he lit the cigar.

Chapter Eighteen

"When did you find me?" Dandy said as he exhaled.

"Half an hour ago..."

He heaved a sigh, running one hand through his hair.

"What happened?" I said, sitting down.

He shook his head slowly, his eyes half closed.

"The whole idea was to let you know I was in the boot before you left the staff car park."

"I don't get it?"

He gasped, massaging his neck. "I almost killed myself."

'What are you talking about? Who put you in my car boot? '

He cocked his head to one side, with great effort. "No one. I let myself in there."

Arching my eyebrows in disbelief, I said, "what are you talking about?"

"Listen," he said, impatiently. "I put myself there, but fell asleep. The idea was to draw your attention to me so you could get me to a safe place before continuing your business, ' he paused, his tone quiet, dispassionate. 'I suppose I passed out. I knew I shouldn't have had an early lunch and four glasses of wine."

"And the bruises?"

"I banged my face trying to get out of the bloody boot " He dismissed with a wave.

"Why would you get in there anyway?"

He hesitated for a brief moment.

"You're being watched - your home, your office, your every move. It was the only way I could contact you without being noticed."

I leaned back in the chair, astonished at his antics.

And with the flair of a military strategist, Dandy began to recount his entire day. He had followed me to Weng Lu 's in Soho. From his car, thirty feet from the restaurant, he had tailed me through a pair of night-vision binoculars. A sophisticated equipment, the kind used by spies, he had bought them from a broke and corrupt MI6 agent years ago, who needed money to pay off his gambling debts.

Dandy also had an extremely sensitive police scanner capable of trapping whispers from forty feet away. Underneath his seat was his favourite Heckler and Koch P7 pistol, detachable silencer and fully loaded with 9mm ammunition. He wasn't taking chances and was fully prepared for the worse as he watched from the relative safety of the car park that night.

Then he described a particularly tense moment. He had watched the ghost- like images - the ponytail Chinese man and me in the greenish light of his binoculars disappear out of view. Worried, he had considered intervening but decided against that. The scanner had failed to pick up my voice.

"Not long after you left the restaurant, a black BMW pulled up outside Wang Lu 's. Four men got into the car so I followed them," he added.

"'Did you see where they ended up?" I asked expectantly.

"I followed them to Canary Wharf."

"Where exactly?"

"Heliport," he said dismissively, drawing hard on the cigar.   "They took off in a waiting helicopter."

"Damn! I don 't like this. There must be a way of finding out who Shadow really is. We've got to stop him before he hurts Lorna." I said with hateful pain.

Dandy rubbed at his face and said quietly. "Can you give them Malik?"

I rose and made for the window. Silence punctuated the room. Without looking back, I told him everything - about Shadow. What he wanted. The blackmail. Judge Pilate. The whole lot.

Turning to him, I limply added   "I'm still waiting to see if Judge Pilate will call me with that vital news that he will release Malik."

Dandy's face was expressionless,

"Doesn't look like the old man is a team player," he said handing me a drink.

"Maybe he needs a little time to think it through."

"We don 't have time," he said emptying his glass in one gulp.   "Does he have any family?"

"I don't think we should do anything rash. He

will come round."

He glared up at me. "If you want me on this case, you've got to work with me."

My mind raced through the deepening crisis. So far, the only thing I had in my favour was Dandy.

I shrugged. "I don't know if he's got any family."

"Never mind. I'll find out myself. Which other devil would rough Malik's case if Judge Pilate weren't there?"

"Judge Forbes."

"I know of him. He is one of the Senior Seaweeds in that organisation. Been around in the system as long as I have," he paused. "A good family man, very fond of his grandchildren. He'll do just fine."

I looked at him alarmingly.

"But you've got to consult me on any decision," I said.

"Relax Phil," he said casually, smoke curling out of his nostrils. "There 's nothing complicated about what I'm thinking. If Judge Pilate won't play, I'll take him out and Judge Forbes will take his place. Simple."

Chapter Nineteen

Next morning, leaving home just after 8am and eventually turning on to the dual carriageway, I noticed a parked black BMW with tinted windows. Stealing a quick glance in the rear-view mirror, I noticed the BMW easing onto the road behind me. There was no elaborate plan to disguise their intent; it was anyone's guess as to what Shadow was up to this time.

I pulled into a petrol station, stopping in front of the pay counter. A female sales attendant shot me a disapproving look from behind the counter, and following Dandy 's instructions to the letter, I waited in the car. A moment later, the BMW drew up at the far petrol pump. Convinced that was the only car on my trail, I got out, entered the shop and bought a car wash token. I could feel eyes following my every move; it was hard to maintain my composure in this awkward situation. I returned to my car, and drove into the car wash situated at the back of the building. I wondered what they might do next, my apprehension intensifying by the second. I knew any slip up would certainly endanger Lorna.

Now in the privacy of the car wash, I jumped out of the car, made for the rear, and pulled the car boot open.

"Are you OK?" I said, helping Dandy out.

"Much better this time around," he replied with humour. He climbed out, dragging with him, a compact briefcase.

"They 're outside," I said almost whispering.

"How many of them?"

"I only saw one black BMW."

"Good. Come on, we better hurry before they get suspicious."

As we quickly settled into the car, I inserted the token and within a few seconds, a red light came on and the machine roared into action.

Resting the briefcase on his laps, Dandy called a number on his mobile phone.

"How far are you from the area?" He spoke into the phone.

Silence.

"Shall we say twenty minutes?"

"Right. One sec," he paused, turning to me. "What part of the world is this?"

"Total petrol station on A4031 heading London," I said loudly.

"Did you get that?" He spoke into the phone again. "Right. See you soon." He opened the briefcase, revealing a range of deadly weaponry. Studying them momentarily, he selected a .45 semi-automatic and a silencer, which he dutifully screwed on to the muzzle of the gun. Then he studied it fondly for a brief moment before tucking it away inside his jacket.

I stirred uneasily. It was hard to know what

was worse - the nervousness knowing that Dandy was planning to assassinate Judge Pilate and aiding it, or the pain of Lorna's abduction.

Deep in thought, I stared ahead as a mixture of water and foams gushed out from different directions engulfing the car.

"I couldn't sleep last night," I said quietly, without looking at him.

"I can tell. I've been there. Life suddenly lost its meaning after my wife was murdered seven years ago," he said impassively.

To this day, it was the one subject that still invoked a pent up fury in him. Dandy regarded his wife's killers as a bunch of butchers, a connotation to the circumstances of her murder - a slow, painful and horrific end.

"It's not sweet when you're on the receiving end of life 's bullshits," Dandy said finally. "No point losing sleep over this. Your wife's still alive and you have a chance to save her, something I never had."

"I still fear the worst."

Dandy did not respond. Instead he watched reflectively as the drier hovered towards the windscreen, stopping momentarily, and then lifting higher above the roof before disappearing in the rear like a masonic hovercraft.

He half turned to me, his eyes steely.

"It's nearly time to part company. The wash is nearly finished," he paused. "Her life's in your hands. All you have to do is follow our plans and she'll have a fighting chance, OK?"

I nodded.

"What's the earliest you can fix a bail hearing?"

"Twenty four hours notice to the prosecution is required."

"Good. Then get one arranged for tomorrow and let Shadow know when he calls."

"A lot will depend on Judge Pilate. Without securing his co-operation on this, any bail application is bound to fail."

"I know that. But make that application anyway, "his voice rose an inch. "If he hasn't phoned you by 10pm tonight, he's called your bluff. Then I'll take him out and plant Judge Forbes in the case."

"What if Judge Forbes . . ."

"Hey! Sometimes the ifs and buts are better left alone." His hand went to the door handle and without looking at me, he added, "I'll stay in touch."

Dandy hopped out of the car with the athleticism of an Olympic sprinter. Clutching his briefcase he disappeared. As the car wash lights suddenly turned green, I made my way through the forecourt and back on to the road.

I glanced in the rear view mirror and sure enough, like a faithful puppy, the BMW was back on my trail.

Chapter Twenty

That afternoon, settling down to a tray of drafts, an accumulation of the past day or so, I started leafing through them. One draft immediately stood out for two reasons. A copy had already been sent to the court and to the prosecution. And it was clear from its content that the person who had prepared it did not show a good grasp of the relevant law and practice, nor did he understand the wide-ranging implications of his ill thought out submissions. I picked up the phone and called the man responsible, Danny Taylor.

"I've seen a copy of the document you sent to the court yesterday on the Mendel's case. It's your signature on the affidavit, right?"

"Yes, Mr. Dias," he spoke softly.

"I find the submissions disturbing, Mr. Taylor. Are you not aware of the Lord Chief Justice's recent Practice Direction on this issue?"

"Yeah. Practice Direction 222/02."

"Your submissions did not reflect that?"

"What I put forward fully complied with that Practice Direction."

"You can't be serious?"

"I'm serious, Mr. Dias."

"Mr. Taylor, perhaps I'm not making myself

very clear. Now listen," I paused. "What I have in front of me makes no direct or indirect reference to that Practice Direction. Instead you made reference to the Practice Direction for an unrelated issue."

"I'm sorry, but I know what I drafted. I cannot be convinced otherwise."

I allowed a few seconds to think, suppressing a growing irritation.

"That aside, Mr. Taylor, you know the procedures. You should've had this okayed by me or by Mr. Ricci before dispatching it."

"I tried, Mr. Dias," he said with a defiant tone. 'You weren't there yesterday. And Mr. Ricci didn't want to know."

"Did you ask Mr. Ricci?"

"Yes. He said he was busy. So I got it okayed by Tobias Sevenson."

I felt a sharp pain in my stomach.

"Thanks for your time, Mr. Taylor," I said quietly and hung up. Then I called Morris Ricci.

"Can you spare a moment?"

"Sure."

"Pop over, please."

I hung up and wondered what to do. Surely, Tobias Sevenson was behind this. But had he alone been behind this elaborate charade? Was Morris Ricci part of it?

Shortly after, Morris Ricci entered my office. Though he managed a weak grin, it was progressively obvious he was troubled. His face looked pale and he was sweating profusely, perhaps in part from excessive body fat.

"You promised to cover for me yesterday."

"I got the adjournment you wanted."

"Yes, you did just that. Thanks. But that 's not my concern right now,"

"What is?"

"Why you turned Mr. Taylor away when he sought your supervision with a very critical part of our department 's work."

"Am I on trial here?" His voice rose sharply.

I studied him intently. He was uncharacteristically hostile, but I tried to mask my suspicion. Appraising the situation, I reached the only logical conclusion; Morris had switched sides.

"No, you're not on trial," I said with obvious disappointment. And pushing the affidavit across the table, I added, "but I think you should look at this."

Hesitating for a brief moment, he eventually stepped forward, picked the affidavit up and started reading it.

"Tobias Sevensen tampered with the content of that affidavit after Mr. Taylor passed it to him to be okayed," I paused. "Literally, he erased all references to the current Practice Direction, inserting incorrect one, to discredit my department and to embarrass me personally."

Morris Ricci stood there staring at me.

"How could that ever be justified, Morris?"

He shook his head imperceptibly.

"I knew he was up to no good." Morris said reflectively. "But it's not what you're thinking," he protested. "He tricked me into this."

"I don't believe this," I said with a raised voice, throwing both hands in the air and swinging the chair to one side. "How could you have allowed him to use us like this?"

"I'm sorry. I . . . I . . .don 't know. I guess I wasn't thinking straight at the time," he said, almost inaudibly.

"I trusted you, Morris."

"I said I'm sorry. I knew I shouldn't have got involved in any of this - with you, with Tobias. Can 't you guys leave me out of it. I don't know what to believe anymore," he paused. "He convinced me you had something to do with Dora's death."

"And you swallowed that?"

"Oh heck, what do I know?"

"That's ridiculous, Morris. You don't think for one moment there's a grain of truth in that?"

"Listen, I don't know what to think anymore. It 's not my bloody business. I just . . ." he stopped and ran a hand through his hair.

Then after a moment's hesitation, he continued, "the morning Dora died, you rang me to see if I'd seen her around," his voice gentle and his stare probing. "I remember looking in the staff cafe for her and discovering she hadn't come in that morning, and I rang you to tell you."

He allowed a long pause.

"What are you getting at, Morris?"

"Now I hear your position for the record is that she'd phoned you that morning on your way here

111

to say she would be off sick. If so, why were you looking for her that morning? Unless of course, she never called you as you claim."

I sat still for a moment, wanting him to go on, but he added nothing more. He looked down intently at the affidavit in his hand, fidgeting with it.

If there was ever a moment in life when no comment was the best form of defence, this was it. I felt like toast. Judging from the way Morris was looking at me, there was little doubt he considered my shocked expression as a tacit admission.

Telling Morris the truth was totally out of the question. How could I confide in a man with his mind already blocked to reason? Clearly he couldn't handle the truth, so what was the point?

Finally, Morris dropped the affidavit on the table and without looking up, said, "No one else knows about this. You can rely on my discretion." Then he left.

I closed my eyes and started thinking things through. Obviously, someone had told Morris about my claim that Dora had phoned me that morning reporting sick. That had surprised me, not least because only Levine and Detective Inspector Des O 'Reiley knew about it. And with understandable disquiet, I wondered which of the two had told him and, why?

***

"Mr. Dias," I heard a voice say. It was distant,

soft and unrecognisable. Quietly, my eyelid flipped back to reveal a figure standing across the table. At first my vision was blurred, but gradually it became clearer.

I sat up. Fully awake, rubbing my eyes for a moment, I immediately felt a sharp ache in my temple.

"I'm sorry, Mr. Dias," Tania Jones said with quizzical expressions on her face. "But I tried putting this call through and there was no answer."

I waved a hand apologetically, massaging the back of my neck and glancing at my watch. Two o'clock.

"Mr. Darlington is on the line and he's not a happy man."

"Never mind him. He was born that way."

"Shall I put him through?"

I nodded.

Tania hurried away. Within a few moments, my telephone started flashing and depressing the button, I said, "Yes Cecil. I hear you're breathing fire."

"Breathing Fire?" He retorted. "That's an understatement, damn it."

"Everyone knows how far you're prepared to receive the Lord Chancellor 's blessing."

He hesitated.

"That was really cheap," he said finally.

"But true."

A gasp of breath rattled the speakerphone.

"Why don 't you just admit you envy my position?"

"Not at all, Cecil. I want a judicial appointment that reflects my ability and professionalism. Your unscrupulous quest for crown and glory is an open secret."

"Unsubstantiated."

"It's self-evident, Cecil."

There was a brief silence.

"What 's not self-evident however is why you're putting us through this trouble."

"Trouble? What trouble?"

"Don't act dumb with me, Phil. You filed a bail application this morning, didn't you?"

"Oh that! That 's hardly putting anyone through trouble. My client is merely exercising his statutory right."

"That may be so. But the initiative was ill conceived and hopeless."

"That 's for the court to decide."

"This is insane," he said with a hint of irritation. "I don't have to be a judge to know he stands a better chance in hell than of getting bail tomorrow."

"So, let him take an early shot at a chance in hell. That 's what you want, isn't it?"

"You bet. Unless he's sensible enough to cut a deal now. Our offer won 't be on the table beyond tomorrow afternoon."

"I'll pass on your goodwill to him."

"You do that." His voice was sharp, defiant. "Just so you know, we 're going to oppose the bail application with all the resources at our disposal. I thought you might like to know that," he said and hung up.

Chapter Twenty-One

'Come in, Phil, come in.' Levine flashed a weak smile from behind his desk, waving me to a chair. He was wearing a shirt and tie, looking pale and tired. For a man who spent much of his time running a delicate high profile firm and controlling the excesses of the brainiest lawyers around, Levine had become a detached figure, almost a recluse. But he maintained strong presence beyond the firm. Rumours had it that behind a row of books in his office was an emergency exit, something he used regularly during normal times than as an emergency exit route, keeping everyone guessing if he was in or out. Not even his secretary would know because she had strict orders not to initiate a contact. Whether this was a myth or not, it worked perfectly well for Levine. He loved the gossips swirling around the place and had an army of spies within the firm who ensured he was up to date with anything that threatened him.

Dennis Dobbs sat in a leather settee facing a small glass coffee table. His hands lay on his thighs in a firm clasp, his expression unpleasant. He was the number two, but was much slower and dumber on the draw, much more likely to be emotional and irrational about his decisions. He was always angry. Although he sometimes held his own, gossips had it that he was not happy with his educational background; the fact that he had risen from rags to riches, from being totally dumb to city wise status, and despite his best efforts he remained way down the list of influential lawyers within the city.

I quickly sensed from the awkward silence and their body language that there had been a heated argument before the decision to bring me in. Hesitating momentarily and trying to be less anxious under Dobbs' stare, I sat across from Levine, wondering what was wrong.

"Mr. Dobbs has just drawn my attention to a small matter. I thought it might be more useful if you could be present," Levine said.

Dobbs made his way to the table.

"This is of the gravest concern to me," Dobbs said. "Can you explain why your department came to a halt yesterday because you suddenly decided to take an unscheduled leave of absence?"

"I'm not directly answerable to you, Mr. Dobbs," I said with a hint of irritation.

"Ah, may be not directly. But I've a right to demand an explanation for an unprofessional conduct which threatens the integrity of this firm,"

"Demand? Hell no. If Mr. Levine is unhappy with my commitment to the firm, I'm sure he will do something about it."I returned.

"That's precisely the problem, is it not. Mr. Levine here, is not prepared to show leadership or good judgement on matters relating to you," he said with a raised voice.

Levine was unusually quiet, his eyes fixed on Dobbs.

"Perhaps Mr. Levine might start showing some leadership around here after reading this."Dobbs removed a folded paper from his jacket pocket and dropped it on to the table in front of Levine. As Levine was reading it, I recognised it instantly. It was a copy of the document Tobias had tampered with. And suddenly my adrenaline surged another gear.

"Anyone could've foreseen this outcome," Dobbs continued, 'because Mr. Dias wasn't there to supervise his juniors, they carried on as best they could. In this case there's irreparable damage not only to the client but also to our standing with the court and the public."

Levine leaned back in his chair, a troubled expression on his face.

I refused to be drawn into the argument. What was the need? How could I prove Tobias had tampered with this document? After all it was Mr. Taylor's signature on it and, besides, the ultimate responsibility lay squarely on my shoulders as head of department. It wasn't looking good. And I knew it.

"There's more." Dobbs said folding his arms, looking intently into my eyes for what seemed like an eternity.

I could almost hear the sound of my heartbeat. Staring back at Dobbs with resignation...hatred, my frustration was at a boiling point. Who the hell did he think he was? I thought.

"Perhaps, you will care to explain why you refused to attend to a client who 'd come here all the way from Ireland. You could've saved the client that inconvenience. You could've spared this firm the expenses. You certainly didn't have to keep him waiting all day in the reception." His voice dropped a fraction, his tone derisive.

"He wasn't kept there all day," I said impulsively, "at least get your facts right for once."

That was a kick to the groin. It hurt.

He considered me momentarily with wry amusement. Then I realize that I 'd stepped into his trap, exactly where he wanted me to be - at his mercy and with my back to the wall. His courtroom witness cross-examination technique had paid off. When you face a wall of silence from a witness, make a wild accusation and you will break through that wall with the force of a volcano. Dobbs had succeeded in getting me to swing wildly at him from a weak point, and he knew only too well that I was there for the taking, however he wanted me. It was for me, a cruel reminder that even the best of us could be manipulated.

"Ah, perhaps not nearly as long," he returned with the glow of a pupil who got an answer right. "But the point is that you made no effort to prevent his disappointment."

"The client was made aware of the cancellation at the earliest opportunity."

"Really? You informed the client personally,

did you?"

"My secretary did. I don't see the point you're making."

"Ah, your secretary. I see. Of course, in your arrogance, you couldn't personally go to the reception and apologise to a client who'd flown across the sea to assist you in a case here?"

I broke gaze with him, pausing for thought. There seemed no easy way out of the present quagmire. At the start I'd resolved how I was going to deal with Dobbs' provocation. Now everything seemed to have spiralled out of control. Yet, knowing the man standing before me, he might not rest until he'd drawn blood. All for what? Why so much fuss about cancelling that appointment? Granted, I should've handled the cancellation a lot better, more sensitively. To that extent, Dobbs was right. But so what? Who wouldn't in my circumstances? Only if they knew my personal tragedy, perhaps they might begin to understand how my preoccupation with Lorna's safety could have clouded my reasoning in a way unimaginable. If only I could bare my heart now.

Slowly, I turned to Levine.

"I take much of the points he'd raised. I've been under pressure lately."

Levine nodded his agreement.

Dobbs cleared his throat loudly. Engaging my eyes for a moment, he finally allowed a cryptic smile. He was almost rubbing his hands in glee. He won. He hung on every moment of my demise. Dobbs, who, not surprisingly, had craved my

119

admonition, was intrigued more by Levine's expression of disappointment than by his victory.

"I will press for all matters raised here to go before the full management disciplinary committee," Dobbs added.

I immediately felt a rupture in my blood cells.

Levine leaned forward, dabbed his baldhead with a handkerchief, "Stop this now, Denis. I think you're over reacting."

"Am I?"

"You've made your point. I don't think the matters raised here are serious enough to go before the full disciplinary committee."

"Don't you now? In my time, certainly under your leadership, I've seen less serious matters referred to the committee."

"Each case is judged on their own merits," Levine insisted. "After much thought, I've reached the view that the seriousness criterion for referring matters to the committee hasn't been satisfied in this instant."

Dobbs raised his chin slightly.

"Ah, you think he's been completely professional in the way he'd behaved towards this client?"

"No, not completely professional," he paused. A slight grin was forming on Dobbs face when Levine quickly added, "but not completely unprofessional either."

"Mr. Dias is in breach of the firm's code of conduct in relation to client care?" Dobbs pressed.

"What I'm saying is that common sense ought

to be applied here," Levine said.   "Phil has a high profile case, of enormous benefit to this firm in terms of profitability and exposure. He certainly . . ."

"It's no licence to treat clients with disdain, " Dobbs interrupted.

"I'm not saying it is," Levine said impatiently. "But I say this; the pressure of this case can't be easy for Mr. Dias. We all know of his near tragic experience at the Old Bailey. That alone would have far reaching consequences on anybody's power of co-ordination and judgement."

Dobbs ignored him, turned to me, his features serious. I kept my gaze away like a child caught between two rowing parents. Then he bent slightly; grasped the edge of the table with both hands and said in firm accusatory voice, "or isn't the truth of the whole matter that you're worried about something else?"

I froze.

"Perhaps you should come clean about her," Dobbs pressed.

"What are you talking about?" My voice was hardly audible.

"Don't feign ignorance with me, Mr. Dias," Dobbs pressed almost snarling. "Shoddy work, loss of focus, the aggressive behaviour?" He breathed down my face. "Are these not signs of a man with guilty conscience?"

I swallowed fast. I was right all along. Dobbs wanted blood; he had me on the floor and was not finished.

"What…are you talking about?" I returned with the confidence of a married man caught cheating with his mistress.

"You don't sound very convincing, Mr. Dias. The whisperings are gathering momentum. Tell us all about it, Mr. Dias."

"Tell you about what?" My heart was beating furiously.

"What really happened to her," he said flashing a vindictive expression.

Rigid and wary, it felt as though blood had drained from my face. I could hear air filtering through my nostrils with the force of a hurricane. Did he know about Lorna? About Shadow?

"Her? Who's 'her'?"

"Dora, of course."

My mind went blank with rage. With lightening speed, I grabbed him, pulling him over the table, my fist crashing into his face. He fell to the floor curling into a ball, trying to protect himself from my punishing kicks.

Then I felt Levine 's hands pulling at mine arm, as he dragged me away from the tall motionless body, blood dripping down his mouth and nose, his eyes, still.

Levine knelt beside Dobbs, lifted his hand and checked for pulse. Quietly, he put the flaccid hand down turning to me, his expression grave.

I stood there staring in disbelief. Never thought I had so much violence in me, I 'd surprised even myself.

Levine looked at me; his face was devoid of

emotion. At least nothing I could discern from the placid expression. There again, he was born that way.

"What were you thinking?" He said.

He bent over Dobbs and turned him over. Blood dripped down his chin from a swelling over his right eye. His body was limp in his unconscious state. Levine picked up his wrist and checked him for his pulse again and turning to me with a stare I 'd not seen before, he said, "You've bloody killed him."

Chapter Twenty-Two

Levine slumped back behind his desk.

For what seemed like an eternity, he did not say anything or move at all. His face was impassive, his eyes almost as glassy-cold as the ones staring out of the dead body on his floor. The only difference between them was that Levine blinked occasionally, Dobbs did not - and never could again.

In that time, we had not spoken to one another, nor exchanged glances. There was hardly anything to talk about. He had a killer within his grasp; I had a witness to the killing. The question was what was Levine going to do? His mood seemed gloomy, even foul. There was no denying that the frenzy of events that preceded this mess, some anticipated and others wholly unexpected, had not been premeditated, but that didn't undermine the seriousness of the situation. Even the mitigation of provocation by the victim was not hard to find. But all that would count for nothing without Levine 's support. How much I needed him now.

For many years he had protected me, his obvious choice to succeed him. Following this revelation he had waged war as never before against dissenting voices within the firm, some grandees and others young. He had fought like a wild beast in defence of relentless attacks against me. He had ridiculed his colleagues including Dobbs during meetings convened to discredit me. He had played around ethics and the rules to suit me. In the process, he had alienated almost all his colleagues within the firm in the quest to establish me as the number one contender for the top job that even some of the objectors had stopped trying to stop him. Grandees that had proved too tough to subdue were routinely retired, only a few pockets of resistance remained but they were no threat. Even Levine understood he needed some opposition in a democratic firm, he didn't want to appear autocratic, and it looked good for the firm to appear representative.

One question took center stage in my mind - what now? What about Lorna?

Pacing the floor, cold sweat dripping down my face, and mouth dry, I could not think straight.

Weary of his punctuating silence, I sat down and looked at Levine. The death of Dobbs seemed to have pushed him over the edge, his loyalty had been tested beyond human comprehension but I wanted to know what he planned to do. Not knowing was no more punishing than knowing. Anything was better than silence.

Leaning forward, he tilted his head to one side.

"Who shall I call first - Mr. Sledge or the police?" He said quietly.

I closed my eyes momentarily as though Mr. Sledge 's name were synonymous with devastation. He was a lawyer; a specialist in murder cases and the best money could buy. Six times divorced father of two grown up daughters, Sledge had built a reputation in the city as a womanizer, and made no secret of it. He was always last out of wine bars every evening, and was often sighted falling over on his way home. Although Sledge showed no self-control over anything in skirts and spirits, he was razor sharp in the courtroom when he was sober. He had the knack of bashing judges to submission, making scintillating speeches to the jury and refocusing their attention from damaging evidence against his client.

"Mr. Levine . . ."

"Please!" He waved his hand dismissively in the air. He was a man in no mood to compromise. "Don't make it any more difficult for me. I can 't cover up for you," he paused. "I cannot do more than to allow you the privilege of consulting with Mr. Sledge before I call the police."

"I don't want you to cover up for me but I need your help now. All I ask is a little more time to tidy up a few things before I can face this." I pleaded.

He shook his head. "Too dangerous. I risk being an accessory to murder. Then there's the wider implication." He said firmly.

"I swear, I'm going to take responsibility for this."

"Then do it."

"I can 't . . . I mean, not just yet. I've got to

126

sort out a few things first."

"I can 't imagine anything more pressing than your present predicament."

"I know, I don 't care what happens to me. I'm more concerned about others. My arrest would end my involvement with Malik 's case. There 's a bail hearing coming up tomorrow and I need to be there, for everyone 's sake. I really need you to stand with me on this one."

"I don 't think this is a wise thing to do," he said reflectively, leaning back in his chair.

I rose on my feet and started pacing the floor again. Surrendering now was not an option. That would effectively disconnect me from Malik's case and how could I then meet Shadow's demands? Surely there would be no point going to prison over Dobbs if I couldn't save Lorna 's life. My pulse suddenly shot up to dangerous levels as I quietly cursed anyone who would dare stop me. Not even Levine, I thought, staring coldly at him. Nothing was going to stand in the way of saving Lorna 's life, I decided.

Then Levine finally sat forward, his eyes hard. He swivelled the chair gently from side to side, staring down thoughtfully at the desk 's surface. It was not easy to decode the facial expression of a man with no emotion, every expression appeared the same, but every expression varied in intensity and purpose. Was he reconsidering? I watched with bated breath as he loosened his tie and undid the top buttons of his shirt.

He lifted the receiver and dialled a number.

"Miss Reid," he said without looking at me. "Cancel all my engagements for the rest of the day. I won 't be disturbed for any reason." He hung up.

"Thanks," I said quietly. "What about this?" I gestured towards Dobbs' body.

"Just get the hell out of here."

***

I darted onto the corridor disappearing into the gents. Staring into a full-length mirror, I examined my reflection. I experienced a whole range of emotions, from fear to the deepest guilt, to an almost uncontrollable grief, and there was the shock, the disbelief. Suddenly a knot formed in my stomach. The cruel reminder that I was now a killer, a fugitive, was simply too much to bear.

Suddenly overcome by the memories of Dobbs' lifeless body on that floor, of the blood trickling down his cheeks, I felt as if my head were spinning, my body paralysed. I closed my eyes momentarily, inhaled deeply, shook my head and abruptly reeled my thoughts in. Dobbs was after all a nasty man; his obnoxious behaviour was crystal clear. Even this reminder failed to rid me of guilt; he did not deserve to die. But nothing could bring him back now and for Lorna 's sake, I could not dwell on it.

I heard the door open and close and stiffened to attention. I caught a reflection in the mirror. It was only a junior, I noted with obvious relief before dashing off.

Quickly, I made my way down the corridor. Nearing the lift, I heard a voice coming from the reception lounge. The mention of Dobbs' name immediately made my blood run cold. Steadying myself, I passed the lift, stopping by the staircase, listening intently.

"I can only apologise, sir." I overheard Tobias Sevenson say.

"That doesn't help us in the slightest," a male voice replied, the undertone of tension in his voice detectable. "Mr. Dobbs understands the significance of today's meeting to the mergers deal. Yet he's chosen to be away today. This is incredible."

"I'm sure there's a good explanation for this," Tobias said defensively.

"What explanation might there be for jeopardising six months of hard negotiations, costing us close to three quarters of a million pounds in legal fees alone?"

"Again, I can only apologise on behalf of Mr. Dobbs," Tobias pleaded. "I'm afraid he didn't leave any instructions as to how we might proceed. I'm sorry I'm unable to help. The conduct of this matter rests solely with him because of the complex and sensitive nature of it. I must add this is uncharacteristic, even his personal secretary knows nothing about his whereabouts."

Retreating quickly to the solitude of the lift, I

felt certain numbness, guilt.

The ding-dong sound of the lift brought me back to life, and stepping off it, I gasped.

"Good afternoon, Mr. Dias. What timing?"

Chapter Twenty-Three

"Bad timing, Inspector, am on my way out, " I returned with a flash of irritation, hurrying towards the staff car park.

"What a shame," he said following me closely, "All I need is a few minutes of your time."

I did not respond nor stop.

"Mr. Dias," he shouted after me. "You know, taking you down to the police station has crossed my mind. But I thought you might feel more comfortable talking to me here."

I stopped and turned. He walked towards me with that familiar boyish grin. He knew what he was doing; he was perfectly at peace with creating bad blood between us in the quest to solve the murder. Since the murders no real progress had been made despite the co-operation given to the detective and his team. They had probed in secret, then prowled openly every inch of the way and they found nothing. If they were murdered, the killer was no novice; he had been careful and methodical leaving very few clues. Despite his best efforts, Des appeared to be no closer to catching the killer; his mood hadn't been helped by political pressure to solve the crimes. The Home Secretary 's re-election depended on the country feeling safe, the mayor of London 's credibility depended on lower murder rates in the city, and both wanted answers from the detectives however trivial or irrelevant, any explanations were enough to calm nerves.

"I'm not under suspicion for these deaths, am I Inspector?" I said.

"Please call me . . ."

"To hell with calling you Des. I ask you this, am I under suspicion for these deaths?"

He reacted calmly to my outburst, his eyes fixed on me.

He finally spoke. "Just routine sir. In this type of investigation, a degree of suspicion usually falls on people who knew the victim or who last saw them."

"I agree. But it 's beginning to look pretty much like I'm your main suspect." The spark in my eyes was obvious. He hesitated.

Then he dropped his eyes and took a step forward. "I have orders to arrest you on suspicion of Dora Simpson 's murder."

I felt a sinking feeling in my stomach. "What?"

He held his hand in the air.

"But there won 't be any need for that if you co-operate fully." He looked very serious now. Even his familiar affable disposition had gone.

"What do you want from me?" I said, barely containing my impatience.

He took two short strides away and leaned against a dirt encrusted Toyota, he didn't mind if his coat gathered more dirt than it already had. His sky blue eyes squinted against the mid-day sun.

"This of course, is routine," he said as he pulled out a notebook and pen from his pocket. "I trust you can clear these matters up for us." He leafed through his notes, without looking up and said "Is it still your recollection that she phoned you on the morning of her death?"

"Yes."

"You see," he began with a ring of cynicism in his voice, "our problem is this . . . a list of calls made from her telephone on that date, which we have obtained from the network providers does not confirm your account. The company's telephone number is on that list, of course, confirming Levine 's account that Dora called him that morning to report her illness," he paused for a moment. "But your number is not on that list." His eyes were searching for an answer.

"That 's my recollection."

"Do you see my difficulty, Mr. Dias?"

"Which is what, exactly?"

"Well, if she called you that morning as you said, your number should be on the itemised statement." A lingering smile spread across his face.

"That conclusion would be correct if anyone could say with certainty that she made the call to me from her home telephone."

"You know," he said nodding reflectively, "I thought that might be one possibility . . . a really clever contribution, Mr. Dias." The inflection in his voice did very little to reassure me. Then he added, "But then there 's the call she made to Levine at 08.24 hours lasting a little over a minute." For a moment he held me in his fixed stare.

I kept my composure.

"If she made the two calls that morning, possibly minutes apart, she could only have made them from the same telephone. Do you see?"

Secretly, I could see that.

"Inspector, that's only one of possible interpretations."

"I know. But this is by far the most compelling."

"You can say that, Inspector. Also compelling is the possibility that she might not have made those calls successively. Perhaps, even half an hour apart - it is plausible she might have made them from different telephones."

He stared at me with a benign grin.

"You know, I can see why you're paid so much." His sarcasm was evident. Then he scribbled a few notes and flipped a few more pages of his notebook.

"Dora 's personal diary for the current year is missing. Have you seen this diary by any chance?"

"No."

"Do you know of any reason why anyone might take her personal diary?"

I shook my head. "Do we know for sure that she kept a personal diary for the current year?"

"No, we don't know for sure. But only Dora herself could say that with greater certainty."

"So why are you pursuing the premise that there might have been a diary?"

"Because, we found her previous diaries dating back ten years."

I shrugged. It was a reasonable assumption. I thought.

"One more thing, Mr. Dias." His voice dropped.

I raised my eyebrows and said nothing.

"Can you think of any reason why anyone might tear off a page from your department's diary, which contained an entry she 'd made the day before she was murdered?"

"A page was torn out of my department's diary?"

He nodded quietly.

"And we know for sure that she wrote on this page?"

"Forensics." His tone was emphatic. "Analysis of the impression on the succeeding page gave us the breakthrough."

I felt dots of cold perspiration on my face. Had Dora mentioned the fax message? How much information had she divulged in the entry? Who tore the page off?

'Inspector . . . '

Des waved a hand in the air. "Please don't ask me what this entry says. I'm not at liberty to do so. All I can tell you at this stage is that she knew about something and someone was uncomfortable about what she knew...if that makes sense. We also know she had planned to speak to a freelance journalist and expected a reward for her troubles. But she hadn't gambled on paying the ultimate price." Des' face was expressionless.

My heart was beating rapidly, my thoughts racing.

"We have obtained a statement from that journalist who could only tell us that Dora seemed frightened and wanted to speak to him urgently. They arranged a meeting on the day she died, but she never turned up. Of course, we now know why."

There was a short pause.

"Do you know why Dora might want to talk to the journalist?"

I shook my head.

He hesitated momentarily. It was the demeanour of a man onto something big, but was keeping his own counsel. I recognized it. Things were suddenly critical, time of their essence. It was like a game of chess. The next move required nerves of steel whoever made it first.

"I want to speak to your wife to verify your alibi," he finally said. His determination was clear. "We've checked with the port authorities and there's no record of your wife leaving the country. Mr. Dias, where is your wife?"

Chapter Twenty-Four

Back at home I sat on the couch, deep in thought. Des Reiley's intrusion was bad enough. The basis of his suspicion, was a combination of circumstantial evidence here and there and he seemed convinced he'd got his man. The lie I told from the start was my undoing, more lies followed to cover the first lie, and so it spiralled out of control placing me in Des' sight. He was clear about that, he wasn't going to be swayed any other direction because of the collective expectation to name a suspect, to arrest a suspect, to keep London safe again.

I reverted to Lorna and wondered for the umpteenth time if she was safe. I checked the time, 7.45pm. There was still not a whisper from Judge Pilate. Had he called my bluff?

Wondering how Dandy had got on, I dialled his number.

"Dandy . . . it's Phil."

"Where are you?"

"I'm at home. Things haven 't gone so good my end."

"Oh no. Don't tell me you've screwed up."

"Phil, don 't worry about that. This line is safe. I've had it checked, so come on tell me, what's happened?"

"You're not going to believe this."

"Try me."

"I attacked Dobbs in Levine's office. I went crazy and . . . well, he's dead."

"Oh fuck no. In Levine's office . . . Holy shit. You couldn't find a more private pad?"

"It 's ok. Levine gave his word. He'll cover up for me until tomorrow. Just in time to wrap this whole business up."

"Does he know about Lorna 's situation?"

"Oh no. No way."

"Did you manage to fix the hearing for tomorrow?"

"Yeah."

"Has Judge Pilate called?"

"Not a word. Any luck on your side?"

"Still on his case," he said gravely. "He's a hard one to track, but we'll hunt him down. One of my boys is holding out in his home as we speak. He was last spotted, driving into court."

"Surely, he can't still be in the court?" I said with a fleeting glance at my watch.

"We'll find out soon enough," Dandy said.

"I'm really worried now."

"You worry too much. You need to remain focused. Meanwhile, don't go knocking any more bodies down. I've got to run." He hung up.

A wave of dark thoughts hit me. Dandy didn't seem so sure. Had the entire plan gone horribly wrong?

My gaze slowly settled on a portrait of Lorna in

the far corner of the living room. It was one of her with sparking eyes, tanned skin, long hair, her full breasts stood against a silky dress. She was smiling with her beautiful teeth. She was only twenty-four years old, then a tenacious prosecuting counsel who made it her goal to lock away all domestic violence criminals. Her fiery temper had stood her in good stead amongst her peers. Once, Lorna was the prosecuting counsel in a case involving a rich Greek who had caused death by dangerous driving. The Greek had mowed down an eight-year old boy and denied he was the driver, only after he hired a clever lawyer to kill the case. There'd been little evidence; even so, it was largely circumstantial. Identification was an issue. Even witnesses who had previously identified the Greek suddenly changed their story, whilst some failed to recollect his identity, others said it was a black driver. There was a world of difference between the two races, the defence case couldn't be stronger, whilst the prosecution case was in tatters. To complicate the mood of the prosecuting team even more, the Greek refused to co-operate with any ID parade. He didn't see the point in handing his head to his enemy, he was in the driving seat and wasn't ready to throw it all away. Frustrated, Lorna relied on the remaining witnesses who could not be bribed to lie, two children, an eleven-year-old boy and a twelve-year-old girl. Although they saw what happened, saw the driver, but they were in shock. The criminal justice system with its paper filling, incessant interviews and re-interviews did little to lift the minors' mood. Not a lot going Lorna's way and she needed more and fast. To make a bad situation worse, she had conniving police officers as witnesses, who swore blind to something they only perceived through reading minds. The Greek 's lawyer proved interminably tough, he was determined to get his rich client off and maintain his recognition in the criminal defence fraternity. Half way through the trial, the defence lawyer had slaughtered Lorna 's remaining witnesses, leaving the police officers dusting their hats and blaming each other for doing such a bad job at falsifying evidence. Similarly, he tore the memory of the twelve year old girl to pieces, so much that she changed her original statement ten times, crying profusely, convinced she might have made them up from watching Harry Potter's films. Lorna was in tears too; such was the degree of devastation. Next, the politicians were united in calling for a change in the law on cross-examination of children in courts, but the public didn't take them seriously. Everyone understood the politics, there was always a knee jerk reaction to tragedies from politicians - that was how they were, more like how they were made. During a short recess, the defence lawyer was having lunch when Lorna walked up to him and slapped him so hard in the face that his lunch flew out of his mouth landing several feet away. "That 's for tearing that little girl apart in the witness box," she said through gritted teeth. "I wonder how much it 's worth getting that man off knowing he killed a little boy," she added before storming out to rapturous applause, but the defence lawyer didn't join in, instead he stared in disbelief. He tried to realign his jaw, and made little success of it. The next day, when it fell on the defence lawyer to cross-examine Lorna 's last witness, the eleven year old boy, through a video link, sad eyes from all sections of the courtroom settled on the little boy as if he were a sacrificial lamb being led to the slaughter. No one had forgotten what happened to the last witness, everyone feared the worse and even Lorna barely looked up. After a momentary hesitation, the defence lawyer said, "James, can you see a screen to your left?" The boy looked to his left nodding almost imperceptively. "Don 't be afraid, James. I'm going to ask you to watch that screen carefully and you will see faces appearing on it," the lawyer said gently. "Would you please say 'stop' if you see the man who was driving the car that killed Andrew." Silence. James watched the close-up shots and suddenly his breathing increased. He was now wearing the face of a child watching a horror film late at night. The defence lawyer said, "James, are you ok? Have you seen the person who was driving the car that killed Andrew?" James nodded tearfully. "Ok, James, you're doing fine. Just this last question and I'm going to get off your back, ok. It's important you're sure it's that person. Which of these faces, is it?" James watched the faces some more. "It's him. It 's that man," James shouted hysterically pointing at the Greek. A loud gasp erupted in the courtroom. The judge banged his gavel twice and then with a baleful stare, waited until the last sound had died away. The defence lawyer turned to the judge. 'Your honour, the defence accepts that the defendant has been positively identified, and I have no further questions for the witness.' The Greek was convicted, justice done. The Greek went to prison and vowed to cut his lawyer's throat and feed him to the wolf. The lawyer was afraid of the threats but he pretended not to care, to his mind he had done the right thing after all justice was seeing the guilty punished. In addition, he got a huge bouquet of roses and a surprise party for his troubles. At the party organised in his honour, before more than a hundred guests, Lorna proposed to her hero, which I readily accepted. And we had remained inseparable since.

Well, until now, I thought with a pang of irritation.

Chapter Twenty-Five

Shortly after 10.00am the next morning, I pulled into a parking space near the entrance of the court. The pressure mounted with each minute that passed. There was still no word from Judge Pilate. No answer to my request. It looked as though judge Pilate had chosen to defend the cause come what might. He would not throw judgement, not even under pain of public humiliation and imprisonment. That was what I feared the most. The hope of securing Lorna safe and well was fading with every passing minute.

Minutes before the hearing, another level of pressure was building up; reality was weighing down on my shoulders thick and fast. Dandy was silent, and he would never abandon his commitment without first telling me. He planned and executed his missions carefully, always mindful of those who placed their trust in him and was keen not to disappoint them. My worst nightmare was unfolding, and fast.

The court was quiet - no journalists, no security barriers, no armed police. This was hardly surprising. Bail hearings attracted no more than a fleeting interest in the media. But a different crowd laid siege to the court. Tourists. Perhaps, tired of prodding the Cathedral nearby and other tourist attractions, and determined to make the most of their holiday, they were embracing a change of scenery. The attendance of members of the public in courts in anticipation of the usual theatrical display of clowns in wigs and gowns was a popular pastime in this city. They clustered around the court's notice board to see if a name was recognisable, if a case made the papers, which was the indication that a case would entertain.

I stopped behind the crowd to check the notice board, scanned a row of listed cases for the day, and located Malik's name. Court number 4.

As I dashed off, I ran into a man standing next to me and apologised. But he didn't acknowledge me, I cursed quietly under my breath. He was wearing a long brown coat and a hat that swallowed half his forehead. A rimless pair of glasses hung loosely on his nose. His grey moustache was well manicured and glossy, curling over his upper lips. He was calm. Then I felt a slight tug at my jacket.

"Hey!" I shouted with furrowing eyebrows.

A few heads turned to look at me, as though I were some freak. I knew what I felt, this man tugged at my jacket, perhaps he was not a tourist, he was probably a pickpocket. Then he swiftly disappeared into the court.

I checked my pocket, and found a folded paper. Puzzled, and quickly glancing around I unfolded it. "Meet me in the gents, now." it read. I was breathing even harder. Was this Shadow? Maybe he had followed me here to monitor the progress on the bail hearing. I quickly left trailing the mystery man.

I approached the court's security desk; the man was not there. Only a frail man, perhaps in his nineties, was waiting to be scanned through security- a stark reminder that the court was taking the escalating threat of terrorism seriously.

A bulky uniformed security guard was standing behind a large metal scanner. He looked as though he didn't want to be there, his face showed the worse kind of fatigue. It was either that or he thought he deserved a better pay for the risk he was taking. Even his body language betrayed a deep-seated discontentment as he waved the frail looking man forward.

Apart from a handful of people loitering beyond the checkpoint, there was little else. There was still no sign of the mystery man.

"Anything in your pockets, sir?" The security guard said, more like a shout at the frail looking man.

There was no response.

The guard shook his head, in utter disgust. He didn't care if anyone found his customer service objectionable, his exasperation and general foul attitude suddenly triggered murmurings from behind me.

The guard swallowed and flashed a stiff smile; he looked less fierce.

The frail man smiled back but made no other effort. He didn't look like a man going anywhere important.

"Is there anything in your pocket, sir?" The guard repeated, and this time, his voice was gentle.

But even that failed to provoke any response from his customer. Instead the frail man stared at the guard, smiling as though he were seeing something no one else could.

I looked back. A long queue had formed and growing. I checked the time and resisted a strong urge to push in front. The last thing I wanted was to keep Shadow waiting in the toilets. Being a man for whom power and manipulation was everything, delays would be dangerous.

"I wonna see Marshall Hall," the frail man finally said, his jaw unsteady. He spoke in a broad Texan drawl.

I considered him with obvious pity.

The guard showed no emotion.

"Empty your pockets, sir" The guard said.

"I wonna see Marshall Hall," the frail man said. "Even the best in the States is no match to his oratorical ability. Last time I saw him, I was fifteen years old. A truly great man, make no mistake about that," he added laughing heartily. But he suddenly stopped when no one else had joined in.

"I don't know a Mr. Hall Just empty your pocket, sir, the guard said gesturing towards the metal scanner. "Any keys, mobile phones, wallets?"

Suddenly the American froze. He inclined his head towards the guard and frenetically ran his feeble hand behind his ear. His hand was shaking. It was not clear if he thought the guard wanted him on the metal scanner. But one thing was certain. He was looking at the scanner with incredulous horror, his hand fumbling behind his ear. Then he turned his head as fully as he could without breaking his neck and engaged my gaze. He was obviously nervous. I gave him a sympathetic nod. Even that didn't seem to calm his anxiety.

"I'm sorry guys," a female voice shouted from the back of the queue. She pushed her way to the front, waving a hand apologetically at a bunch of angry faces. "I'm sorry," she told the guard. "He's my grandfather. I didn't know when he wandered off. He's always embarrassing me. Would you believe this? I've been searching everywhere for him. Sorry guys." She flashed an uneasy smile before slapping a hearing aid in her grandfather's ear. "Stop losing them," she snarled.

Then the security check continued much quicker, much to everyone's relief.

As I made my way down the hall towards the gents, the frail American waved at me.

"Hey buddy. Is Marshall Hall here today?"

"Sorry, am running late," I said without stopping.

"Grand-dad, I'm not gonna keep telling you the same thing over and over again. Marshall Hall died sixty years ago," his granddaughter shouted into his earpiece, her frustration evident.

Chapter Twenty-Six

The toilet was spacious, well lit, with a set of urinal systems fastened onto the wall. A large mirror towered above a row of sparkling sinks reflecting the lights. There were three lavatory cubicles in the far right corner. The room was empty except for the middle cubicle that was occupied.

I hesitated momentarily, my heartbeats were faltering. Suddenly, the cubicle opened an inch and a pair of eyes scanned the surroundings, the movement seemed more urgent than casual, yet there was something about the purpose that was mischievous.

"In here," a voice said quietly.

I responded with the same urgency and hurried towards the cubicle, careful not to draw attention to myself. Though I worried about my safety, there was no time to put things into perspective. One moment I was relieved and excited that Shadow had made contact with me, with that some hope of getting Lorna back safe and well. The next moment I was fearful for Lorna knowing that judge Pilate was not playing ball. The hope gave me courage and suppressed all fear.

The cubicle thrust wide open.   "Come on,"

Dandy waved me on.

"Oh my God!" I let out a suppressed gasp, standing there for a time, transfixed. His disguise was perfect. Even as I stared intently at him, he looked nothing like him. Something between an ageing scientist and a moneylender would be a fitting description. The initial surprise soon gave way to disappointment and relief. On one part, disappointment because it wasn't Shadow after all, the one person who would have led me closer to Lorna. On the other part, relief because Dandy was here at long last to tell me whether his plan had worked, if not what else we might do to make judge Pilate comply with our demands.

I hurried into the cubicle.

"You fooled me," I said, closing the door and leaning on it.

"Got no choice. You're being followed. At least this way, we can stay a step ahead," he said, almost whispering.

"Listen, we haven't got all day. Have you heard from Judge Pilate?"

I shook my head.

He hesitated.

"What's wrong?" I said.

"No one has seen the old man in the six to twelve hours."

"You think he's in hiding?"

"Your guess is as good as mine."

"He can't just . . ."

"Sssh!" He pressed his index finger on his lips.

The door clicked shut. Footsteps faded in the

urinary area, and there was a brief silence. There followed the familiar sound of a belt buckle rattling, then the sound of a zip being undone. Silence. He broke into a song, something between the hum of bees and a roaring lion. He paused and burped loudly. "Aah, that's better," he muttered, then more singing. The urinary system flushed. He zipped up, followed by the same rattling sound. He ran the tap, and moments later, the hand-drier went off - finally the footsteps faded towards the door, which opened and clicked shut.

"It's not safe in here. I've got to run," Dandy broke the silence.

"Tell me. What do you think has happened to him?" I asked anxiously.

"Not a clue. All we know is he didn't return to his house last night. And he didn't make it to court this morning."

I looked at him expectantly.

His shoulders shot up and down. "Maybe he's killed himself."

"You think so?"

"My guess. Maybe it was all too much for the bastard," Dandy said with a hint of aggression.

I thought for a moment.

"What do we do now?"

"Stick with the plan. That's why I'm here. If he's anywhere in the building, I'll find him. He won't make court alive." His eyes were steely cold.

"How about Judge Forbes?" I said.

"That's sorted. He's going to hear the bail

application, and he understands what he must do."

He looked at his watch.

"Are you sure . . ."

"Sssh," he interrupted again.

The door opened and clicked shut. Slow but determined footsteps echoed towards the cubicles. Suddenly, our cubicle door was being pushed in. Gently at first, but it soon became more forceful.

For a moment, we stood motionless. Dandy was calm; his eyes were alert as he listened intently.

"Open the Goddamn door, Marshall Hall. I know you're in there."

Chapter Twenty-Seven

"Phil."

I stopped, half-turning.

Cecil Darlington walked grim-faced towards me, his assistant dutifully trailing along. He was wearing an impeccably tailored single-breasted suit and looked more like a successful bank executive than a lawyer. He was pale and tired, but displayed no visible discomfort. His manners were somewhat less assertive, almost uninspiring and his smile, benign and insincere. The smell of some strong aftershave quickly pervaded the hall.

"Morning."

"Morning."

"We have to talk," Cecil said.

"Now?" I glanced at my watch.

"I'm afraid so."

"OK."

"The conference room over there is empty," he said, and turning to his assistant, he added, "I'll talk with Mr. Dias alone. Please let the Clerk know we're here."

When we were settled in the conference room and the door was closed, he leaned on the wall, his hands folded above his stomach. He gazed momentarily at the floor. There was nothing to look at but the wall, a table and two chairs on either side, but he seemed far removed from reality.

I drew one chair and sat down. For a moment, I looked at him. I had no idea what he wanted. Whatever his motive, it was a dramatic start to the morning and he was doing well at it.

"It's just been brought to my attention that Judge Howard is unavailable," he said finally.

I managed a straight face, trying hard to suppress my delight. I inclined my head to one side.

"You make it sound as if it's a hopeless situation."

"Oh no no. Not quite hopeless," he said quickly.

"So?"

"But it's unsettling somewhat," he said.

"Unsettling?"

He nodded.

"How so?"

He hesitated for a few moments, trying to suppress a certain anxiety.

"Come on Phil. It's not hard for you to see how his absence presents some difficulty," he said.

"Difficulty? What difficulty? You mean the court can't arrange a replacement for him?"

"I didn't say that," he returned with a hint of exasperation.

"Then I'm missing the whole point. What exactly is the difficulty?"

"Judge Forbes is going to hear the case. Quite frankly, we find this objectionable." His demeanour was now ruthless.

"Why?"

"I don't think Judge Forbes can handle such a case of extreme sensitivity and importance. That's why." His voice was firm.

"Nonsense. He's much more experienced than Judge Howard," I protested.

"That may be so. I give you that. But there's much more to being a judge than mere experience alone, you know."

"Of course, I know. The ones in your pay roll, you mean?"

He closed his eyes momentarily as if he were having trouble swallowing something.

"Listen, the point is this. Judge Howard has followed this case from the beginning. He knows the facts and issues in this case."

"Don't be silly, Cecil. A bail application involves no complex application of the law. Even lay magistrates make decisions every day on bail applications," I said.

He flashed a mean smile and thrust his hands deep in his pockets. His head tilted back in a sudden gesture of defiance. "I'm not prepared to let a liberal judge like him preside over a case of this significance."

"What are you afraid of, Cecil?"

"Am not afraid of anything. You miss the point, pal." His voice rose sharply.

"No, I am not missing the point. What you're looking for is a competitive advantage, and Judge Howard is the only one you can trust to give it to you, right?"

"Nonsense. What do you know about how this establishment is run? Listen to me. The real heroes are the likes of Judge Howard. People like him have made great personal sacrifices to safeguard society against the criminal fraternity you seek to protect. So don't come up with that conspiracy bullshit. He's a hero, my hero, your hero." He was now a picture of a snarling bulldog.

There was an awkward silence.

He closed his eyes and ran his hand through his hair. Darlington had always been a fiery person, especially when he was rattled, a trait that didn't particularly bother him because it was in his DNA. This time he seemed more troubled than usual and he wasn't the sort to betray his inner thoughts. It could be a number of things. The fatigue from preparing Malik's case, the trauma of Judge Pilate's inexplicable absence, or the dread of Judge Forbes hearing the bail application. Any one of these was enough to set him off.

"I'm sorry. I didn't mean to raise my voice," he said quietly. "Our differences aside, we've got a situation to deal with here. I'm going to ask for an adjournment if it's OK with you."

"Hell no." My response was emphatic.

He considered me for a moment, his shoulders sagging and his chin was buried in his chest. He was unfazed. I could tell instantly that he was planning his next move. It was in his genes to go down fighting. Now he seemed as though he were struggling to find the words to define his next move. He just stared.

A rap on the door interrupted the meeting. His assistant entered, avoiding eye contact with me. She seemed a little anxious, and turning to her boss, she managed a sad smile.

"The usher has indicated that the judge is ready," she said and made a quick retreat.

***

The usher, a middle-aged woman, was waiting in the hall when we finally joined her. She quickly glanced at her watch, muttered "morning" in a bad-tempered way and made her way towards the stairs. We filed after her up the stairs, through the long corridor, passed Judge Pilate's chamber and finally entered the last room on the landing.

The room was bland. Apart from a desk, four chairs encircled a coffee table, and little else. The usher opened the window and adjusted the blinds.

"I'll let the judge know you're here," she said quietly and walked away.

I sat across from Darlington who was gently massaging his temples. His anxiety was understandable. He and Judge Forbes were like cat and mouse. For many years, Darlington had been careful to avoid appearing in his court. Now, this. Judge Forbes would welcome this opportunity to chastise him for all those years of backstabbing and dishonour, and nobody understood this better than Darlington himself. He knew he was about to receive as much as he had given for a long time.

I checked my watch and immediately got a hostile glance from Darlington's assistant. She didn't seem naturally obnoxious. But she'd been in the trade long enough to know how to play her part. Now, her team was sinking and bad attitude towards me was all she could offer to show solidarity with her boss.

Then there was a light tap on the door. We all rose to our feet as the door swung gently inward and Marcia swept through, clutching a bundle of papers.

I froze to attention, wide-eyed.

Judge Pilate bounced into the room with the athleticism of a youth, and sat behind the desk. He gave us an imperceptible nod as he spread his papers on the table.

It was difficult to ignore the pounding in my chest. Even prickly heat had formed on my temples. I stole a glance at the other side. The expression on his assistant's face summed up their relief. Her eyes sparkled with delight. Even Darlington seemed stunned for a moment - genuinely surprised. The dour expression on his face had gone. Instead, a sadistic smile curled treacherously in the corners of his mouth like a mischievous brat as he slowly turned to me.

Where the hell did he come from? I thought, staring blankly ahead, like a hypnotised patient.

Chapter Twenty-Eight

Judge Pilate looked calm as he thumbed through the documents on his desk. He took a few moments and scanned through the papers, with the seriousness of a man who had the weight of the world on his shoulders. He turned a few more pages, some he read with deep concentration, and others he showed little interest over. Only the occasional squeezing movement of his forehead showed he was taking in information. Finally he took a deep breath and looked around. He leaned back in his chair, his eyes blinking rapidly, looking from one face to another. When he engaged my gaze, his disdain was obvious.

"Yes, Mr. Dias." His voice was steely.

I explained as carefully as I could why my client should get bail. His right to bail. The fundamental right to liberty. The Prosecution's objection to bail on grounds he was a flight risk.

I paused, breaking his gaze momentarily. "I've not been shown a shred of evidence to support the Crown's position." I paused.

Judge Pilate was staring at the floor. He had a distant look in his eyes, and I couldn't tell if he was listening to me or thinking about something else.

"Does his lordship want me to take the court through the affidavit?" I said deliberately.

He did not respond.

I studied the judge for a brief moment and cleared my throat loud enough to bring him back from what seemed like a deep reflection. Then realising the spectacle he'd caused, he shifted uneasily. His lips pursed firmly and he quickly assumed control. He quietly arranged the papers on his desk. Not that they were a mess in the first place – he was just doing anything to deflect attention from this uncharacteristic lapse of concentration. Then he looked at me expectantly.

"My lord, would you like me to take you through the affidavit?"

"No," he said gravelly. "I've been greatly assisted by the affidavit. I will come back to you if need be. Thank you." Then he turned to Darlington. "Yes."

Under the doleful gaze of the judge, and with an encouraging grin from his assistant, Darlington leaned forward in his chair. He quietly waved aside a prepared text being offered by his assistant, and with a firm, resonant voice, he started to unravel his argument against bail.

Yes, the defendant had a statutory right to bail. Yes, the Crown recognised the defendant's rights to liberty under the 1998 Act. But no, bail would be inappropriate. Malik Henman was a flight risk. The seriousness of the offences was such that a substantial custodial sentence would be likely. Then there were his international connections. The

159

sophistication of the crimes hadn't been seen since the infamous train robbery. Trial was imminent; he would fail to turn up if released.

He had access to huge wealth. More than enough to stimulate a third world war. Intelligence had tracked the money from banks around the world, onward to a bank in the Bahamas, then to Switzerland, where no one could find it and the money trail stopped. How could he be trusted? Bail had to be refused, he paused.

For a moment, it seemed he would never stop. Every conceivable theory under the sun had been minutely dissected with clarity and, with force. Throughout his submission, he had raised questions about this and that, nothing of significance, just unsavory records served up to make Malik appear as if he were going to unleash a terror of Armageddon proportions.

There was silence. If Judge Pilate had listened to the submissions, there was little evidence of it. He didn't move, he barely flinched but maintained a blank stare across the room.

There was no way of knowing how the judge was thinking. In the ensuing silence, I sat on the edge of my seat, sweating profusely. Had he already decided to refuse the bail application? How would Shadow react if that happened? Would he kill Lorna?

As if on cue, Judge Pilate removed his glasses and examined them for a moment.

"Mr. Darlington, isn't the main flaw in your argument that you cannot produce a shred of evidence to support your submissions that this defendant is a flight risk? Does it not follow from that, that this difficulty as it were, would make your position untenable" His eyebrows furrowed as he looked expectantly at Darlington.

Darlington allowed a moment and adjusted his tie. "My Lord, we accept there's no concrete evidence to support what we assert against this defendant," he paused, "however, when all the circumstances of the case: his international connection, the international dimensions to the offences, his limitless resources, the gravity of the offences being alleged, are viewed as a whole, they collectively form the evidence to conclude he is a flight risk. And that in my opinion, my lord, discharges our burden of proof under the relevant law."

Judge Pilate reclined in his chair, wiped his lenses and put them on.

"I understand that, but surely, all that is no more than mere accusatory at this stage. At best, a set of facts which is yet to be tested under cross-examination," Judge Pilate said.

Darlington's face turned crimson.

"My Lord, it may not have been tested, but it's evidence nonetheless," he said.

"I agree it's some evidence, otherwise the case would not have come this far. But it's hardly sufficient ground for denying bail to this defendant. Nothing to suggest he has previously failed to appear to answer any charges, is there?"

Darlington exhaled loudly.

"I invite my Lord to consider the totality of . . ."

"Mr. Darlington," Judge Pilate called quietly, his voice gravely, "I'm not persuaded by that argument. I ask you again. Is there any evidence that this defendant has previously failed to appear before any tribunal?"

"No, my Lord. But . . ."

"Thank you, Mr. Darlington," he said and made a brief note in his notebook.

Then Judge Pilate looked up and engaged my eyes. He took a long hard swallow and then clasped his hands. My heart dropped.

"Regardless of the Crown's apparent difficulty, the basic instinct must be to refuse this application given the likelihood of a substantial custodial sentence." His face was straight.

I felt as though someone had punched me in the solar plexus. Even moments later, the chilling words resonated in my head. My heartbeat drummed an unsteady rhythm as I stared back at him, wide-eyed like a dead fish. Not that I hadn't expected some hostility from him, yet when he suddenly turned against me, the anxiety, the fear was as raw as if I'd been taken by surprise. Judge Pilate was as slimy as he was evil - even two faced. Like most lawyers, I'd been through it many times before. The first attack on the prosecution was always going to be a facade, a window dressing for the record, saving his worst contempt for the defence. And for the second time since the hearing, I wondered how the hell he managed to slip through Dandy's net to make it to court.

I sank back in my seat, a picture of a man in despair. Though Judge Pilate's mind seemed closed to persuasion, I had no plans to give up easily.

"My Lord, your decision must be guided by the relevant legal principles." I managed to say, crossing one leg over the other, I continued. "There's a presumption of liberty unless a defendant has done something adversely to warrant the misapplication of this presumption in his favour. Certainly in this case, the crown has adduced no evidence to justify misapplying the presumption of bail."

There was a brief silence.

Judge Pilate shook his head, scratching his cheek lightly. "I'm persuaded by the Crown's argument that the presumption of bail ought to be disregarded in the circumstances of this case. Surely, a man of immense means such as the defendant, facing a substantial prison sentence if convicted, must be a flight risk. Do you not see that, Mr. Dias?"

"I do not agree, my Lord. However if your lordship is concerned about this, your lordship may impose a sizeable security as appropriate." He shot me an over-the-lenses stare and said nothing.

"Perhaps," I continued, "your lordship may wish to impose a reporting condition as well."

Judge Pilate's eyes narrowed. The silence that followed seemed age long. And like a deer putting up one last brave struggle against its predator, I braced myself. Most pressing, though, at the moment, was keeping Lorna's only chance alive. Suddenly, my expectations grew. Judge Pilate was paying some attention, not sure how much. But it was enough to restore some courage. Or was it a figment of my imagination?

"If your lordship is so minded, my client is prepared to lodge half a million in court as security. Also, my client is prepared to report daily at a local police station if your lordship so wishes. His passport is already with the police," I paused.

A long pause, and Judge Pilate who seemed in no hurry to talk, straightened himself. His eyes were dark, his face drawn and his hands still firmly locked together in front of him. Another moment passed, and a further moment dragged on. Everyone watched the judge in pained apprehension. Everyone was still but impatient, surely, there was a limit to how long we could sit here and stare at him.

"After careful consideration of both arguments for and against granting bail, I have decided, reluctantly I must add, to grant the application on conditions along the line suggested by counsel for the defence . . . namely, first . . ."

I sat in stunned silence as the judge delivered his judgement. Apart from feeling relieved, I showed little else. The moments of uncertainty and anticipation had eliminated any elation. In truth I was eager to leave the room, to leave the court and pass the good news to Shadow.

Judge Pilate eventually spat out his last words, gathered his papers and without so much as a fleeting glance at us, he shot out of the room like a man destined for hellfire. Marcia trailed him.

Darlington was slumped in his chair, looking more tired than he'd done before the hearing. He was shocked. Even his assistant seemed in a trance. She just stared and stared at the table where Judge Pilate had pronounced his judgement a moment earlier.

Finally, Darlington rose from his chair and walked up to me, his hand thrust forward.

"Congratulations," he managed with a grin, a sudden squinting around the eyes and a shrug of his shoulders. I took his hand and nodded.

"Well, I was wondering . . ."he said.

My mobile phone started to ring, stopping Darlington in mid-sentence.

"Excuse me," I said, moved away from him a few strides, flipped the phone open and said, "Hello?"

"Bravo, counsel! Congratulations!"

I stiffened momentarily, but quickly regained my composure, because Darlington was scrutinising my every move. How on earth did he know about the verdict? I swallowed nervously.

"I can't talk right now," I said.

"Don't worry about that jerk in front of you. You will have no more business with him after today," Shadow said.

I glanced up at Darlington. Then I stared at the

open window for a brief moment. How strange? Where was Shadow?

"Anyway," Shadow continued, "you need say nothing, just listen. You're a few instructions away from being reunited with your wife. First, the half a million pounds security is being wired to an account as I speak, so there is a statement to show the court."

Cold sweat had formed on my forehead.

"Secondly," he continued, "a black limousine is waiting outside the court, next to your car. You will join it to pick Malik up from the prison. Is that clear?"

"Yes," I returned quietly.

"Good. Oh, by the way Counsel, you were brilliant in there a moment ago. For me, you're the modern day Marshall Hall," Shadow said with suppressed laughter and hung up.

Chapter Twenty-Nine

The black limousine stretched across two parking bays, with tinted glass windows designed to impress and provide much needed privacy whilst in reality it attracted a lot of unhealthy attention to it. Shadow could care less about that, though he seemed to live his life in the dark, he was large, his actions audacious.

As I approached the limousine, the window lowered and a gruff voice called "get in." I slid into the soft-leathered seat and slammed the door. The strong smell of a cigar hit me. To my left sat a solemn-faced and noncommittal man, his left hand ominously inside his jacket, he wore a white turtleneck with a large gold chain hanging down. A baseball cap covered much of his grey hair. His eyes were invisible behind dark glasses. He looked in his early fifties, stocky build with the flair of a top-notch mercenary or an ex-soldier.

"Hello," I said, straightening my tie. For a fleeting moment, I thought that I'd said something wrong. It was the way he stared at me, cold and expressionless. His lips then parted a fraction into a grin, revealing a row of pearly teeth for a man his age.

"We figured you could ride with us," he said

offering me a cigar, which I quickly waved aside. He lit one and exhaled a thick smoke. Then he spoke to the driver in a foreign language and suddenly the limousine eased into the late morning traffic heading south of the river. He leaned back in his seat as the privacy window rolled up.

Forty-five minutes later we pulled into the Visitors 'car park of the High Security prison. We had a clear view of the main gate. We sat there in silence watching as Securicor vans went in and out of the prison, prison officers entered and left.

"Make yourself comfortable, Mr. Dias. Drink 's in the fridge."

"Am good, thanks."

He drew thoughtfully on his cigar.

"I trust you know what you must do. If not, I'll answer any queries now. We don't want any hiccups. We expect a professional job at this stage of the operation," he said.

"Why are you telling me this? You think I've come this far to mess things up?"

He raised a hand more to stop me in my tracks than an apology.

"Please don't take this the wrong way. We've been in this business long enough to know that most problems occur at the late stages of operations, however well planned," he declared, "and there are reasons for this. One is that people get excited quite unnecessarily and lose their heads. Once Malik comes out of the gate, you will escort him to us. It's as simple as that. Then we will take it from there. Job done"

"I'm aware of that."

"Good boy. Any mistake will cost dearly." It was a veiled threat; no explanation was required.

"And how will I get my wife back?"

"One thing at a time, Mr. Dias. Beyond what I've told you, I know nothing. I'm sure Shadow will let you know what arrangements he's made to reunite with your wife. It's not my problem," he added "Anything else?"

I didn't respond and stared out of the window.

***

Like a retired general calculating his next move, the grey-haired man kept a perpetual watch on the entrance, only glancing surreptitiously at his watch.

A moment later, a black BMW pulled into a space beside us. Two middle-aged men in suit sat impassively in the car, a female sat behind the wheel. She looked in her late thirties, casually dressed in a jean shirt and a baseball cap. They were all wearing dark glasses. If they noticed the imposing presence of the limousine, they didn't show it.

The grey-haired man turned to me and flashed a grin.

"I believe you have something to pick up from that gate over there," he said nodding towards the prison entrance.

I kept a straight face. The thumping in my heart cage was gathering momentum. How would Malik react to this? What if he refused to come with me? My legs suddenly felt as if they were heavier, perhaps even numb. Then I thought about Lorna and a wave of strength shot through me. I would have to see this through for her, I said under my breath. It would not be long now and all this would be behind us. First, however, I had to deliver Malik to Shadow and that was the hard part.

I got out of the car wincing in the mid-afternoon sunlight. As I strolled leisurely across the car park toward the prison entrance, I felt eyes watching my every step.

The gate slid noisily back and a dishevelled looking figure limped into the sunshine as if pushed, squinting at the sun.

I waved at Malik and quickened my steps.

"Hi," I said breathlessly greeting him with a firm handshake; I could tell instantly that he had things on his mind. He was pale faced and calm. If he was afraid, he didn't show it. Instead, he gripped my hand more firmly, grinning, an insincere kind of grin that didn't do much to inspire me. But whatever he was feeling now was too late. He was out, and no longer protected by these prison walls.

"Counsel," he called quietly, "Judas was generous enough to betray his master with a kiss, all I'm getting is a miserly handshake," he said.

Chapter Thirty

"I'm sorry." My voice was almost inaudible.

Malik shrugged and dropped my hand as if he suddenly realised that I were suffering from leprosy. He had the expression of a man as deep in thought as his problems. There was nothing to show that he was angry. But even that did little to dispel my guilt. There was a sneaking perception that he was secretly calculating his next move. He suddenly looked unhealthy. His forehead and nose were heavily veined; his eyes were bloodshot and rapidly darted from side to side.

"Why, counsel? Why? I trusted you," he said with a frightening calmness. His eyes engaged mine fiercely and scanned me. "For money? I could've paid you any price to keep your trust."

I did not respond. Instead I looked away, thoughtful. The grey-haired man had been right about possible hiccups even at this late stage of our mission. Had I been foolish to underestimate Malik? Had I counted my gain too soon? What if he should run back and seek refuge with the prison officers?

Finally, I quietly engaged his eyes again. With the confidence of a disgraced politician, I said, "I didn't do it for money."

He considered me with narrowed eyes.

"So why did you do it?" There was a slight inflection in his voice, which only intensified my anxiety.

I exhaled heavily. "Listen, what I've done is inexcusable. It's cowardly. Until now I never fully understood the biblical Samson's weakness over his wife Delilah."

His eyes widened a fraction.

"But Counsel, Levine assured me at the outset that you don't have a family," he said.

"I know. Levine lied to you...he wanted this case badly."

He threw both hands in the air. "Shit," he said. "I wouldn't touch you otherwise. Damn."

As he tilted his head to one side, he let off a suppressed gasp and ran his hand through his hair. He turned away from me and took two short strides towards the prison wall, his head inclined as if in deep reflection.

"I misjudged you, misjudged everything," he said quietly.

"Am sorry," I managed to say.

"That's no use to me now. I wouldn't have hired you dead if I knew you had a wife. Because I know men like you are fucking easy target for the mafias."

There was a brief silence. Then he turned and looked at me, a mysterious smile hung in one corner of his mouth.

"I'm so so sorry," I pleaded.

He shrugged.

"You did what you had to do." He said stonily. "So where are they waiting?"

I nodded towards the car park behind me.

He shot an eye in that direction and pursed his lips thoughtfully. 'Well, I suppose you've got to deliver me now."

Suddenly, he shifted his gaze to an approaching car. His face lit up, his eyes sparkled and a defiant smile spread across his face. "Hey, look who's here."

I turned and stiffened to attention as a marked police car crawled towards the gate. My pulse rate increased and my hands trembled. I closed my eyes for a moment, more in utter daze than in any genuine contemplation. My mind was blank.

The police car stopped in front of the gate. From the corner of my eye, I noticed there were two uniformed officers in the front; a third was angling in the rear seat. They too were staring curiously at us.

"Don't they turn up when you really don't want company," Malik purred, walking towards the police car. He grinned mischievously glancing back at me occasionally.

My heart stopped. I could almost test my bile as I swallowed repeatedly, a cold shiver streaming down my spine.

"Excuse me officers," he called as he crossed over to the obese police officer behind the wheel.

Stunned, I stood there like a ghost trapped in a blaze of sunlight. I stole a quick glance over my shoulder and met Malik's gaze. Should I run? I

173

heard myself thinking. In the end, I just stood there watching helplessly as Malik finally leaned towards the police officer. Then he looked at me for a brief moment, stern-faced as if he were appraising me. He reached into his jacket pocket and pulled a cigarette.

"Got a light please, officer," he said with a wry smile.

Chapter Thirty-One

Finally the prison gate opened and the police car quietly disappeared behind it, and even then I was still transfixed, motionless, my nerves showed no sign of steadying. The feeling of hollowness in my stomach remained as life gradually returned to my face amidst a huge sigh of relief.

Malik smiled as he walked towards me. He seemed at ease, as if nothing had happened. But the joke was not just on me, because beyond where I stood there was a trail of panic then suspense. Again, he wore that familiar impenetrable shroud of mystery, only smiling knowingly as if to say he was in control. Why hadn't he sought help with the police? I mused.

I instinctively looked over my shoulder in the direction of the car park, and could only imagine their anxiety. There was little doubt even in the atmosphere of heightened tension that Malik was the treasure and he was in control of his destiny.

"The reason you're here is you want to trade me in for your wife's life. Yes?" Malik said dispassionately.

I did not answer, instead, held him at my fixed stare.

"Tell me, why I should let you have your own

way on this?" he added.

I felt a sudden chill down my spine. More so because he had sounded normal. There was neither strain nor anger in his voice. Had he something up his sleeve? I knew how unpredictable Malik could be and that worried me even more. Even Shadow, in spite of his intelligence, had got this part wrong. Allowing Malik this much latitude was not the smartest thing he had ever done. Even control freaks like Shadow had their weaknesses, I thought. Malik had made me see that.

What was ironic, about Malik's question was that I had found myself suddenly tongue-tied. I had always operated under pressure, and yet, even by my usual high standard, this was all a little much to cope with. In fairness to Malik, the question was not unreasonable or imposing, but the awkwardness lay in its simplicity. How could I tell him that Lorna's life was worth saving and his was not? I was ashamed, and more exhausted than any trial had ever made me. Yet, there was much left to do.

When I did not answer, he considered me for a moment, a sad grin on his face.

"You're a selfish man," Malik said "I guess you've made that clear. But there is a bigger issue here than your wife's life, that's for sure."

"What do you mean?" I asked.

'Come on, walk with me,' he said stabbing out his cigarette, his eyes dark and cold. And without another word, he started walking away from me.

Then I followed, painfully aware that this was not in the game plan. Not in the least. There again, who could've predicted an easy ride with Malik? Shadow should've allowed for something going wrong, and what a time to learn a lesson.

Quietly, I cursed my misfortune; everything had been going so smoothly until now. Shaking my head, wondering where this was leading, I stepped into pace with him.

We made our way to the public road, and for a moment, neither of us spoke. The sidewalk was deserted apart from an old man cycling towards us.

I peered back and received a slight panic. The BMW was crawling after us, on the outer side of the dual carriageway, followed by the limo, each driver doing their best not to draw attention. I wondered what they would do next. But more so, I wondered where Malik was headed. He did not display any urgency, though his face was tightly set.

At first, I had tried to consider calmly what Malik's game plan was. In the end my anxiety gave way to wild speculations and doubts. Was he planning to string me along as a human shield? With sudden alarm, I wondered if Malik was slipping through my fingers. My anxiety, never long sustained, diminished and certain boldness replaced it.

"So what will you do now?" I asked.

He looked up at me and said nothing.

"At least you can tell me where we're going." I added.

177

"What's the rush?" Malik said without looking at me. "Somehow, I know you will follow me wherever I go."

I did not reply knowing how true those words were.

Malik smiled. "How about you buy us lunch?" he said walking into a nearby cafe.

Noise levels abruptly reduced to suppressed murmurs, eyes glancing inquiringly at us. I had never felt so out of place before but Malik was at ease. He didn't look at all nervous.

The muscles around my face twitched nervously as the BMW and the limo drew towards the cafe. None of this seemed to make any sense. Surely Malik had noticed them and yet he had shown no anxiety, certainly no attempt at resisting capture. But despite my quiet elation at this, another thought depressed me. Guilt. A certain emptiness. I was conspiring to endanger the life of my client, something that flew in the face of everything I had been taught. The fact that the initial plan hadn't worked straight away had given room for reflection, for soul-searching, for guilt whatever the prize. The release of my wife safe and well was the prize worth pursuing I reminded myself steeling my resolve.

The cafe was half full and noisy, little more than shabbily furnished workmen's hang out. Not that I had a choice. The room was stuffy and smelt of fried onions.

A fat woman in her fifties wearing a heavily stained apron stood behind the counter. She considered us methodically; Malik as usual didn't seem to take any notice as he sat beside the window staring outside.

"What you like?" The woman was now towering over us, holding a pen and a notepad. Her face was screwed as if she could do without the distraction.

"Toast and black coffee." Malik said.

"We've finished serving breakfast," She returned.

"Coffee then," Malik said.

She rolled her eyes and didn't bother scribbling on the note pad.

"You?"

"Coca-Cola, please." I said.

A few minutes later, she returned with our drinks.

Malik sipped his coffee and considered the two men now leaning on the limo outside. Their stance alert, like bodyguards straight out of a Hollywood film. They drew attention from all corners, not least because their conspicuous interest in the local cafe was bizarre. Even the diners in the cafe had noticed too, followed by more conspiratorial murmurs and yet more surreptitious glances. Yet there was not a trace of concern on Malik's face. He seemed determined to keep everyone guessing, to keep everyone sweating. Finally he lit an electronic cigarette and blew the smoke out slowly.

"To us." I said raising my can.

He slammed a palm on the table. "Wrong time

for sarcasm," the impact was like a gunshot, looking pointedly at me, his features set. Suddenly a new tension permeated the room. The hum of conversation stopped as attention intensified around us. Only the buzz of traffic outside intruded faintly. It was evident to everyone now that this was no ordinary meeting, no ordinary people.

A moment later, someone hurried to the counter, paid his bill and left. A few others followed, and within seconds, the cafe was empty, except for two men who remained on the edge of their seats. The fat waitress watched nervously from behind the counter.

"I wish this were a toasting encounter," Malik continued, his voice low but serious, 'I chose this filthy place for a purpose, not least to make a point." He paused, his eyes swept across the room.

I swallowed quickly.

Malik's face tightened even more. He appeared about to say something forcefully, and then changed his mind. Instead he took a shallow breath.

"Take a look around you and tell me what you see."

Hesitatingly, I scanned the room. "At what specifically?" I asked.

"Food. Left-over food" He said quietly.

"Just what do you have in mind, Malik?"

"Across Europe alone, fifty million tonnes of food are binned every month, yet the average consumption is less than 75 calories a day in most developing countries. Did you know that one child in five dies before its first year in Sierra Leone, Sudan, Zaire, Senegal, Mali, and Burkina Fasu? I can go on and on," he paused as if to allow me time to think. "There, infant mortality is as high as forty three per cent compared to less than 1-5 per cent in the West. In general, life expectancy is less than thirty years in Africa." His voice had a direct no-nonsense sound to it and somehow I knew he had much more to say.

I suppressed the urge to ask what any of this had to do with me. Malik had already displayed one outburst too many, it would be pointless to provoke the next.

"At this alarming death rate, more than half of African continent will be wiped out by the next millennium." He said.

"And who do you blame for all this?" I asked.

"The entire western civilisation. You and me." He said.

"In what way?"

"In what way?" he retorted. Then he drew on his e-cigarette and for a moment, watched the smoke curl lazily upwards. "Too many to recount in the time we have. In short, the developed countries are safely through. But now they have moved the goalpost. Exploitation is rife; they manipulate the markets to gain unfair advantage over the weaker nations. New face Colonialism has replaced the old - state sponsored private security companies fuelling wars so they can trade arms for diamonds and other rich mineral resources. I know because I was part of the global network that was filtering the proceeds through a web of off-shore accounts for corrupt government officials and presidents," he said with clenched teeth. There was something about the last sentence that seemed to have touched his nerves. Suddenly, he didn't look angry any more: He looked as though he were in pain. He stared thoughtfully at the burning cigarette, and when he finally looked up again, his face was firm. There was something sinister about him that made me feel uneasy.

"Counsel, the high standards of living you enjoy have been bought at the cost of terrible human suffering; malnutrition, river blindness, yellow fever, Aids, leprosy and now, mass emigration from that continent. They need our help," he said quietly. "This is why I no longer want to be part of the exploiting force. I want to help but so many organizations, governments, want to shut me up."

I weighed the issues he'd raised. No doubt he was versed and passionate about them, but still, I could not see how they might influence the dilemma we faced. The reality remained that Shadow's men were lurking outside, and why would Malik choose this moment to discuss world politics? So what if the world was unfair? And so what if the strong would keep the weak in perpetual poverty and misery? What in the devil's name had any of that got to do with me, with rescuing Lorna?

"I'm sorry, but I can't figure out where you're

driving at, how this is anything to do with me."

He looked me in the face.

"Do you seriously expect me to believe that? You have no idea, no idea at all?"

"I have no idea what this has to do with these people waiting out there. For God's sake, what the hell is going on here?" I said.

"You should've asked that long ago before you got yourself mixed up with Shadow. I said this before, I say it again, you're a selfish man. You're clueless."

I flushed with anger. "Have you finished?"

"Not quite. Just beginning." He sat up, his voice dropped to a whisper. "Years ago, the Russians devised a highly classified biological and chemical solution to curb human population. It's the most ingenious invention I know. But the problem is: it's irreversible once applied, and has the capacity to wipe out a country the size of Great Britain within a decade."

"No kidding." I regarded him with fresh curiosity. "Is this one of those crazy inventions intended against the Americans during the cold war?"

"No."

"No?" I retorted.

"It was intended against the Chinese," he said.

"The Chinese? Why?" I asked.

"It was in the Russian strategic interest to do something about the escalating Chinese population. The ratio of Chinese army to Russian army is one hundred to one and rising."

183

"That doesn't justify this brutal invention."

"You see it that way. Then again, you're not Russian." Then he added, 'perhaps not ethical, but an entirely legitimate precautionary measure. And in case you've forgotten, let me remind you that every country has a skeleton in their cupboard. What's the big deal?"

"Just the fear that all this biological and chemical warfare will fall into wrong hands, especially in the hands of terrorists and rogue nations."

Malik smiled.

"Your concern has come a fraction too late," he said.

My attention sharpened, and like a bubble from underwater, the first hint of trouble emerged.

"What?"

"If it's any comfort, this latest Russian invention is in safe hands. For now at least."

"Whose hands?"

"Mine."

I considered him for a moment. His face was taut, expressionless. There was nothing to suggest he was anything but serious.

"You? You mean . . ."

He interrupted with an affirmative, dismal nod and moistened his lips.

"That's the whole point of all this." He gestured contemptuously to the limousine. "We bought the classified formula for the deadly solution from some corrupt Russian General years ago. Now they want it back."

"Who's "we" that bought this formula?"

"Monza Network. The organisation I represent."

A spasm of fear seized my entire body. "Network?" I gasped quietly. As each revelation struck an uncomfortable note, I could barely reconcile in my head that Malik was head of a terrorist organisation. Was the man in front of me a wanted terrorist?"

I glanced through the window. The two men watched unobtrusively. One of the men said something. The other nodded.

"Are you alright, Counsel?"

I rubbed my temple frantically. "All right? That's an understatement. I don't understand any of this. I mean, if what you're saying is the Russians want the formula back, why would they try to kill you in court? That doesn't make sense."

"I know. Except the Russians didn't try to kill me. The Monza Network did. They sent that hit-man to the court."

"I don't follow. Your organisation tried to kill you?"

He nodded.

"After acquiring the formula, there arose a deep division in our organisation about the way forward. Majority favour an outright terror campaign against the West using our newly acquired biological warfare. Their objective; to systematically obliterate the West from the globe," he paused and gazed outside for a moment. "For them, it's pay back time. I understand their anger;

185

I understand their craving for revenge. Equally, I have voiced my objections to the proposed use of our new power in this way. Two wrongs cannot make a right. Instead, I have proposed a middle position."

"Which is?" I said more out of exasperation than anxiety.

"To threaten the West with its use but not use it unless absolutely, I repeat, absolutely necessary," he said.

"That's a blackmail," I said.

"For lack of a better word, yes. But that's legitimate and all the powerful governments use it against the weaker ones. Today, diplomacy has been replaced by blackmail, threat of force and sometimes by force. The only remaining superpower uses them very well to keep Iraq, Iran, North Korea etcetera in check. The Russians do the same. So do Britons. Why shouldn't we?"

"Don't ask me. All this is beyond me." I sat back.

"I realise. But it's surprising how quickly people adapt," he said with a piercing stare and weak smile.

"You have two dangerous organisations after you for the same thing. That sounds like being in a quagmire to me."

Malik said nothing.

"The question, I guess, is who do you want to negotiate with?"

"The Russians," he said with a determined blaze in his eyes.

"What do you want from them?"

"Fair play in the way the powerful nations pursue their strategic interests around the globe," he leaned forward. "I want a global bill of rights, an end to the exploitation of the weaker nations, a ban on illegal arms sales to warring nations in African, Asia and Middle East, implementation of fair trade policies, transparency in banking, publishing foreign accounts and property of all African and Arab despots and seizing their assets unless they can account the source of the funds, criminalizing foreign companies conniving with corrupt government official to loot public funds and mineral resources, putting corruption in Africa, Asia, and Middle East on the G8 summit."

"How do you hope to achieve all this?" I asked.

"By making Russia force the hands of the big players in the UN Security Council: the Americans, Chinese, Britons and the French. Counsel, this is the deal. As soon as they can pass this bill in the UN Security Council, provide a legal and military framework to enforce the bill, and we can monitor its effectiveness for 5 years, we will return the formula. How about that?"

I shrugged. "Who's "we"? You say your organisation is not with you on this?"

"I mean you and me."

"You're crazy? No way I'm getting involved with any of that." I said.

Again there was the piercing stare and little else. He sipped his coffee, drew hard on his e-cigarette and exhaled noisily. Then he removed a

187

folded note from his pocket and pushed it discreetly across the table.

I picked up the note and started reading with nervous astonishment. When I had finished reading it, I looked him in the face.

"I'm not sure. I'm not sure I can do this."

"Oh yes you can. For your wife and for all those victims of the West's exploits."

"Are you blackmailing me?"

"No. But we can do this the hard way or we can move things along fast." He interlocked his fingers and considered them for a moment. Then he rose, his expression solemn, and offered his hand. Reluctantly, I took it.

"The gentlemen are waiting. Goodbye, Counsel," he said and walked out.

Outside, the men guided Malik into the limo and drove off.

My mood was subdued - the strain of uncertainty, of painful anxiety, as I stared incredulously into space.

My mobile phone rang.

It rang a few times, my pulse increased with each ring. Finally, I answered it.

"Well done, Mr. Dias" Shadow said, "I suppose it remains for me to keep my side of the bargain. I'll call back in . . ."

"Cut that bullshit. Where is she?" I snarled angrily.

"Calm down."

"Don't tell me to calm down. You've got your man, now you let her go," I said.

"I'm afraid there's a security issue to be sorted out. But we will soon make arrangements for her release,' Shadow said.

"You're buying time for your men to get away. Listen, I don't give a damn about what you do, I just want my wife back. Now."

"You're getting worked up unnecessarily. In any case, make your way towards City airport. I'll call back in a little while and let you know exactly where she is," he paused. "Oh, by the way, your car is outside," he added and hung up.

Moments later, I steered speedily through traffic heading east on the A406 motorway. The note Malik had given me was on the passenger seat, I had memorised his instructions. I wondered if I should keep the note in case my memory failed. No, I thought. Reassured that I'd had the details covered, I tore it up. I checked the rearview mirror to see if I was being followed. Everything seemed OK. Even then, caution remained the operating word. Then one after the other, I threw the pieces out of the window.

Suddenly the phone rang again.

"On my way there," I said impatiently.

"Mr. Dias," the caller said.

"Oh Tania," I frowned. "Look, this is not a good time. I'll get back to you."

"I'm sorry, Mr. Dias, but . . ."

"Tania," I interrupted angrily, "can't this wait till I get back?"

"I'm afraid not. The detectives are here and want all partners back in the office ASAP."

I felt a stab in my stomach.

"Something wrong?"

"Mr. Dobbs was found dead in his car. The police think he may have been murdered," she said.

Chapter Thirty-Two

Now my nightmare was twofold: the discovery of Dobbs' body in his car followed by a murder investigation, then there was the growing sense of anxiety over Lorna's safety. Both were deep and engaging, it was hard to gauge which one was more pressing. With detective Des' claws already encircling around my neck over the previous murders, his resolve to arrest and detain me would only be that much stronger.

Driving down the North Circular road towards the docklands, my concentration wavered. I fought to keep my mind from swirling. Surely, now it would be much more difficult, if not impossible, to convince the detectives that Dobbs' death was anything but murder. No doubt, forensic examination would reveal the impact to his skull and find it inconsistent with a car accident, assuming this was what Levine had intended. Whatever his intention, this was an error of judgement. Moving the body from the scene might have destroyed the half chance I had of successfully arguing manslaughter. Had Levine done me an irrevocable harm?

Fear churned my stomach. Why had Levine placed the body in the car where it would be easily found? Maybe this had been a knee jerk reaction, his first concern being to safeguard the firm's image I reasoned.

I stared helplessly ahead. Nothing made much sense. Every conceivable rationale for Levine's decision seemed pathetically inadequate.

The nagging questions made my temples throb even more.

I decided with a hint of irritation that what I thought was not important. What was the point trying to make sense of it if I couldn't do anything about it?

The mobile phone rang again, jerking me back to life. "Yes." I said.

"First, about the financial reward for your . . ." Shadow said.

"I don't want your money, damn it. Where is she?" I shouted.

Shadow hesitated for a few seconds.

"Alright," he said finally. "Your wife is at 3 Pinkerton Drive, Docklands. I would like to take this opportunity to thank . . ."

I dropped the phone on the passenger seat. Glancing at the clock on the dashboard, I assessed the journey time. It would take at least twenty minutes or so to get to Pinkerton Drive. Suddenly a sense of optimism overwhelmed me. I depressed the accelerator launching the car forward and within a few seconds the speedometer was showing 100mph. The 500SL squealed around a bend, veering wildly. I struggled with the steering wheel and eventually steadied it, and glancing again at the speedometer, I realised I was doing 145. I eased my foot from the accelerator and instinctively looked in the rear-view mirror.

"Shit." I exclaimed as a patrol car, with its blue light flashing, shot into sight.

Braking, the car swung slightly, before I slid into the slow lane now down to sixty.

The patrol car filed in behind me. My heart thumping, I finally pulled up on the hard shoulder.

The police car pulled up behind me. A female officer was in the passenger seat; a male officer sat behind the wheel, his eyes hidden behind dark glasses.

Relax, this is nothing, I told myself. Just don't try anything stupid and they will go away, I heard myself thinking.

A moment later, the woman was bending over by my window. I rolled the window down and managed a nervous smile.

She smiled back.

"Good afternoon, Sir. Is this your car, Sir?"

"Yes. Is there a problem, Officer?"

"And you are, Sir?" She insisted.

"Phil Dias."

"You were travelling over 140 miles an hour." Her gaze dropped to the mobile phone on the passenger seat.

"I wasn't using the phone," I protested.

"The flip is open, Sir."

"Yeah. I just forgot to shut it."

She raised her eyebrows.

"Well, are you going to report me for

speeding?" I said trying but failing to conceal my impatience.

"One moment Sir." She retreated two feet.

I heard her checking my personal details on her radio. I glanced at my watch. Quarter past two. Anxious, I adjusted the rear-view mirror, and saw the woman officer listening to the radio with a puzzled expression, then darted back to the male officer. They talked for a moment and the woman nodded. She walked back to my car and bent down by my window.

"Step out of the car, Sir," she said firmly. The stress in her voice set off a panic button in my head.

"Sorry Officer, I can't."

Thrusting the gear forward, I slammed my foot on the accelerator. The car roared into action like a rocket, tyres squealing and a smell of burnt rubber permeating the interior. A frantic glance in the mirror brought the woman officer into focus; she was running back to the patrol car and speaking into the radio at the same time.

The patrol car chased me with its siren blaring, and blue light flashing.

***

Five minutes later a few more police cars had joined the chase. I tried to concentrate on the driving. Yet fear punctuated my thoughts, the fear that Lorna might not be at Pinkerton Drive. What suddenly gave rise to this feeling was unclear. I turned off onto a slip road, following the directions

194

instinctively.

The town was small. Almost no traffic and only a few pedestrians.

I turned left at the traffic light and up a steep winding road past isolated houses flanked by a dense tangle of trees and shrubs. In the distance, sirens wailed, but checking the mirrors, I saw no police cars.

I veered past a gate and braked. The car swerved sharply right, and then left before I gained control. It was a cul-de-sac. Beyond that, there was nothing except dense bushes. I slowed down.

To the left was a farm. Without much strength to think, I drove straight into a stable; several bundles of hay fell on top of the car covering it. The engine sputtered and stopped. It was suddenly pitch dark and in the silence that followed, there was the strident wail of sirens, and a hovering sound of a police helicopter above.

Sweating profusely, I anxiously waited.

Chapter Thirty-Three

When the noise had faded, I pushed the stacks of hay out of the way. Apart from occasional flapping sounds, it was otherwise quiet. I took a cautious peep at my surroundings. There was no one about. Even so, I waited a few moments longer appraising the situation. A privet hedge formed a fence behind the stable.

I ran up to the hedge and crouched behind it. Then after a few moments, I peered out over it, and there was a beautiful house set in expansive grounds. A warning sign read "Beware of Dogs". I felt a rush of adrenalin. I scanned the rear of the house. Two large windows stood on either side of a door; one was half open.

Taking a deep breath, I moved cautiously towards the windows and managed to get a view of the interior - a glamorous kitchen. No dogs were in sight. Or at least not in the kitchen.

I listened more intently. Nothing. Only the distant sound of the police helicopter greeted me.

I pulled the window open and climbed into the kitchen, landing on the marble floor with a faint thud.

The kitchen smelt of fresh lemon and lavender. Nothing seemed out of place; the surface was sparkling. Fastened to the wall was a wooden cabinet, they looked new as if they had never been used.

I looked in the cabinet and found a set of kitchen knives. My apprehension somewhat diminished, a certain sense of determination took hold, and then it quickly changed to excitement, then fear in equal measure. There was a disquieting anticipation that more surprises lay ahead.

Clutching a kitchen knife, I headed through the house.

The ground floor was large, divided into two, each exquisitely furnished. In one part was a set of settees over-looking a large TV screen. The other room had a set of handcrafted chairs, oak wooden artifices stood in corners.

The staircase wound steeply upwards, which led to a pair of transparent glass doors. I started climbing the staircase, taking each step slow and steady.

Halfway up the stairs, I stiffened to a muffled noise. I held my breath, listening. I couldn't be sure where the noise was coming from. I waited for a moment, till I was sure, even then I was more confused.

I followed the direction of the noise until I reached the glass doors at the top of the stairs. A swimming pool met my gaze through the glass doors; the light green water was still, glinting in the lights. The surface around the pool was wet.

Hesitating briefly, I finally pushed the door

open.

A naked man lay on a woman moving rhythmically in excitement, each movement urgent and mindless. Suddenly, he started thrusting forward, groaning.

She wrapped her hands around him staring lazily at the ceiling. She too was groaning, with pleasure.

'Oh!' She cried and in a unified movement, turned her head to one side and noticed me. She let out a loud gasp, her expression frozen. Though her unsuspecting partner continued for a few seconds longer, he too soon slowed down, and suddenly all movement came to a halt.

She just lay there blinking at me. I wasn't sure what shocked her more, my presence or the long blade in my hand.

Misjudging her mood, the man tried to kiss her. But she quickly shoved him out of the way. Now frowning at the rebuff, he studied her expression for a moment, and then followed her gaze to me.

He gasped.

His face turned crimson, then white as he frantically rolled over and grabbed a towel in one quick movement. He tried to scream, but no sound came out. Only his mouth opened and shut in quick succession.

Chapter Thirty-Four

"Please don't hurt me," the man spluttered. He was lean-faced, short hair, with thin lips. He stared pleadingly at the blade. "She forced me. I swear she made me do it," he protested. "Oh shit. You've got to believe me. She told me you ain't coming back till late."

"Shut up!" she screamed at him, a hint of frustration in her voice.

Her voice was steely, assertive. Apart from the initial shock, she had shown no weakness. She was stunning, probably in her early forties. She had a well-toned body, and large full breasts.

"I swear Sir . . . I swear she forced me. I ain't been up here before."

"Ssssh," I pressed the blade against my lips.

He muttered a few more words, slumped on the floor in a foetus position, mumbling to himself.

Turning to her, I said, "Get dressed."

She considered me momentarily, and then sat up. No trace of fear in her eyes. She seemed resigned to her fate, much like a prisoner on death row awaiting death, showing nothing but arrogance having since come to terms with destiny.

Hesitating briefly, she went across, took a jean shirt and slipped into it so the hem just about covered her buttocks.

She turned and looked at me. When I didn't say anything, she sat on the edge of a seat and crossed her legs.

"Now what?" Her voice was cold. "He sent you to kill me, didn't he?"

"What are you talking about?"

"He sent you. My husband damnit?"

Then it clicked.

I studied her face for what seemed a long time. There was no doubt that I would need her help, I desperately wanted her help. She stared back at me, unfazed.

In life, people were driven to extra-marital affairs for two reasons. One was the risk element, a by-product of boredom, and a desire for excitement. The other was the pleasure element, an insatiable appetite for sex, perhaps also, a desire to fulfill a sexual fantasy of some sort. I wondered in which category she belonged. Was she the risk taker I needed to get me to Pinkerton Drive?

I went with my gut feeling, lowered the blade and forced a smile.

"It's not what you think. I'm not here to kill you. I'm not going to harm you." I said.

She remained expressionless. It was as though she couldn't be sure if I was serious. Her eyes were suddenly dark and enquiring. Even the man, now sharpened his focus on me.

Her gaze dropped to the blade now hanging loosely in my hand.

"Oh, that. I'm sorry." I dropped the blade in

one corner. "Trust me. I'm not going to harm you."

There was a long pause.

"So what do you want?" she said quietly.

The sound of the helicopter was growing louder. I looked at her, and then walked over to the window.

Suddenly she rose. "You'd better step away from the window," she said and drew the blinds. She reached for a pair of jeans. Turning to the man, she said, "Get back to work." Her voice had a trace of contempt. Even then, the man would not budge. He was still shaking. He looked up at me, and then sensing no objections, frantically gathered his clothes and shot out of sight.

She fumbled between clothes before pulling out a pair of knickers.

"My husband comes home from work at eight o'clock." There was a hint of fatigue in her voice now. She pulled her hair into a bun and lit a cigarette.

"I'm not planning to stay. I've got to reach somewhere as soon as possible."

"So who's stopping you?"

"The police."

"I can see that. But I can't see why you won't wait around a few hours till the area is clear," she said.

"It's much more complicated than that. That's why I'm here. I need your help."

"Don't start taking liberties just because you witnessed my indiscretion," she said.

"I won't take advantage of you. I won't force you to help me if you don't want to," I said.

"So what exactly do you . . .?"

The doorbell rang stopping her in mid-sentence.

"Excuse me," she said almost inaudibly. She stubbed out her cigarette and straightened her jean trousers. She walked past me, and turned, "Stay here," she said forcing a grin, as if to reassure me.

I moved anxiously closer to the glass doors and listened. My pulse rate rose sharply. Could I trust her?

Pacing the floor like an expectant father outside a labour room, I heard a door open downstairs. I paused and listened. A surge of irritation rushed up my neck when the helicopter sound returned drowning the conversation downstairs. Moments later, the noise faded back in the distance.

" . . . Have a good day, Mrs. Quail," said a voice.

"And you too, constable," she said.

Then the door slammed shut.

A couple of minutes later, she returned upstairs with two drinks, her expression, quizzical.

"The whole area is crawling with cops." She said as she handed me a drink. "You must have done something really naughty."

She sipped her drink in front of a mirror, watching me in the reflection. "I hear there are police checkpoints everywhere and police helicopters searching the area. You'd be a fool to try leaving."

"I must get to Pinkerton Drive urgently."

She turned. "And how will you get there?"

I shrugged. "I've got an idea, but I'll need your help to make it work."

"How?"

Swirling my drink, I swallowed in one gulp. "Drive me there."

"Me?"

"Please. This is really important."

"You're crazy. I can't. Isn't it enough I'm putting my neck on the line shielding you here?" she said with a raised voice.

"OK. OK. I understand. But can I borrow your car?"

"The keys are downstairs. By the way, no one lent you the car. You broke in here, saw the keys and took them, right?"

"Sure. Thanks," I returned quickly.

I reached for the door.

"May I ask, what's so important that you're prepared to risk getting caught for?" She said.

"My wife was abducted a few days ago. She's at that address and she may be in great danger. That's why, Mrs. . . . ."

"Quail," she said. "I'm sorry I didn't realise it was something as serious as that."

"Don't be sorry, you've done enough. I know it must be difficult for you. Thanks again for your help."

"No, no. Wait. I don't know why I'm doing this. It must be your lucky day." She forced a weak smile. "And what do I call you?"

Chapter Thirty-Five

After a long absence, Mrs. Quail returned.

"Change into these. They have a description of the clothing you're wearing. Meet me in the garage when you're done," she said heading towards the door.

"Can I use your phone?" I called after her.

"You may. But don't answer any calls. It might be my husband. There's phone in the room opposite." Then she left.

I quickly changed into my new outfit, the jeans were baggy, but the belt held them in place. Even then, it was still loose around my waist.

I checked the mirror. I looked like something between a local angler and an animal rights protester, especially with the baseball cap and the dark glasses. But despite the distaste, it contrasted sharply with my former description, providing me an ironclad disguise.

I quickly phoned Dandy.

"Yeah. Who's this?"

"Hi, it's me. Listen . . ."

"Hey you listen for a change. What the fuck is the matter with you? I've been dead worried. You don't answer your phone, you don't call me. How the fuck am I supposed to know anything if you don't talk to me?"

"I'm sorry. I left my phone in the car."

"What the fuck for? Your wife's life is on the line and you leave your phone behind. What were you thinking?"

"Listen, I've got a situation here."

"What's new?"

"I'm just leaving to get Lorna."

"Great. Where is she?"

"3 Pinkerton Drive."

"And where are you now?"

"Around the corner from that address."

"So what are you hanging around for? Go get her then."

There was a short pause.

"Oh! You smell a rat or something?" Dandy added quickly.

"The police are crawling all over the area looking for me."

"What for? Oh shit! That bastard set you up?"

"Oh, no, no. Shadow had nothing to do with that. I got stopped speeding on my way here. I guess they carried out a routine check and found out I was wanted for the murders at D&L."

"Oh shit. All right. Here's the plan. Keep your ass off the street whatever you do. We don't want you screwing up, you hear me? I'll go pick her up."

"How far are you from here?" I asked.

"Forty five minutes away, traffic allowing. An hour tops."

"Oh no. Can't wait that long. I'll have to take

a chance on it."

"Too risky. You hear me. Too risky," Dandy said.

"I've got no choice."

"Yes you have. All you've got to do is wait another hour max. I'm leaving City airport as I speak and should be with Lorna within the next hour."

"City airport?" I asked.

"Long story. In short, I followed Shadow's men just after they took Malik hoping they would lead me to Lorna. But they headed here where a private jet was waiting for them." Dandy said.

"Did you find out where they were taking him?"

"To hell by the look of it. Information I got suggests the plane was bound for Russia. There's more. The men who drove you to collect Malik from prison are members of the Russian diplomatic corps."

"Oh my God," I exclaimed.

"Don't worry about it. Who cares what happens to Malik anyway. He probably screwed them up in the past, now they're screwing him back. We'll get your wife back and you can look back on this whole thing as a bad dream. Now what's the deal? Are we doing this your way or my way?"

"Can't wait an hour when I can reach her in five minutes. Don't worry about me, I'll be fine. Do me a favour."

"Uh uh."

"Can you pick us up from there?"

"Consider it done. What was the number again?"

"3 Pinkerton Drive."

"Got it," he said and hung up.

***

Inside a large, square windowless garage, Mrs. Quail sat behind the wheel of a new jeep, her index finger tapping the steering wheel.

I thought about her and how she must be worried. Cursing my irrationality I wondered if it had been one big mistake after all to persuade her to take this risk.

I got into the passenger seat. Feeling a little cramped, I adjusted the seat.

Peering into the rear mirror, she reversed the jeep out of the garage and down a gravelled drive towards the road.

Three minutes later, the road levelled out and ahead, we could see a traffic jam.

"Traffic here at this time of day is unusual." She said as she peered anxiously ahead.

A pang of fear shot down my spine.

"I don't like this. I'll get out here."

"No, no, wait. There's a car coming."

I frantically checked the side mirror. A Ford Mondeo was closing up behind us.

In front, we could see why the traffic was tailing back; police officers were stopping and checking cars.

"Shit. I've got to get out now." I quickly scanned the surroundings, my stomach turning with apprehension.

"Too late now. You will only draw attention to yourself," she said.

"Doing nothing is not an option either."

"It is now. Stay with me."

With increased caution, Mrs. Quail followed the traffic, maintaining a greater distance from the next car. She lit a cigarette and exhaled. About twenty meters from the checkpoint, she veered off the road and along the grass verge speeding past the checkpoint.

"What are you doing? You will draw attention to us." I said between clenched teeth, my heart clanging furiously against my ribs.

"Just watch me."

"Watch you? This is crazy," I said quietly.

"Just hold on to your seat," she said.

We screeched round a bend and through an open gate into a field. She drove close to the edge following the tree line. Looking back, I saw two police cars stuck in the mud, wheels spinning and sirens blaring. With a sudden jerk of the steering we turned down a cinder path and back on to a road, twenty seconds later, we screeched to a halt outside 3 Pinkerton Drive. And without looking at me, she said, "you are on your own from here."

"Thanks." I got out and watched her drive away.

I quickly scanned the area. A quiet neighbourhood with a good distance between houses, and each neatly hedged.

Immediately, there was the strong sensation I was being watched from somewhere. Fighting to control the flutter in my stomach, I turned to number 3, a conservatively built house.

Hardly containing my anxiety, I rushed up the driveway. Reaching the front door, I pressed the doorbell and waited, not sure what to expect. Curtains were drawn. Not a movement. Now the only noise I could hear was my faltering heartbeats. My head was swimming in all directions with fear. Would one of Shadow's men answer the door and lead me to Lorna? Perhaps, they might just let Lorna get the door herself. What a moment that would be. The elation... The relief. I would lift her off the ground and carry her home, and no one would hurt her again.

I pressed the bell again.

Nothing.

I backed up and looked through the windows, but not a movement. I swung around and headed back to the front door and jammed the doorbell.

Now panicking, I tried the door. It was unlocked. I cursed myself for not trying this sooner. Pushing the door open, I rushed inside.

BOOM!

The explosion was deafening.

The flash of blinding light.

The pain was excruciating. Everything was suddenly out of focus. Breathing was difficult and strenuous. Blood seeped from my nostrils and mouth, followed by an acute pain in my chest and head.

My eyes slowly rolled back, then calm, total darkness.

Chapter Thirty-Six

Later that day, not far from the events of the Docklands, Shadow stood passively in a luxury penthouse suite eyeing the splendid view of the Thames and the London Eye. Deep in thought, he wandered over to his computer and studied the screen. Sliding into a leather swivel chair, he rubbed his eyes and took a deep breath as he turned, slowly exhaling. He stared at a blank cinema screen in the corner.

Shadow was amazed at how suddenly things had changed. Not long ago, he'd watched Malik live on video link being removed from this country on the Boeing 747. That accomplishment far compensated for the difficult years he'd spent hunting him. And now mopping up this long and complex operation was at the front of his mind.

Shadow always tried not to think too much of those things he had no influence over, concentrating instead on what he wielded in abundance. Power. That never failed to lift his mood, as though he needed constant reminder of his worth in gold. Power was to Shadow what drugs were to an addict.

He swung his chair in an arc stirring with some contentment. Despite everything, trapping Malik was one of his most significant and proud achievements. Not least, because he had manipulated one of the best democracies in the world, he had penetrated the best judicial system in the world. Now he could boast of his exploits like never before; never had anyone gotten to the very heart of the British judiciary before. And soon, his clients in Russia would gladly take delivery of the man they too had sought, and for whom they'd spared no expense.

Head bowed, eyes closed, Shadow quickly returned to the present. At this moment, he was not completely in control of his world; he had to await confirmation from his foot soldiers that the mopping exercise had been successful too. No evidence should be left behind, no witness allowed. Such was how it had always been from time immemorial.

He lit a cigar and flicked the match missing the ashtray by a whisker. Then he drew hard on the Havana, savouring the taste. He had no idea if Dias was dead or alive. Surely, the man must be dead, he reasoned. That much he expected from a six pound bomb strapped somewhere in the house and primed to go off on his entry. No man could survive that. Impossible. Not even if he was the luckiest man on the planet.

Shadow started pacing the floor with short quick steps. This much was clear. His integrity was on the line. Until the mop-up exercise was complete, neither he nor his clients would rest. Then he stopped by the window and stared out, his hands interlaced behind him. The river Thames was quiet except for a few tour boats. The million-dollar view had always been a welcome distraction when he was tense. He loved it at this pent house. He always came here to get away from it all, to relax. But not this time. Instead, he held a slight irritation mixed with impatience, and he quickly retreated again into himself like a wounded animal. He hated waiting for news, especially the news that he had helped to make. Life was strange, he mused quietly.

The phone buzzed shattering the silence.

Shadow dashed across, depressed a button turning on the speakerphone.

"Yes," he said irritably.

"Eyeball here, Sir. Is it OK to speak?"

"Yes . . . yes. What is it?"

"We've picked up a sound. We're enhancing it now, Sir," said the caller.

"Hold on. I'm just putting in my earpiece to listen in too," returned Shadow.

There was a moment's pause.

"Can you hear that Sir?"

"No... no. This had better not be another hoax." Shadow pushed the earpiece deeper and held his breath. "What's that?" he said impatiently.

"We think it's breathing, Sir," said the caller.

Shadow immediately turned the speakerphone off and leaned back in his chair listening intently through the earpiece. Then as clear as a bell, he heard a woman say, "Drink?" He recognised the voice as the same one he'd heard talking with Dias earlier.

Shadow heard a shuffling sound. Then a faint thud.

Silence.

A popping sound, followed by a clank of glasses.

There was another silence.

"Hmmm."

A rapid breathing ensued. Then muffled groans that rose steadily as the breathing intensified. Moments later, a mild scream filled Shadow's earpiece, followed by a loud throaty groan which also reached a crescendo. And suddenly there was calm.

A rather protracted silence, and then, "Hmmm… that was great," the female voice said. "I'm surprised you still rose to the occasion after what happened earlier with that intruder."

"Shock of my life, that's all. That ain't nothing," a male voice said.

"Oh, now you can talk," she teased and laughed.

"What's that supposed to mean?"

"You're a coward really. He could've killed me and all you wanted to do was save your own neck, you idiot."

"What did you expect? There I was banging another man's wife, stoned out of my fucking head. Then there was that blade, like a Samurai sword. Naah! I said, no way I was getting slashed because of a shag."

"A real man would've stood up for me."

214

"Fuck sake. Against that blade? I'm no Swarzzenegar, you know. Besides I freaked out because I thought he was your husband."

She giggled. "If my husband were that handsome and hunky, would I be looking at you?" She giggled some more.

"He ain't coming back, is he?" the man said.

"Not as far as I know. Why?"

"He left his suit behind."

"Oh that. It's going in the bin before my husband comes home."

Staring grimly in the space, Shadow removed the earpiece and leaned back in the chair. His features tightened. He wasn't sure what made him angrier; the incomplete mission or the uncertainty. Though the whole incident left an indelible mark on Shadow, what grieved and worried him most was what his clients might make of the blunder.

Shadow knew there was only one other source of information, and with some hesitation, he painfully switched on the TV.

Chapter Thirty-Seven

An hour after the explosion, parts of the ground were still smouldering, the damage was colossal.

No one seemed more struck than Josh Adams, who was restlessly pacing the scene of the crime. He was in his late thirties and twenty-four stone. It wasn't the scale of the terror that perplexed him, after all he had seen much worse during the IRA campaign, but rather it was the target. Rarely was a residential area on mainland Britain the focus for terrorist cells. But there was something else on his mind.

Josh Adams stopped to the first ring of his mobile phone. "Yes?"

"The property's squeaky clean," said the caller.

"Whom is it registered to?" Josh Adam's relief was evident in his voice.

"Arthur Stones. A pensioner," returned the caller.

"Do we have anything on him?"

"Not a thing. My guess is he doesn't exist."

"Don't guess, pal. Get to the bottom of it and come back to me." He hung up, less tense than he had been. No security concern on the address also meant he could safely rule out Al-Qaeda cells. In turn, that would mean no CIA or FBI involvement in the investigation. Josh Adams had nothing against Americans; he just didn't like taking orders from them.

The area was still cordoned off. Fire trucks, ambulance vans and police cars lined the street. Two helicopters were hovering noisily above, combing the area. Forensic experts scurried about in the frenzy, with the sporadic crackle of radios. Even in the commotion, there was one question on everyone's mind; how could anyone survive the blast?

Josh Adams bent over the exact spot where moments earlier Dias had lain, encircled by a team of paramedics. Now only a pool of congealed blood on the ground remained.

"Mr. Adams," a voice shouted above the noise.

Josh turned and quickly rose. "Afternoon, Mr. Quail. Some horrid scene here."

Jasper Quail ignored him, glancing round. He was head of anti-terrorist branch at Scotland Yard.

In his early sixties, he had greying hair swayed neatly back. He was casually dressed, his Nike baseball cap made him look like a character out of Dallas.

"Oh shit. Of all places in this country, they chose my neighbourhood." Mr. Quail said to no one in particular.

Josh shrugged. "I suppose this is as close as it gets. Don't worry, Sir, we'll hunt down those responsible."

Looking around, Mr. Quail took in more details. Fear had never played any part in his professional judgement. But this was about to change. Not only was he wrestling with the rationale behind this, he was also painfully aware of the consequences. Whatever the reason was, it appeared to have put Mr. Quail in a state of deep unease. He knew that fear would soon spread to his influential neighbours like a wildfire.

Mr. Quail turned to Josh. "What have we got?"

"Not much. It's early days yet. But I've run a check on the property." Josh paused to slow his breathing down, something he did frequently when he was nervous.

"And then?"

"It's clean." Josh scooped a heap of sweat off his forehead. "One Arthur Stones owns the property. His identity is in doubt. But the boys are following that up."

"That's not good enough. Find out who bought this house. Someone paid money or with a cheque for this. Go trace who sold it. Was an estate agent involved? I want answers, Josh. I want them fast," he said flicking his fingers, and then walked away.

"You don't get it, Sir." Josh threw both hands in the air and followed Mr. Quail. "The trail on the owner is cold. I suggest . . ."

Mr. Quail stopped abruptly stopping Josh in mid-sentence. He made a forceful, self-controlled gesture in a vain attempt to remain civilized.

"Somebody please tell me I'm imagining this," Mr. Quail snarled. "Don't go cold on me now, Josh. I need information. Anything. Get a

218

description. Some bastards paid good money for this property and blew it up. That's not normal, is it, Josh?" He shouted.

"No."

"Good. At least we're agreed on that." Then he moved closer to Josh. "The whole world wants answers fast. We've got to have something to say to look like we are in control of this situation. Anything. Don't let them know we are bum...I know we are but don't let them know or we both go down too. Don't let me down, big boy?"

Josh nodded his agreement. "OK. There's one more thing. The press."

"What about the press? That's the least of your problems right now. Tell them there was an explosion, which may be a bomb. One casualty and we're investigating. Do you know more?" He shouted.

"No Sir."

"Then move it."

***

Des Reiley arrived at the scene, weaving his way anxiously past columns of security personnel until he finally stood at shoulder length with Mr. Quail. For a moment, Des appraised the damage, his stare intense.

"What the hell was he doing here?" Reiley's voice was a little more than a whisper.

"Who?" Mr. Quail returned.

"Sorry. Just thinking aloud," Des said.

219

"Noted. But who do you mean?"

"The casualty."

"You know him?" Mr. Quail turned fully to him.

Reiley nodded quietly, still staring ahead. "We're interested in him."

Mr. Quail shot him an evil eye. "What else do you know about this guy?"

"He's a suspect in two murders we're investigating."

"Has he got a name?"

"He's been identified through dental records as Phil Dias. He's our man."

"Active?"

"No, no. He's a lawyer."

There was a short pause, as Mr. Quail studied him, his face creasing into a frown at Reiley's terse responses. Mr. Quail had never liked him and both knew the feeling was mutual. Until now, their paths had never crossed, himself busy tracking down terrorists and Des Reiley, engrossed with chasing after murderers. The difference was distinct, and Mr. Quail had hoped it would stay that way. It was not to be; here he was standing with a colleague he would rather strangle if given half a chance. Now the realisation that they might be working together on this case, albeit in a short term made his heart sink.

Then, Mr. Quail smiled. But the smile was false and he sensed that Reiley knew it too. The truth was that Reiley's presence had depressed him. He was still depressed even now; though he was relieved Reiley had provided some useful information on the casualty. He would need to put personal feelings to one side, he reasoned, if he was to get anywhere in solving the case.

"This lawyer, Phil Dias, what was he doing in this area?"

Reiley shook his head thoughtfully. "We've no intelligence on that."

"Oh ok,' returned Mr. Quail with some sarcasm. "Let's start with something much simpler. How come you got here so fast, Mr. Reiley?"

Chapter Thirty-Eight

It was not only those at the momentous crime scene who maintained a keen interest on the case. A few hundred metres away, Dandy sat in his car glued to binoculars, listening to the police frequency radio with painful apprehension.

Dandy's face set grimly, he wondered if Dias was dead. Nothing in his imagination had prepared him for this. What traumatised Dandy wasn't the fact that they'd tried to eliminate Dias - he'd suspected that, but that he had hoped he could have stopped it. If anything, he was prepared to put himself at risk for his friend. Why the hell not, he thought?

Anxiety about his friend's safety persisted amid growing hope that he was still hanging on to life. At least so he willed. Now he would have to wait much longer to see if he could get wind of where the air ambulance had flown Dias. The trouble was all effort to trap the information on the scanner was futile. In the end frustration set in and tired creases around his eyes said the rest.

Hopeless as it seemed, Dandy reassessed the situation with fresh curiosity. Instinct told him that if Dias were still alive, he wouldn't be the only person interested in his whereabouts. He felt a chill all over his body, now the urgency to find him first, grew ever more intense.

Dandy sped away, checking the time. It had just gone four PM. His forehead wrinkled into a thoughtful frown. He knew a number of top hospitals where they might be headed. The trouble was guessing the correct one on so little information and quickly.

He pursed his lips reflectively, then removed his mobile phone and dialled.

"Come on," Dandy snarled angrily as it rang and rang.

A few more rings later, the line finally crackled into life and a male voice shouted, "Yeah."

Dandy's brows shot up an inch. "Hey Mucho. Listen good. I've got a situation here . . ."

Chapter Thirty-Nine

At Silicon hospital, Dr. Tim Reid and his team waited on the rooftop of the twenty-five floors complex. Two armed officers stood guard, scanning the helipad and the surrounding area with rapt attention.

Dr. Reid, a tiny bespectacled figure with dark hair and a trace of grey at the front, was wearing a dark suit underneath an oversized white coat, a stethoscope hanging round his neck. Lines across his forehead betrayed certain unease.

"They're here now, doctor," a nurse announced.

"Thank goodness," Dr. Reid said checking his watch. He had a sense of relief when the helicopter finally came into view, though commonsense told him the relief was only temporary, and the stress would soon return.

They rushed forward as soon as the helicopter had landed, taking delivery of a mobile stretcher on which Dias lay unconscious. An intravenous tube dangled off a pump. A bloodstained bandage was wrapped around his head and an oxygen mask over his face.

As they wheeled him swiftly towards the entrance, Dr. Reid checked his pulse. The doctor's features immediately signalled concern, then irritation. He hadn't counted on another long night. His eyes were already burning with fatigue. He'd been working non-stop for eighteen hours, and needed rest. But there was little chance of that. The struggle for the top position of consultant had never been fiercer.

Dr. Reid pushed his head back, then stretched it right and left to try to take some of the tension out of his neck.

"Anything else I should know about?" he said to one of the paramedics, gesturing for the medical record.

"Sustained life threatening injuries. His pulse is weak and had to be monitored," the paramedic said.

"Hmm." Dr. Reid grunted, reading the note.

'And he was unconscious throughout,' added the paramedic.

They hurried past a set of glass doors set in polished brass frame, reaching along a wide and brightly lit marble-panelled corridor that had landscape paintings on the walls.

Dr. Reid's face tightened even more as he studied the record, much of which made for a gruesome reading; dangerously high blood pressure at 180/140, the 140 per minute heartbeat and his respiratory rate intense, a suspected internal bleeding in the brain - possibly a punctured membrane, the irregular rhythm of the four heart chambers. When he finally looked up, he was in no doubt about the enormous task facing him. He must save the patient. He knew that

Scotland Yard's interest in the casualty meant only one thing; they wanted him to live to tell the tale. And he would have to keep him alive if he hoped to retain his reputation.

"Thank you guys," he stopped abruptly. "I'll take it from here." Now clutching the medical record to his chest, he joined his team in the elevator headed for the sixth floor.

Chapter Forty

Shadow moved to the window and lit a cigar, staring out, and anger still burning in his eyes. He checked his watch for the umpteenth time. It was coming up to four-forty. He was exhausted, mentally and physically. The waiting for news had been protracted, beyond anything he'd imagined, his patience stretched. Worse still was his growing sense of helplessness - a situation he'd thought would never visit him again. Not so. Because, for the second time in his career, he would agonise over a project, wondering if a mission had succeeded or failed. It was only at times like this that he came face to face with the reality of human imperfections. Something almost always went wrong despite careful planning and he loathed that part of human shortcoming.

Shadow returned to his desk. Now the emphasis quickly shifted. The question was no longer whether he survived but how to buy his silence if he did.

Quietly, he weighed his options, and a dreary cloud lifted from his features. He still had the woman, he thought, and if all else failed, there was always the bait card to play. He would not let her go after all, at least not yet, until Dias was dead.

227

And if Dias set the police on his trail, he further reasoned, he would kill her.

Shadow reached for the phone, dialled a number and instantly got through to the secret location where Lorna was being held.

"Yep," a male voice said.

"How is she?" Shadow said.

"Okay."

"Is she still agitated?"

"She's more relaxed now. The last dose of valium is still working."

"Has she eaten?"

"Not much. Had one bite on a sandwich, that's all. Only because I told her she would be going home today."

There was a short silence.

"What's wrong? She's going home, isn't she?" The man added curiously.

He was Shutz Ritz, an unusual breed. He was as ruthless as he was cold, and the last thing he wanted was to be holed up in the middle of nowhere entrusted with looking after a hysterical woman. Bored stiff, he had looked forward to her release. Nothing in his imagination, had prepared him for this low-keyed assignment, he was used to popping brains and chopping up dead bodies, not woman minding.

Shutz Ritz was an international assassin. No one had done more to enhance the organisation's reputation in Europe, something that had earned him the position as head of Security-Europe. No wonder Shadow trusted him with highly sensitive

228

operations such as this, and to that extent, he was trying to come to terms with his present situation. Only he and Shadow knew where the woman was, and whilst this demonstrated his seniority in the organisation, his patience was now running thin. And that would be such a dangerous thing to happen to a man with his mind always set on one thing; wrecking lives.

"Something wrong?" Ritz pressed.

"She won't be going home just yet." Shadow disclosed.

"What happened?" Ritz said quietly.

"There's a hiccup. We can't verify if her husband died in the explosion or not. Until we can get the whole picture, she stays."

After a moment's hesitation, Ritz said, "Whatever."

"I'll let you know if anything changes. He's becoming a pain in the ass."

"If only you listened to me," Ritz added. "I could've popped him with much less fuss."

"Maybe so. But the risk was too great, and the last thing I wanted was to get MI5 involved."

"We could've used a local hit man."

"I stand by my decision. That's that." Shadow's voice raised a fraction, followed by a momentary, awkward silence. "Keep her from all news sources."

"That's under control."

"Good." Shadow hung up and took a deep breath, satisfied he hadn't let the discussion get out of hand. Even though he didn't always agree with Ritz's thinking which was generally hot-blooded

229

and extreme, he often found himself secretly persuaded afterwards. Ritz had the experience of the gutter, which Shadow lacked. Whilst Ritz was a wild animal, Shadow had been tamed although he was deadly too. Although there was little between them when it came to brutality, Ritz edged a notch because he was raw and didn't see things on the basis of what was good or bad – he instinctively chose bad, but he made decisions on the basis of what was required. With the benefit of hindsight, Shadow knew Ritz was right. That what was required was a local hit man to finish Dias off without exposing the operation to risks, and why hadn't he thought about that, he frowned.

The inter-com buzzed and he flicked the button angrily. "Yes."

'I think you want to watch Sky News, Sir," the caller said.

Shadow turned on Sky News, and was immediately drawn to the caption on the corner of the screen that read, "breaking news - bomb explosion," and turning the volume up, he leaned forward. The news coverage was brief; there'd been a bomb explosion in the docklands area, no information on casualties, police conference to follow soon, no terrorist group had claimed responsibility, and undisclosed police source would not rule out Al-Qaeda cells.

Leaning back, Shadow's face creased into a faint grin, having read between the lines. The news blackout on casualties didn't fool him, it made him wiser.

Chapter Forty-One

Shortly before seven-thirty PM, Dr. Reid finally emerged from the Intensive Care Unit onto the brightly lit corridor and locked the door behind him. He was clutching a clipboard with what looked like a medical file. Standing there as if he found their presence objectionable, he pursed his lips at Mr. Quail and Reiley.

The two police chiefs nodded imperceptibly at him.

"Dr. Reid, I take it you know Superintendent Reiley?" Quail said.

"I do," Dr. Reid returned quickly, a hint of impatience in his voice. He didn't need any introductions. Over the years, he'd become familiar with most police chiefs in the course of their enquiries, usually to do with murder cases, serious assaults, and casualties of IRA bombs around the city. His professional relationship with most of them was awkward. Though he understood it was in the nature of police work to be self-centered, he was often irritated by their insensitivity towards seriously ill patients on whom they relied for evidence. He disliked the culture of disregarding patient care in favour of crime detection, earning him a reputation amongst

231

detectives as extremely stubborn and unfriendly.

Reiley backed up against the wall, staring coldly at the doctor.

"How's it looking, doctor?" Quail said, looking as concerned as he could without making it too obvious he was pretending.

"I'm sorry to disappoint you, Mr. Quail." The sarcasm was not lost in the soft tone of his voice.

"He's going to make it?" Quail said.

"You mean will he live long enough for you to speak to him?" Dr. Reid said.

"Look Doctor, we have a job to..." Quail snapped.

"You damn well have a job to do," Dr. Reid said. "Just spare me the boring details about your duty to protect public, therefore it doesn't matter at whose expense that damned duty to society is performed,' he spluttered, pausing to catch his breath back. In the awkward silence that followed, Dr. Reid was aware of sweat forming on his forehead. Avoiding Quail's gaze, the doctor rubbed his chin.

"Now Mr. Quail," Dr. Reid continued, 'I take it you guys want to know what I'm going to do with this patient?"

Quail didn't respond, there was no point. Asshole, he cursed under his breath. It was a bad day as it was without stirring the doctor's prejudices too, he thought heaving a deep sigh.

Dr. Reid grinned. "All I can tell you about this patient is that it's not looking too good, and I . . ." he paused to a bleeping sound, raising his hand apologetically. He unhooked the beeper from his waist, pressed a button and checked his message. His brows narrowed, and then he looked up again at Quail. "Sorry about that," he added replacing the beeper. "As I said, it's pretty grim at the moment. We're monitoring him closely whilst tests and x-rays are carried out. What happens next will depend on those tests."

Quail scratched his head. "Doctor I wonder . . ."

"Don't even think about it. He can't even breathe on his own let alone talk to you."

Quail put his hands up in the air. "OK. OK."

Dr. Reid forced a grin again, glancing at his watch. "Gentlemen, you must excuse me. I need to contact the reception urgently."

"Sure, sure. Oh one other thing," said Quail. "My men will keep guard outside his door round the clock. So, for security reasons, you must let us know the medical staff that are allowed access to this ward."

"That can be arranged. Excuse me," Dr. Reid said and hurried away.

Halfway down the corridor, Dr. Reid entered a room with a "staff only" sign posted on the door. The medium sized room had a desk and two chairs, and standing over the desk, he called the reception. A female voice answered after several rings.

"Dr. Reid here. You bleeped me. What's the urgency?"

"There's a man here to see you. He insists it's urgent, doctor."

"I'm busy with a patient. Can't see anyone right now."

"I told him that already."

"Then tell him again."

"He's not listening doctor," she said with a ring of indignation. "Oh yes. He said to tell you that the fish had swum out of the ocean, he said you should understand what he means."

"Something like that anyway,' she added with a trace of curiosity.

Dr. Reid slumped into the chair, staring blankly into space. His hands trembled as he tried to maintain a firm grip on the receiver.

"Hello, hello, doctor. Are you there?" The receptionist called.

"Yes." Dr. Reid's voice dropped, almost inaudible. "I'll see him."

Chapter Forty-Two

Now the bomb explosion had attracted national media coverage, and Shadow was certain that Dias was alive. As to where he was receiving medical attention, he was less sure.

Shadow cradled his brandy glass in both hands as he watched a hastily called press conference on the TV. He listened as Mr. Quail announced that a full and swift police investigation was under way to catch the criminals behind the explosion. On behalf of Scotland Yard, Mr. Quail appealed for information, ruling out any Al-Qaeda involvement, he ignored questions from the press and made his way out.

"Hmmm" Shadow changed the channel, and for the first time that evening, pictures of the crime scene spooled through. No 3 Pinkerton Drive had been reduced to a pile of rubble, the rear supporting columns of the building were ripped out and the front view levelled. Much of the debris had been burnt black by the intense fire. Security personnel still peppered in the background and forensics team was still milling around the scene.

"Lucky son of a bitch," Shadow grunted.

The images suddenly disappeared, replaced by

the newsreader and the reporter who had split the screen between them.

"Tom, do we have any more information about the bomb explosion?" One newsreader said.

"Not a great deal, Francis. Scotland Yard is not saying a lot. But we are told another press conference will be held tomorrow morning. Over to you Francis."

"So Tom, there's been no official confirmation of any casualties?"

"No. But we've had an unconfirmed report of a casualty. A man is said to have been airlifted to hospital and is believed to be in an intensive care unit as we speak. Scotland Yard has neither confirmed nor denied this report. As I said, this is an unconfirmed report. Back to you in the studio, Francis."

"Has any group claimed responsibility for this? Any ideas as to who might be responsible?"

"As far as we know, no group has accepted responsibility for this, although Scotland Yard has not made any official statement. But we have gathered from sources close to the investigation that they are still keeping an open mind about . . ."

"Tom, we must leave it there. Sorry to cut you short. We've run out of time. Tom Jeffries reporting from Docklands where a bomb exploded this afternoon."

Shadow turned the TV off and reached for the phone, he dialled a number and waited.

Ritz's unmistakable gruff voice came alive instantly. He too had been following developments, and he knew Shadow would consult him on how the next action might play. For Ritz, the buzz of espionage was in putting right a bungled operation - because it nearly always involved killing. He took great pleasure in snuffing out people.

"Yep?" Ritz said.

"You heard the news?"

"Down to the last detail," Ritz said coldly.

Shadow hesitated for a moment. "Put our best on this one. Seek out and eliminate."

"When by?" Ritz said.

"Tonight. Delay is dangerous. Failure is not an option."

"You got it."

"Who do you have in mind?"

"The best," Ritz replied calmly.

Shadow grinned, leaned back in his chair and said no more.

Chapter Forty-Three

Dr. Reid slipped into the elevator unnoticed heading for the main reception on the ground floor. He was still recovering from the shock following the announcement of his visitor, even his heart continued to miss a beat, a cruel reminder of the nightmare that awaited him. Someone he'd known long ago had resurfaced and he could almost bet his last penny that it wasn't a social visit. That much was sure.

Reaching the ground floor, he entered his office. He slumped behind his desk facing the door, and lifted the receiver, "Dr. Reid here. Please direct the gentleman to my office," he said and hung up.

Several moments later, the door jerked open. His visitor hadn't even knocked. But none of that surprised Dr. Reid because the man he knew never had been a prospective candidate for the world's most courteous man.

Dandy stood at the door for a few seconds, his steely cold eyes riveted on Dr. Reid.

Swallowing hard, Dr. Reid let out a few gasps of breath, forcing a nervous grin as he tried to duck out of Dandy's intense cold and penetrating eyes.

Dandy stepped in and shut the door behind him.

Dr. Reid stared up at him, analysing him. It was ten years since he last saw Dandy and had hoped it would be the last. The two had struck a genuine friendship that quickly crystalised into a brief criminal enterprise that almost wrecked Dr. Reid's life and career. Between them, they masterminded insurance fraud netting several millions of pounds. It was simple. Dandy brought in a shipload of dead bodies from war-torn Albania; Dr. Reid gave them fake IDs made up from the hospital's database of deceased patients. Then a substantial life insurance policy was arranged for each dead body which was cashed in soon after, usually after the insurance company had made due enquiries. With one of the best surgeons certifying the deaths, there were few eyebrows raised. Like all good things, it soon turned sour. An alert insurance executive under threat of losing his job got lucky. Whilst on a routine enquiry of a beneficiary named in one such policy, he recognised Dandy from an earlier transaction. Alarm bells started ringing and the scam was uncovered. Dandy was convicted, shunning the prosecution offer for him to dump Dr. Reid in it. The doctor was home and dry; he hadn't used his own seal in any of the fraudulent claims. But Dandy wasn't so lucky because, the judge mindful of his determined loyalty to his friend gave him ten years imprisonment. Dr. Reid had since paid Dandy a quarter of a million, a gesture of his gratitude. That was ten years ago. That much money brought him two promises from

239

Dandy. First, Dandy would keep his mouth shut about the doctor's involvement in the scam. Second, he would keep his distance from the doctor for eternity.

Disgusted at the ominous presence of the figure from his past, Dr. Reid quietly confirmed what he'd long suspected.

"What are you doing here?" His voice was barely audible as though a tennis ball had wedged down his throat.

Dandy sat across from him. "Hardly a way to welcome an old friend who's done so much for you."

"I paid for it already, damn it."

"I agree," Dandy said calmly.

"You promised to stay away from me. You gave me your word of honour. Not much of an honour, is it? Because I'm staring at you right now, damn it."

Dandy reclined in his chair, his features deep set. His contempt was all pervasive.

Dr. Reid swallowed rapidly, breaking his gaze. His expression became solemn. He loosened his tie a little and waved his hand apologetically, staring away.

"I wouldn't be here if I could help it," Dandy said quietly.

Dr. Reid looked at him. "Let's not waste each other's time. It's a bad time. I can't raise an awful lot right now. We've just moved into a bigger house . . . that's cost me an arm and a leg. Quite frankly, I don't want to sound ungrateful or

240

anything but . . ."

"I don't want your money," Dandy interrupted, and hearing a faint sigh, continued, "listen, you do me this favour, and I'm out of here. I swear I'll be out of your life for good. I mean it."

Dr. Reid eyed him with obvious suspicion.

"What favour?"

"The patient in the intensive care unit is my friend. His name is Dias."

"Yes? He's under my care."

"Unless I remove him to a safer environment quickly, he will be killed." Dandy pleaded.

"I don't understand. You mean ... Hold on a moment," he paused. "You're asking me . . ."

"Yep. That's all I ask and I'm out of your life for good."

"That's crazy . . . that's insane," Dr. Reid said running his hands through his hair. His lips quivered with tension. "This is stupid . . . I mean it's impossible. There's a huge security presence around this guy 24/7."

"I know. But I've got a plan to get round that," Dandy said staring intently into his eyes.

Dr. Reid shook his head. "I don't know . . . I really can't think straight right now." He rose and paced the floor, beads of sweat forming on his forehead. "Who's this guy anyway?"

Dandy didn't respond immediately, his face devoid of all expressions as he wondered if he should trust his old friend.

Finally, he told him as much as he needed to know.

Chapter Forty-Four

A man in his early forties hesitated momentarily in the doorway of the lobby at Silicon hospital. His brown eyes darted cautiously from one corner to the next as he made a mental appraisal of everyone. Sensing no obvious danger, he shifted his gaze to the reception.

The lobby was scattered with people, mostly women and children. The overall picture was grim - the occasional shrieks from children, the familiar cry from hungry and restless babies, pale looking adults reeling from exhaustion after hours of waiting, frail and non-temperamental old people bracing themselves against boredom and anxiety. There were also grief-stricken faces fretting over their loved ones, not sure whether they would live or die, whether the illness was temporary or terminal. Then there was the pungent odour of perspiration, medicine and antiseptic pervading the air.

The man marched across the brightly lit lobby towards the reception desk, his shoes echoing as they hit the floor, attracting stares from across the lobby. He was aware he looked distinguished. He'd planned to look different. It was part of a coherent plot.

He stood in the short queue at the reception counter. And while he waited his turn, he discreetly scanned the lobby again. This time he was checking to see if anyone had taken more than a casual interest in him. He would know if someone did as he was trained to spot even the best of them – plain clothes policemen, decoys, the whole lot. He would know if there were security personnel mixed with civilians. But all he could discern from the small crowd were disinterested, anxious faces.

Nothing suspicious, he thought. Then he noticed a woman sitting in the far corner and engaged her stare for a moment, he nodded but she didn't nod back, resentment written all over her face.

Satisfied he wasn't being watched, he turned to the counter.

He looked at a female receptionist who was looking exasperated in a vain attempt to satisfy her patients. Poor thing, he thought, the NHS was increasingly under pressure from more people living longer, refusing to die, and out living their contributions. Money was tight, and the organisation's answer was to cut staff putting a tiny workforce under constant pressure.

Finally she looked at him and nodded, and he responded with a faint smile. She blushed and quickly adjusted the fringes of her hair as she became conscious of the penetrating brown eyes watching her. Her concentration faltered somewhat. She couldn't remember the last time anyone showed any interest in her. She was used to rude enquirers, not to mention depressed doctors battered by excessive working hours, who wasted no time in venting their frustration on her and others.

He rested his briefcase on the counter. "Hello," he said softly trying to sound clear and not ordinary. He knew how effective first impressions could be and he wasn't about to waste the opportunity.

"How may I help you?" She said smiling.

"I hate to trouble you … I know how busy you must be. I'm a consultant at Kings' hospital and I know how much pressure our staff are under."

She smiled even more.

He straightened up. "I've been called to assist in a complicated operation on a patient called Dia. Perhaps you can save me time and tell me where he's located in the building."

"Sure," she said taking a position in front of a computer. A few moments later, her brows narrowed. "What did you say the name was?"

"D.I.A." he spelt it slowly and waited patiently. He was used to this process already - his third enquiry that night.

"Sorry I can't seem to find Dia on the computer," she said dutifully browsing the screen.

"I hope I've recorded the name correctly," he said, pulling out a small sized diary and flipping through the pages. "Perhaps, you will be kind enough to check if there's something remotely resembling that name."

She concentrated on the screen again. "There's Diakim, Dias, Dianne . . ."

"Oh, I don't know. I shouldn't take up your time much longer. There seems to be some confusion. I'll phone my office and get the full details," he grinned satisfaction. Third time lucky, he mused.

"Sorry I couldn't be of much help," she said defensively.

"Oh no. You've been most helpful," he returned with a wink.

As the receptionist returned the wink smiling broadly and invitingly at him, Shultz Ritz left the reception area and disappeared into the corridor knowing he was a hair's breadth from his target.

Chapter Forty-Five

Dr. Reid was still staring into space long after Dandy had finished explaining the plan, head cocked to one side, he rubbed his chin with his index finger. His first reaction was one of horror, then indignation. But as he slowly regained his composure, he mauled over what he'd heard, and even then, nothing made much sense. The whole thing reminded him of characters straight out of Mario Puzo's book, and taking a deep breath, he sat back down folding his hands in even more contemplation.

"I still think this is unwise whatever the justification," he said finally.

"Some things don't make sense but they are necessary nonetheless," said Dandy. "I suffered a long stretch in prison to protect you. It didn't make sense but I did it anyway."

The lump in Dr. Reid's throat shot up and down. Dandy leaned back, displaying no emotion. He was defiant, his determination evident in the way his head tilted backwards.

"If a friend is not worth losing an arm for, he's not worth having," Dandy added quietly.

Dr. Reid shifted uneasily. He knew the last sentence was personal, an indictment of him, and he needed no further prompting of the history, the era of greed that had now returned to haunt him. He suddenly assumed a picture of a man with nothing to lose.

"Two things you need to know. First your friend is still unconscious and his condition is critical. Results of tests will not be ready for another twenty minutes or so. It may well be he'll require brain surgery. So wherever you intend taking him must have adequate medical facilities to meet his needs, or he'll die," Dr. Reid said.

"Hmm." Dandy stared distractedly. Though he'd arranged to move Dias to his friend's private clinic, he hadn't considered this, and the clinic had no facilities for specialist operations. That much he knew. But he would have to choose between the devil and the deep blue sea.

"We'll take the chance. The alternative is more frightening," Dandy said finally.

Dr. Reid shrugged.

"Anything else?"

"Security. He has round the clock police protection."

"I know," Dandy said. "I'm aware of the armed guards. Here's the second plan."

Chapter Forty-Six

Ritz stood patiently in front of the elevator on the ground floor, his destination was the intensive care unit on the sixth floor. He knew from experience that no one survived such a blast that was not nearly mashed up, and such casualties were nearly always kept in the intensive care units. That was standard practice in hospitals, and he was sure it would be the same in this one.

Moments later, the doors opened with a ding-dong sound and a doctor hurried out of the lift and past him, stethoscope dangling around his neck.

Ritz's interest deepened when the man stopped at the far end of the corridor, unlocked a door and disappeared from view.

"You look as if you could do with some direction?"   Dr.   Reid   interrupted   Ritz's concentration, slipping into the elevator.

Ritz turned and forced a benign smile.   "No thanks. Just got carried away for a moment."

"I know the feeling. We all do these days. You coming?"

"No thanks. I'll take the staircase. Need the exercise," Ritz said.

Ritz waited until the elevator had started ascending before moving quickly down the corridor. He stopped in front of the door the doctor had entered moments earlier, and peering left, then right, he quietly turned the doorknob and slipped in.

The doctor was sitting behind a desk with his eyes closed, his hands clasped behind his head, and swinging to light classical music. Reaching inside his suit jacket, Ritz pulled a Heckler and Koch PP7 9MM pistol and screwed on a silencer. He pointed it at the doctor and cleared his throat.

The doctor opened his eyes. At first, out of focus, then making sense of his vision, he let out a suppressed gasp and jumped to his feet. His expression was frozen.

"Ssssh. Easy now," Ritz said calmly. "Easy does it, and nobody will get hurt. You hear me?"

The man nodded quickly, his eyes glistening with wariness.

"To stay alive, you just need to tell me the access number for the intensive care unit on the sixth floor."

"We use a security swipe card," he spluttered, swallowing rapidly, his hands clasping, unclasping and clasping again as if he were suffering from a manic disorder.

"OK. Relax. You're doing just fine. Now place your security swipe-card on the table," Ritz said waving the gun lightly.

The doctor quickly fumbled in his breast pocket, unhooked a chain strapped to a swipe-card and dropped it on the table.

"Where's the key to this room?"

He pointed towards the door. "It's there."

Ritz smiled coldly.

"Please don't hurt me," the doctor pleaded, his back to the wall.

"Sorry, but you have a lousy taste in music." Tightening his finger on the trigger, his eyes narrowing into slits, Ritz fired a shot - the sound of a champagne cork popping. The bullet pierced through his forehead throwing him backwards from the impact. He hit the wall with a loud thud before slowly slumping to the floor. His lifeless body sat in an upright position, legs sprawled forward, hands crossed, and head tilted to one side and a hole the size of a coin was visible on his forehead.

Ritz replaced the gun inside his jacket and set down the leather briefcase on the table, and opened it carefully revealing a 4000 lb. bomb. Glancing placidly at his watch, he then primed the bomb to a hand-held detonator before shutting the briefcase.

Ritz unhooked a white jacket hanging on the wall and slipped into it. Then he scooped the security swipe-card, the key and the stethoscope off the table and calmly appraised the situation for a brief moment. He had everything he needed.

Out in the corridor, briefcase in hand he locked the door and headed towards the elevators rather pleased with himself. He was happy to be back doing what he loved doing best.

Chapter Forty-Seven

On his way back to the ICU, hands thrust in his coat pocket, his head drooped, Dr. Reid's mind swirled. He thought about Dandy.

He played back Dandy's plan in his mind. He was still the master planner he'd known years ago - a pure genius, he thought. Dandy's mind represented the greatest threat to human race after nuclear bombs. He'd been surprised to find the old man still possessed such enormous stamina. But it was the old man's display of calm, his alertness under pressure that amazed the doctor the most.

The first part of Dandy's plan had been easy for Dr. Reid. He'd swiftly recalled from the mortuary the last male patient who'd died under his care. He wasn't surprised to learn it was still laying outside the fridge. Shortage of space had been a problem for some time. Besides, no one was likely to raise an eyebrow because there was nothing unusual about the request. Sometimes, dead bodies were recalled and carved up for body parts without the knowledge of their unsuspecting relatives. All this, of course, so another patient might live. There was another reason besides. Sometimes, bodies were recalled at the request of police pathologists, which fitted in with Dandy's plan.

Dr. Reid's only other problem would be to keep his cool under the alert eyes of Quail and Reiley. His pulse was beating faster than normal, and reaching the entrance to the ICU, he looked at them and grinned. Everything is fine, he heard himself saying in his mind.

"Trouble?" Quail said, and shot a glance past the doctor.

"No, no," Dr. Reid said, his eyes shifting from one man to another. "But there's a development."

Quail's features dropped suddenly. "What is it? Bad?"

"Tests show a serious brain hemorrhage," Dr. Reid said.

Quail turned away and faced the wall, his fist clenched. He gritted his teeth as he resisted an urge to punch the wall.

Reiley cleared his throat. "So doctor, what's the plan?"

"Must operate straight away. I've arranged for a specialist brain surgeon to perform the operation," said Dr. Reid.

Quail turned. "And his chances?"

Dr. Reid shot him a disapproving look. "Excuse me, gentlemen," he said walking away.

"Don't walk away from me, damn it," Quail shouted angrily, shoving the doctor back and pinning him to the wall. "Don't you fucking disrespect me, you son of a bitch," Quail snarled.

"Stop it," Reiley shouted, throwing himself between them.

Quail shook himself free of Reiley's hands.

"Don't lay your stinking hands on me," Quail snarled at Reiley too.

"Look doctor," Reiley said quietly, "I'm sorry. This is a bad time for all of us. He's under pressure to get a result and Dias is all we've got right now. Forget this ever happened, right?"

Dr. Reid straightened his jacket. "I'll get the patient ready for the operation," he said and disappeared into the ICU.

Moments later, two nurses emerged from the ICU wheeling Dias in a mobile bed, followed by Dr. Reid.

"Gentlemen, we're going to the operating room now," Dr. Reid said.

"We're coming with you," said Reiley, nodding at two armed guards.

"It's on the seventh floor," Dr. Reid said, trailing his team.

Quail followed, his downcast eyes had a certain hollowness that bespoke the pain of fading hopes. It was all too clear that the expectations that Dias might recover and speak to them were now a little too optimistic. Perhaps not soon, probably not ever.

Chapter Forty-Eight

Hiding in the operating theatre, Dandy and four mercenaries he'd hired to assist him were now uncertain and dispirited. Only one thing happened which was not in the plan. Delays. They'd been waiting for Dr. Reid, and Dandy was fuming, his anxiety infectious.

"I don't like this," Dandy said glancing up with frustration at Viper. He studied the untidy balding nondescript man across from him.

Dandy guessed he was in his mid-forties. He looked like a small-town butcher, without a care in the world. Stocky and constantly chewing gum, he stared back defiantly. Viper's motivation in life was money.

"I'm talking to you," Dandy said.

"Cut it out, you fool," Viper growled.

"Maybe I am a fool. But right now, I'm paying you to give your best in this operation. You hear me. And that includes giving your opinion when I ask for it."

"My opinion?" Viper snarled. "Fuck you, you frail fucker. The only thing I fancy giving you is a kick up your ass."

"You foul-minded bastard," Dandy snarled drawing his gun at Viper but he didn't bat eye.

Suddenly Dandy stopped, staring into three semi-automatic pistols pointing in his direction. His eyes, now fiery, darted from Viper to the mercenaries then to Viper. Even so, Dandy was unfazed.

"Put that fucker away, you gutless mother fucker," Viper said chewing more rapidly. "You should've listened to me. We were all for storming the ward, taking out the fucking guards and removing your friend. But you said no. You had a better idea, huh? Now you start losing your nerve, you do it alone. Don't ask my fucking opinion. You ain't getting fuck all."

Dandy lowered his gun. Wearing a surgical suit, shower cap and reading glasses, he looked more like a space scientist than a brain surgeon. And as the woman and two men stared sharply back at him, Dandy had the feeling of being a deer amongst a herd of lions. Tension gnawed at his stomach.

"It's alright, guys," Viper said with a wave, and they reluctantly tucked their guns away.

Dandy turned and paced the floor. And checking the time, he wondered if something had gone wrong. He moved towards the far corner stopping beside a mobile bed on which lay a dead body. An oxygen mask was placed over the corpse's face and an intravenous tube attached to its arm. Dandy felt pressure lift from his shoulders. One thing, at least, had gone to plan. Though on close inspection the dead man bore no resemblance to Dias, it was enough for their purpose, he

255

thought.

"I think they're here," Viper said in a muffled voice.

Dandy turned, listened and nodded. They quickly slipped on their masks and converged around the operating table. A lamp above the table provided the only light.

There was a cautious knock.

Dandy looked at Viper and raised his thumb; Viper nodded his agreement.

"Remember, nothing stupid," whispered Dandy.

"Shut the fuck up and get the door," said Viper.

Without another word, Dandy opened the door, standing in the doorway. He quickly scanned the entourage.

"We'll take it from here, doctor. The room has been disinfected and ready for surgery," Dandy said pulling the mobile bed into the room. Viper and the female mercenary immediately took over. "Of course, you may observe the proceedings from the observation room next door."

"Sure. Oh, just one more thing," Dr. Reid said. 'Mr. Quail here is in charge of the security arrangements for this patient. He will be present for the duration of the surgery."

Quail nodded, but Dandy didn't reciprocate.

"Anything else, doctor?" Dandy said checking the time.

"Two armed guards will be stationed out here. No one will be allowed in unless security cleared," said Dr. Reid. He turned to Quail. "Do you want to add anything to that?"

"No," Quail said. "How long will the surgery take?"

Dandy shrugged. "Three hours max?"

"Doctor, there's a situation here," Viper interrupted.

Dandy spun round. "What's the matter?"

"We're not getting any reading from the monitor. The equipment is not working properly," returned Viper.

"Shit. Have you applied the anesthetic already?"

"That was the first thing we did. He's gone to sleep."

"Oh gosh," Dandy gasped.

"Calm down," Dr. Reid said, "let's get him to room 12 instead. Now."

Quail swallowed rapidly. "Oh my God."

Dandy turned to his team. "Come on. Transfer the patient to room 12. Quick," he shouted, stepping aside as the mercenaries sped past, wheeling the mobile bed down the corridor. The security personnel followed with dogged alertness.

When Dandy and his team finally disappeared into room 12, Dr. Reid headed towards the observation room.

"You coming?"

Ignoring Dr. Reid, Quail turned to the armed guards. "Nobody's allowed in that room unless you clear it with me first."

Chapter Forty-Nine

Ritz took the elevator to the sixth floor, stepping into the corridor; he looked to his right, then left, noting the ICU. His eyebrows furrowed slightly. Lack of security outside the ICU was all too auspicious for his liking. In normal situations he would be pleased he was not in any danger, but he was not feeling lucky. Instead there was a pervasive sense he might be walking into a trap.

Reaching in his pocket, he removed the swipe security card and ran it through. The automated door buzzed and he pulled it gently, standing in the doorway, his face impassive, he took a swift scan of the room that was separated into three sections by curtains. The only sign of life was the blipping sounds of life support machines.

The grey floor, white wall, acrid smell and the inferior leather-topped desk in the center made a somber impression. Aside from that, the room was well lit.

Ritz was alert. He moved cautiously into the room stopping by the desk to listen. At that moment, he heard a movement. The curtain drew and a plump female nurse emerged, clutching a pressure cuff.

She saw Ritz and let out a suppressed scream.

Her eyes widened and everything slipped from her trembling hands landing noisily on the floor. Reacting to the disturbance, a male nurse rushed out from the other side, halting abruptly as he noticed Ritz.

Ritz gave the male nurse a quick glance. "Do what I say and nobody will get hurt. Now, get on the floor," he gestured towards the floor with the gun.

They quickly dropped to the floor, liquid forming a pool underneath the female nurse. Springing forward, Ritz reached the curtain in the far right and drew it wide open. An old man on a life support machine lay with his eyes half-closed.

Ritz moved to the center cabin and drew the curtain. It was empty. He checked the far left cabin, and found a young boy on a life support machine. The boy was in tears. Turning away slowly, Ritz wondered momentarily why the boy was crying.

He returned to the center of the room. "Where is he?" His voice was sharp. His raucous command made the female nurse tremble even more. She took a fleeting glance at the gun, squirming a little.

Flicking the safety button off, his cold penetrating eyes riveted on her, Ritz said, "For the last time, where has he been taken?"

She swallowed, and shut her eyes mumbling a silent prayer.

"Don't tell him anything, Fiona," the male nurse cried.

Ritz's eyes darkened. Thoughts mirrored on his face: contempt mingled with disgust. Turning the gun to the male nurse, he squeezed the trigger. Two muffled shots rang out in succession. The first made a hole in his forehead, the other tore out his throat, sprinkling blood everywhere. His body writhed and then lay still.

She shrieked, looking pleadingly at him.

"Sssh."

"They took him . . . they took him upstairs for an operation," the female nurse cried

"Where's the operating room?"

"Upstairs.. Um. . Um... on the seventh floor. Next floor up. Dr. Reid is . . ."

But that was all she had chance to say before a single bullet to her temple splattered her brain across the floor.

***

As Ritz made quickly for the door, he heard the old man groaning. He stopped and walked back to the cabin.

"Were you talking to me, old man?"

The old man just stared.

Ritz studied the life support machine for a moment, but couldn't make sense of its complicated graphs. His features turned into a wistful expression; he was never one to be patient with modern technology. Frustrated, Ritz aimed the pistol at the old man, and then hesitated when he noticed that the old man's mouth had curled backward into a pleasing smile. He stopped and considered him.

"Ah, I get it now, old man. You want me to snuff you out," Ritz said quietly.

The old man smiled even more broadly.

Ritz returned the pistol inside his jacket and moved closer to him. "You should've said, old man," he said, almost whispering. "It's a pleasure. I'll fulfill your wish as painless as possible," taking a pillow from under his head. He switched off the life support machine. "Relax. Soon you will feel no more pain." He placed the pillow over his face and pressed down. Instantly, the frail body twitched violently, then more twitching and the body gradually stiffened. Ritz smiled. It was the sweetest killing he'd done because he had been invited to do what he loved doing most in life. For the first time in his life, he had done a noble thing, he mused. He had performed a civil duty, he thought.

Ritz let go and staring briefly at the lifeless body, he noticed that the old man's fist was clenched with his thumb held up.

He grinned. "You're welcome, pal."

The old man's gratitude had jolted him. He'd never seen anyone so happy to die. He wondered if there would ever come a time when he didn't want to live anymore. Yet he supposed it made no sense, if living was reduced to agony and pain. Hesitating, he looked in the direction of the boy, and remembered the tears in his eyes, and Ritz concluded it was his tacit wish to die.

He pulled a pillow from under the dead man's head and moved towards the boy. He'd never killed a child before, and now shrugging off a sense of unease, he braced himself. He was being charitable, he reasoned.

Lifting the pillow over the child, he noticed that he was not breathing, and the tears had dried on his cheeks leaving lines. The life support machine had already been switched off.

Chapter Fifty

Dr. Reid, flanked by Quail and Reiley, watched the surgery from the observation room. A glass window separated them, from which they had a clear view of the body lying on the operating table, with Dandy and his team in attendance.

As the three were glued to the activities, Dr. Reid was painfully aware his breathing had increased. Sweat beaded his face. Secretly, he vowed never again to cross the threshold into dishonesty.

Reiley was also less buoyant. His features were sunk, and despite a great show as a tough cop, he only managed the composure of a captain in a sinking ship. He too had been under pressure to produce results on the D&L murders, and rumours were already brewing amongst Fleet Street journalists. He knew it was only a matter of time before their patience would run out and questions asked about the investigations into the murders. Besides, peer pressure was another source of Reiley's headaches. Heavily criticised by colleagues for ditching the traditional methods of crime detection, he'd made more enemies than Saddam Hussain. He remained an avid advocate against the Force's unwritten policy - where you couldn't find the culprit, get the closest suspect and cook the evidence.

True to his professional calling, he'd since ignored mounting pressure from his bosses to arrest Dias, favouring instead the fairer process of finding reasonable suspicion before arrest. Now convinced he'd finally collated enough evidence to arrest and question him for the murders, Reiley was hoping he would get his chance in the end. Like many before him who'd been on a slippery slope to oblivion for the professional sin of incompetence, he knew Dias's death might end his investigation, and with that, his career in the Force. With no formal qualifications with which to launch straight back to the labour market, that would leave him two options, either to resign to earning peanuts for the remainder of his life working in the murky business of private security, or join the underworld risking a long stretch in prison. Grimacing at the grim choices, Reiley said more prayers than he'd done in his entire life.

"You mind if I smoke?" Quail said.

Dr. Reid shot him a disapproving look.

Quail exhaled noisily anyway. The steam had built up inside him for some time now. Not even his training, or his twenty-seven years of experience in the force had prepared him for this anxious moment. He understood more than most, the burden on his shoulders, especially in the current climate of fear of terrorism. He knew everyone would need reassuring - the public, the tourist industry, the politicians, the media, and how could he reassure them unless Dias could survive the operation and help the investigation, he reasoned?

"You think he will make it?" Quail said calmly.

Dr. Reid shrugged. "It depends on who scares him the most - you or the devil."

Quail shot him a contemptuous look.

"My guess is, he might find the devil a better company," Dr. Reid said. "But don't worry, if anyone can save him it's this man. He's the best in this business,' reassured Dr. Reid, and for once, he'd told them the truth.

Quail folded his arms. "I hope you're right. I hope you're fucking right, because I need this guy to live."

Silently, they watched the sudden panic in the operating room; Dandy's attention had been drawn to the monitor.

Quail's face turned red. Something was wrong, he thought. Instinct had warned him that Dias might not survive the operation. Jesus! He gasped. His stomach cramped. He stepped closer to the glass window almost pressing against it, his features underlining his deep fear. Helpless, he watched the frantic activity. Pained astonishment creased his face as the team placed a defibrillator on the body and shot 150kh voltage of electric shock through the body. Quail watched the process repeated several times then suddenly, all activity ceased.

There was a brief silence. Dandy finally locked

up, his expressions subdued. Quail knew they'd just lost a vital witness.

"You son of a bitch," Quail snarled.

"Calm down," returned Dr. Reid.

"You bastard! We would've spoken to him if it wasn't for your stubbornness."

"I'm not having this conversation all over again. You know . . ."

"I know fuck, you son of a bitch." Quail was livid.

"I didn't kill him. I tried to save his life," protested Dr. Reid.

"Like fuck you did, you bastard. You piece of shit."

"I'm not going to take any more of this," Dr. Reid said, as he walked out of the observation room slamming the door behind him.

"Come back here, you piece of shit," Quail shouted after him.

Reiley stood speechless staring down at the operating room. He saw Dr. Reid and Quail enter the operating room. Quail was still ranting, his hands flying everywhere. Then he watched as Quail bent over the body and felt for a pulse at his wrist and neck, the expression on his face confirming it.

Reiley's gaze slowly shifted to Dandy and his team. They looked devastated. He watched them filter out of the room leaving Quail and Dr. Reid alone.

Reiley backed away from the glass window and slumped in a chair, exhausted and disappointed.

He wondered what life would be like outside the force. His mobile phone rang, and he ignored it. What was the point?

But the phone would not stop ringing, adding to his frustration and finally he answered it. He immediately recognised the voice as that of his Chief Constable.

"Yes?" Reiley grunted, not bothering to show the usual courtesy for his boss.

"How is it going?"

There was a short pause.

"Are you there?" The caller said.

"Dias died, a few minutes ago."

"Oh shit."

" I'm sorry."

"You will be," the Chief Constable said sharply. "Take it from me. Put Quail on the line now."

"He's not here. I mean he's with the medics in the operating room."

"Then fetch him, you idiot,' Chief Constable barked.

Reiley's anger bubbled to the surface. "No, you fetch him yourself, you wanker."

"I beg your pardon."

"You heard, you deaf wanker," Reiley added and hung up.

Chapter Fifty-One

"Well done guys," Dandy said as they settled back into operating room 15. He removed his mask; so did the others. "We'll be on our way as soon as our getaway transport is here," he added moving anxiously to the mobile bed. He checked Dias's pulse, heaving a sigh of relief.

Dandy dialled a number on his mobile.

"Yep." A voice said against a noisy background.

"Cooper?"

"Hold on."

There was a short pause.

"What's up?" A voice shot in life.

"How long will you be?" Dandy said.

"Fifteen minutes tops. We're on route to pick up your doctor friend. If you don't need him now, we can make it straight to the hospital and lift you guys in eight minutes."

"No, no. I need the doctor on board," he turned to look at Dias. 'He definitely needs one as soon as possible. Get Dr. Braithwaite on board."

"You got it. Fifteen minutes."

Dandy hung up. "Guys, our ride will be here in fifteen minutes." He checked the time. "I suggest we start making our way to the roof-top." He turned to Viper. But Viper was paying little attention; his head inclined and was focused on cleaning his .38 automatic.

"Viper?" Dandy prompted.

Viper looked up.

"Any objections to waiting on the roof-top rather than here?"

Viper shrugged. "It makes no difference to me."

He turned to the others who slowly shook their heads.

Viper turned to Dandy. "No-one gives a fuck."

"Then we leave immediately. You two push the patient. Viper, you take care of the intravenous tubes and other equipment. I'm the doctor. I'll be right behind you," he paused. "There's one more thing."

Few eyes bothered to look up.

Dandy looked at Viper. "I want this as bloodless as possible."

"Bullshit. I won't compromise my safety, or that of my men, full stop." Viper's voice was defiant.

"Fair enough. But I insist, no shooting unless absolutely necessary."

"Shut the fuck up. I don't need a lesson on rules of military engagement - certainly not from you." Viper moved towards the mobile bed, lifted the back of his shirt, and concealed the pistol inside his waistband. Then he turned to the other two. "Listen up guys. You know the score. Now let's do this."

Chapter Fifty-Two

Dandy and his team made their way through the hospital corridors, attracting occasional glances from passers-by. They looked like any other team of medics pushing their patient to surgery. Dandy, ever vigilant, not only had the police to worry about, but also Shadow.

As soon as they settled into the lift, Dandy pushed a button marked 'H'. He checked the time. If all went to plan, Cooper should be landing about now, he reasoned. Then he surveyed his team quietly. They all seemed cool but reflective, and Dias was still unconscious. He knew that unless he could see a doctor quickly, he might die, and all this would be pointless.

Suddenly, the lift doors opened and they made towards the heliport. "Shit. Where the fuck is he?" Dandy said.

"What's going on here?" Viper growled.

"How the hell should I know? Just shut up." He scanned the rooftop. In the corner stood the hospital's air ambulance, and immediately, his mind went into overdrive weighing up the alternatives.

"Shit. We've got company," Viper said softly, "an armed guard is heading our way."

Dandy flinched and spun round to face the guard who was armed with Heckler and Koch.

"I'll take him," Viper whispered from the corner of his mouth.

"No, no." Dandy muttered, his face now dripping with sweat.

Just then, the thumping of rotors slicing through the air caught everyone's attention.

"Well, there's your ride," the guard shouted placing one hand on his cap.

As they hurried towards the helicopter passing the guard, Dandy said, "Thanks officer."

They lifted the mobile bed on to the chopper securing the wheels. Within seconds, all climbed aboard and the chopper finally lifted effortlessly into the night sky.

***

On the seventh floor, Ritz found two armed guards seated outside operating room 12. His face creased into a faint grin. He knew the long search for Dias had finally come to an end; it now remained for him to pass security to reach his target. After that, he would earn that long coveted holiday to South America before taking over his new post as director of operations. His adrenalin suddenly shot up, as he looked at the guards knowing they alone stood between him and his goal.

Ritz quickly assessed their alertness to less than four on a scale of ten. Perhaps it was fatigue, or poor training, but whatever it was, Ritz was encouraged.

The guards looked him up and down, their interest intensifying with each step he took. The briefcase incensed them more than anything else, as they quietly rose to their feet.

Ritz stopped within a few feet from them and smiled.

"Who are you, sir?" One of the guards said, stepping forward.

"I'm the registrar. I know Dr. Reid is attending a patient up here. I wonder if you would kindly ask him to see me immediately. It's rather urgent."

"You have an ID, sir? Sorry, just routine."

Ritz smiled. His gaze momentarily shifted to the other guard,

"I said could I see an ID, sir?" The officer said.

"Sure." Ritz quickly removed his pistol and shot him in his forehead knocking him backward. Then he turned to the second guard. "One move and I'll kill you. Now drop your gun."

"Okay, okay," he said, dropping the gun.

"Where is everyone?"

"In there," the officer said quickly.

"Are there are other armed guards in there?"

The officer nodded.

"Alright. You do what I say, and you won't get hurt. We're going in there together, slow and easy. You take the lead," Ritz said.

As they entered the room, Quail, still remonstrating with Dr. Reid over Dias's death, turned, "What the hell do you want?"

Ritz pushed the guard further into the room and shut the door behind him.

"Armed police. Drop your weapon, now," Quail announced pointing a gun at Ritz.

Quietly, Ritz set the briefcase on the floor and opened it. "I only have to press this button and the whole building will come down. Take a pick, your way or mine?"

Quail swallowed and quietly replaced his gun. "What do you want?"

Reiley, having observed the intrusion, was suddenly in the room. He brandished a gun and shouted, "Armed police. Drop your weapon."

"No, no,' Quail said quickly to Reiley, "don't shoot. He's carrying a bomb. Put your weapon away, Mr. Reiley."

Reiley's eyes steeled. "I don't trust this guy."

"What choice have you got, you idiot?' Quail said. "If you do it your way, you will take all of us down. Put the Goddamn weapon down."

Reiley was already sweating. He glanced at the briefcase, and watched as Ritz held his thumb over the remote control he was clutching in his palm. He hesitated a moment. In reality, the risk was too high. He also knew that his first duty was to ensure public safety, and reluctantly, he finally lowered the gun.

Ritz, however, was less considerate. Almost instantaneously, he spun round and shot Reiley in the forehead, and then he shot the guard in the head spurting his brain tissues across the room.

Quail gasped. "Oh shit. Oh shit."

Ritz's eye fixed on Dr. Reid who was now trembling in the far corner. He held his hands together, staring back at him with pleading eyes.

"Doctor, can you identify your patient?"

"Phil . . . Phil... Dias. He was Phil Dias," Dr. Reid said.

Ritz looked at him quizzically.

"He is dead," Dr. Reid added.

Ritz made his way to the table checked the nametag, then the pulse, and turning to Dr Reid, he shot him twice, once in the forehead, then in the heart.

"Oh shit. Who the hell are you?" Quail said with unsteady voice.

"You ask too many questions," Ritz replied as he pulled the trigger.

***

Ritz peered round the room staring coldly at the lives he'd snuffed out, not a hint of remorse in his eyes - a deadly assassin through and through.

Leaving the room and locking the door, he made his way to the elevators. Time was of the essence now. He finally found the lift with a blue "H", pressed the button and stood back watching the lights ascend from the second floor up to the seventh. The doors rattled open, and standing side by side were two paramedics holding large green cases.

As Ritz stepped in, he noted the blue "H"

badges on their jackets, and moving behind them, he waited until the door had shut before pulling out his gun and prodding the female in the back. She let out a gasp.

"Don't either of you try being a hero, and you will live. Now slowly turn around."

"What do you want?" The blonde haired woman said trembling with fear.

The male paramedic stood frozen to the spot. Ritz noticed a patch around his groin and knew he would have no problem with these two.

"All you have to do is walk me to the chopper, and everything will be fine." He prodded the female medic again. "If we're challenged, you will say I'm a medical advisor on an emergency call out. Remember, both your lives depend on it."

When the lift doors opened, Ritz saw two armed guards standing together by the walkway.

"Right! You know what to do. Start walking to the chopper."

As they made their way up the gangway, one of the armed guards dropped his cigarette and crushed it into the ground with his black shiny boot.

"Everything all right, guys?" The guard said.

At that moment, the second guard nudged his colleague and whispered something, and with that, both guards dropped their gaze to the male medic's groin.

"Is anything wrong sir?" The guard asked sensing the tension in the male medic's face.

Now shaking uncontrollably, the male medic

275

suddenly bolted across the roof. One of the guards quickly drew his MP5 up to eye level, the other guard instantly dropped to one knee and covered the female and Ritz.

"Don't move," the guard shouted, and taking his eye off Ritz for a few seconds, two thuds hit him, one in his cheek, and the other in his forehead. Blood and white tissues were strewn over the wall behind him. And before the second guard could do something, Ritz already had him in his sights. His throat exploded as two bullets ripped out his larynx. He dropped to his knees gurgling and spluttering followed by two more bullets which double-tapped side by side on his forehead.

Ritz grabbed the female paramedic, pushing her to the ground; he quickly scanned the rooftop, releasing the empty magazine. With the speed of a professional combat officer, he slammed a full one home.

"Let's go," Ritz snarled, making across the roof towards the helicopter. The thumping of the rotors got louder and reaching it, he pulled the door open. "Get in," he shouted.

The pilot spun round, stunned, he threw his hands in the air. "Please, I'm just a pilot. Don't hurt me. Please . . ."

"Shut the fuck up. Do what you're told and you'll be all right," Ritz shouted, settling beside the pilot and placing the briefcase behind. "Let's go. Head west."

The chopper lifted into the night sky and flew

across the city. Twenty minutes later, Ritz spotted an empty park, and shouted, "Put it down near the playground."

The pilot brought the chopper down with a gentle bump. Ritz flung open the door, and turning to the pilot and the female medic, he said, "I told you I'd let you live," and with that, he jumped to the ground, crouching and running until he was safely away. Then he stopped and watched the chopper lift back into the air climbing to three hundred feet.

Smiling knowingly, he pressed the remote control he was clutching in his palm. "Damn it. That was a designer leather case. What a waste," he said as he watched the sky light up above him.

Chapter Fifty-Three

"Son of a bitch. You almost got us killed."

"What?" The pilot shouted without looking at Dandy who was sitting beside him.

"What took you so long?" Dandy shouted again.

"Oh that? Don't blame me. Blame that fucking twat in the back - the bloody doctor or whatever he calls himself," the pilot said.

Staring ahead, Dandy sat back and lit a cigar.

"Sorry you got rattled, old man," the pilot continued. "I reached the fucking doctor on time but he wasn't ready. He was attending a meeting, and I almost kicked his ass when he stumbled out at last."

Dandy sank further into his seat and exhaled deeply. Staring distractedly at the battery of buttons across the dashboard from under heavy eyelids, he felt his anger dissipate slowly. He grimaced at the eccentricity of his doctor friend, wondering if it had been a mistake to involve him. Dr. Braithwaite had built a reputation as one of the best private physicians ever, his availability being subject to status only. His patients ranked amongst the world's wealthiest, and almost exclusively criminals. He was popular for his discreetness and his dogged commitment to his patients. His patients knew that if anyone could keep them from six feet under, it was Dr. Braithwaite. And if he couldn't, which happened very rarely, then death would've wanted them badly.

Dandy peered into the cargo area where Dr. Braithwaite was attending to Dias, his stethoscope swinging with the hypnotic rhythm of a pendulum.

"How's he doing, doc?" Dandy shouted.

"I'll be happier when we get him to my clinic," Dr. Braithwaite returned.

Dandy could see the anxiety etched on the doctor's face, and suddenly felt his body go light as the helicopter started to descend. Out of the window, he could see thousands of tiny lights flickering with every colour of the rainbow. He watched as the helicopter hovered towards a circle of blue fluorescent landing lights, beside which stood Dr. Braithwaite's clinic, a splendid Georgian mansion set in ten acres of beautifully manicured lawns.

As they landed with the grace of a butterfly, Dandy marveled at the magnificence of the estate, a view he'd never seen before. Secretly, he admired the vision and achievement of a man who'd transformed himself into a royalty status amongst dishonorable men.

Rushing down the path were two nurses pushing a mobile bed. With the rotors slowing down, Dandy opened the door and bent down, making his way round the helicopter to open the cargo doors. First out was Viper, who scanned the

279

immediate area. Dr. Braithwaite followed him. Slowly, Dias was lowered down onto the bed, with their heads lowered, the nurses headed up the path towards the clinic.

Dandy put his thumb up to the pilot, and turning to Viper, he shouted, "well done. Mucho will pay you."

Viper smiled and jumped back into the chopper.

Dandy watched as the helicopter gradually lifted back into the night sky and disappeared out of view.

***

It was nearly midnight when Shadow's safe line finally rang. It had been a nervous night even though Shadow knew Ritz was the best in the business. He had completed a number of high profile jobs, but Shadow was aware of his obsession with killing, something that had threatened the security of operations in the past. In truth, everyone had a weakness, but his was an unusual ruthlessness, Shadow reasoned.

Shadow finally took the call after a few more rings. "Hello, Ritz, I've been waiting for your call."

"I just got back not long ago."

"What's new?"

"Job done."

A momentary silence followed.

"Sure? Target is disabled?"

"Permanently."

A thin smile broke across Shadow's face. "Well done. Our clients would be pleased. Now, get some rest and we talk again tomorrow."

"Yep"

"Oh, before you go. Just to let you know that the chief security position is yours if you want it."

"Wow, what can I say?"

"Yes would be appropriate."

"Cheers. So, what now with the woman?"

"What do you think, Ritz?"

"She's outlived her usefulness."

"Hmm. Does she pose any security risk?"

Ritz hesitated for a moment. "No."

"She doesn't know why she's been abducted, does she?"

"No." Ritz said between clenched teeth.

"Then we spare her," Shadow said gravely; it was a command. "Sedate and return her to their house tonight," he added and hung up.

Ritz made his way downstairs, searching in his pockets; he pulled out his ski mask and pulled it over his head. He entered the room. In the corner, was a double bed with a small lamp casting just enough light for him to see his way across. He stopped for a moment, staring at Lorna, his breathing faster, his thoughts more sinister.

Suddenly she stirred, unable to move her hands that were fastened to the bed, and turning her head, she cried, "Who's there? Please untie me." She sobbed weakly.

Ritz sat on the side of the bed, placing his hand on her thigh and slowly pushed his hand under her dress.

"No . . . no . . . Please...Please don't hurt me," she cried.

"Shsss. I'm not going to hurt you. You will be good now and I'll let you go home tonight. How about that?" Ritz whispered to her.

She didn't answer, but stopped protesting and cried some more. Faced with a stark choice, knowing her life depended on getting it right, she sobbed quietly.

Now aroused even more by her powerlessness, he pulled her dress up to her waist revealing a pair of G-string knickers. He stroked her, gently at first, then vigorously, groaning and suddenly, as if in a fit of anger, he ripped the G-string off and pushed himself on her. She gasped with pain and sobbed even more.

Chapter Fifty-Four

Next morning, a new Ford Mondeo swept along the short path leading to Dias's house, the silhouette of trees made patterns on the glass, the tyres made crunchy sounds towards the drive. There were two men and a woman in the car.

The woman, in her late thirties, was driving, squinting through the windshield at the piercing glare of the rising sun. The man, who was sitting next to her, was also in his thirties, wearing sunglasses and dressed in a dark suit.

Jed Warren, Assistant Head of Mainland operations of MI5 was the third man. He sat passively in the back seat looking out of the window. In his mid-forties, bespectacled, bony faced and clean-shaven, he too was wearing a dark suit. He was a shy, rather quiet family man. He always dreaded any assignment that was under the media scrutiny. The agency was by its very nature secretive, and he would rather it stayed that way. Besides, he was pensively aware of the magnitude of his task - any assignment passed for his urgent attention was bound to be dangerous. He was now growing in reputation as Mr. Fix-it of the agency.

Though he hated the publicity associated with his position, he nonetheless relished his growing international stature. He had intelligence, he was cunning and now there was financial reward.

Jed Warren reached the door and pressed the doorbell. Tugging lightly at his tie, he turned and looked at his colleagues, who looked back but said nothing.

Moments later, the door opened slightly, held in place by a security chain, eyes peeping anxiously through the opening.

"Hello. Who's there?"

Jed Warren produced his warrant card. "MI5, can we come in, please?"

There was a short pause, then the door closed with a thump and opened wide in quick succession, Lorna stepped aside holding the door ajar. Her vision was out of focus, she was reeling from hours of sedation although she didn't know why she was feeling this weak. But she put it down to her ordeal, her body was fatigued and that too was natural, she thought.

"Mrs. Dias?" Jed Warren said as politely but firmly as he could without making things worse. Public relations duty was after all his greatest strength.

She gave him a long cautious look, and then turned her gaze to his colleagues. Her stomach cramped a little.

"Yes?" she said weakly.

"My name is Jed Warren. These are my colleagues, agent Troy and agent Zoë. Mrs. Dias, we need to speak to you."

She squinted at a throbbing headache.

"Are you all right, Mrs. Dias?" Warren said.

She nodded slowly. Hesitating for a moment, she started walking back into the house. She led them into the lounge and didn't notice that Troy was missing.

"Excuse me," she said leaving the lounge, aware her every movement was being carefully analysed, the memory of her abduction was playing on her every thought. Then there were the unanswered questions. How had she got back home? How long had she been lying here? Had Dias left for work before she returned home? She pondered some more. She would have to get a message to him quickly. She needed his support. And pausing, she wondered if Dias had involved the MI5 in his desperation to rescue her. Why the MI5? She mused, when the police were all they needed?

She picked up the phone in the bedroom and dialled Dias' mobile. It was switched off. Her brows narrowed. She checked the time. Seven fifty nine am. She called his direct line and it rang and rang, and now exasperated, she replaced the receiver gazing thoughtfully into space. Why was he always unavailable when she needed him most, she thought with some irritation? No, she was not going to tell the MI5 anything until she'd spoken to her husband, she concluded.

Meanwhile, Jed Warren and his team were still standing in the lounge, scanning intently at anything that might remotely help their investigation. At first, Warren was secretly disappointed. There were no telltale signs of their involvement with organised crime. No photographs of ostentatious lifestyles with foreign dignitaries. No rare foreign ornaments displayed.

But something else kept Warren's interest active - Lorna herself. He had noticed the bruise on her wrist and she seemed roughed up, yet there was calmness about her mannerisms that portrayed a woman at peace, perhaps it was her composure, perhaps it was a façade, Warren thought. Though nothing gigantic considering the nature of the enquiry he was conducting, nonetheless it was something he had to bear in mind.

Lorna returned, a glass of soda in one hand and cupping four paracetamol in the other.

"How may I help you, Mr. . . .?"

"Warren." He took his glasses off and folded them. His brown eyes suddenly glazed with pain. "Mrs. Dias, I'm afraid I've got bad news for you. Your husband died last night following a bomb explosion in central London."

Lorna's knees buckled and the glass slipped out of her grip, followed by the tablets. A feeling of panic zipped through her body as she struggled to stand. Now barely in control, her face ghostly white, she stumbled backwards.

Jed Warren quickly surged forward catching her just in time, her eyes fixed in wild stare. He put his arms around her back and legs and lifted her up. He carried her across the room and lay her down on the sofa. Standing back, he watched her eyelids slowly close as she slipped into unconsciousness.

Chapter Fifty-Five

Dandy sat beside Dias listening to the monotonous bleep of the life support machine. Occasionally, he wandered over to the window to admire a view of beautifully manicured lawns. Though tired and bored, he refused to leave Dias alone.

Dr. Braithwaite entered with two other doctors and a nurse, and without a word, Dandy left the room. He wandered down the corridor to an open plan waiting room and slumped into a leather armchair.

Twenty minutes later, Dandy was woken by the sound of clinking glasses, and rubbing his eyes, he tried to make sense of it.

"Brandy, old chap."

Dandy slowly turned. Dr. Braithwaite stood by the drinks cabinet, mixing brandy.

"God. You look like hell. I think I'd better prescribe you some sleeping tablets," Braithwaite said.

"Hmmm…how is he, doc?" Dandy said running his fingers through his hair.

Dr. Braithwaite stared down at him for a moment before moving slowly across the room. He stopped at the window staring out. His manner was one of subdued optimism. As he admired the greenery, he knew better than to give much hope too soon. Dias was still critically ill. Though the patient had shown some improvement, it could still go horribly wrong.

Finally, he turned slowly. "He's making slow but steady progress."

"But he's going to pull through, doc?' Dandy said swallowing. Dr. Braithwaite ignored him and pushed the rest of the brandy down his throat.

***

"Something's not quite right," Jed Warren said as he walked around the room studying the photos that hung over the fireplace, his gaze fixed on one of Dias. He wished he could animate the man in the photo and get him to tell all he knew. He suddenly snapped back into reality as Lorna stirred.

He turned to Troy. "What do you think?"

Troy shrugged. "She's not stupid, sir. I think she knows more than she is letting on."

"What do you think, Zoë?"

"I'm not quite sure, sir. She's done nothing to arouse my suspicion, sir," Zoë said.

"It's not everyday you get a knock on the door from MI5, yet she didn't bat an eye, she wasn't intimidated. It was as if she was expecting us."

Zoë looked over at Lorna who was now murmuring but still unconscious.

"The bruise on her wrist looks quite recent,"

288

Zoë said.

"Hmm," Warren grunted thoughtfully, pacing back and forth. "The question is, who did that to her wrist and why? We know it couldn't be her husband. Finding out how she bruised her wrist will begin the story for this investigation?"

Troy nodded quickly.

Warren shifted his gaze to Zoë.

"Yes, sir."

"Good." Warren breathed. "Early signs are the people behind all of this are ruthless and experienced and from now . . ."

Troy cleared his throat stopping Warren in mid-sentence. They turned to Lorna who was trying to sit up, both hands covering her face. The events of the last few days had taken their toll on her, now she had the added pain of losing her husband, so she thought. All she wanted now was to be on her own, life was not worth living any longer.

"Mrs. Dias, I'm sorry about your husband but there are some questions we need to ask you," Warren said.

Lorna didn't answer; instead, she turned to look at the photo frame above the fireplace.

Warren cleared his throat and continued. "Mrs. Dias, we believe a criminal gang probably with international connections might be responsible for your husband's death."

She shifted her gaze to Warren.

Warren continued, "We also believe that he was the intended victim of a bomb probably originated from Russia. When they realised he survived the explosion, they sent a professional hit man to the hospital to finish the job. In the end a number of security personnel and hospital staff were also killed."

Lorna dropped her gaze to the floor, her hands trembling and tears rolling down her cheeks.

"Mrs. Dias, do you know who might want to kill your husband?"

She shook her head without looking at him.

Warren reflected briefly. "Mrs. Dias, you understand that your life is in danger so long as these people remain at large. You must tell us anything you know that might assist this investigation."

"I don't know anyone who would . . ." she stopped, overwhelmed with emotion. "I don't know."

"Mrs. Dias, how did you get the bruise on your wrist?"

Lorna looked up at Warren. "Please leave now."

"Mrs. Dias . . ."

"I said, leave now," she shouted.

Warren removed a card from his wallet and placed it on the table. "Call me anytime day or night if you want to discuss this. I'll stop by tomorrow morning," he said and left.

As the Ford Mondeo pulled away from the house, Warren turned to Troy, an expert in covert operations, especially in planting listening devices.

"Well?" Warren said from behind dark glasses.

"One bug's in the Porsche and the other in the

lounge, sir,' Troy said.

"What about the jeep or are we going to leave it to lady luck?" Warren said.

"She can't. I immobilised the jeep, sir," Troy said.

"And it's trackable through satellite as well?"

"We can track the movement of the Porsche, sir."

Warren let out a deep breath. "Good. Now get the surveillance team on the phone."

Troy pushed the armrest down revealing a Nokia phone embedded in it. He quickly dialled a number and pressed the hand-free button. After a few rings, a deep voice echoed round the car, "Control room."

"Hello, Troy here. I've got two active. Do you read their signals?"

"Yes. We've been monitoring them. Just usual activity, nothing to report."

"OK. I want to know as soon as she makes any significant move," Warren said.

"Yes sir. Will do."

Chapter Fifty-Six

"Dandy. Wake up."

Dandy stirred, his eyes half open, squinting at the bright daylight. He felt a sharp headache and instantly frowned. He couldn't have slept for a long time, he thought. He could tell because his eyes were still heavy and his body ached. He grumbled a few curses turning and tossing in the settee, and suddenly stopped. He was sure he'd caught sight of a human form. His eyebrows narrowed as he looked more closely. He was right after all. Standing at the entrance to Dias' room was Dr Braithwaite. Then Dandy remembered where he was - in Dr Braithwaite's clinic, not his home, and quickly sobered. He sat up engaging the doctor's gaze.

"What the hell's wrong?" Dandy asked, scanning the doctor's features for hints. "Oh Jeese. Don't tell me he's . . . " he stopped, running his hand through his hair. It was something he did often to make him relax momentarily. His breathing was suddenly reduced to irregular gasps, perspiration forming on his forehead. "Damn, is he dead?" he shouted jumping to his feet, "Is he? You son of a bitch, you talked me into getting some sleep and you let him die," he snarled, "you creep. I brought him to you coz I wanted him fucking alive, not dead, you creep. You incompetent piece of . . ."

"Shit?" Dr Braithwaite interrupted, laughing. Dandy collected himself and reassessed him. "You may go in there and see him now. I think he needs to see a face he can recognise," he added grinning mischievously.

At first, Dandy just stared. Then the corner of his mouth slowly curled into a smile.

"Don't keep him waiting. I've told him you're here and he's expecting you, I hope." Dr Braithwaite said.

Dandy rushed past the doctor and entered Dias' room, and immediately their gaze met. As Dandy knelt beside his friend clasping his hand, Dias wondered what the hell was going on.

**

Meanwhile, Lorna lay curled up on the sofa, staring blankly into space. She was calmer now. It had taken a few hours for the news of her husband's death to sink in. In that time she had wept, unable to make sense of it all. She had also scanned the teletext hoping she might find the answers she sought. But apart from half-baked speculations about international conspiracy linked to the case, nothing was making any sense to her. She knew her husband well enough to dispel all this as nonsense, and surely, it must be the MI5 making this up as they went along, she reasoned.

Fighting back tears, Lorna drew strength from her resolve to escape to somewhere far away, where she would eventually die and be forgotten, perhaps be reunited with Dias in the next world, then the cruel hand of fate could no longer deal her a bad hand. Then she would no longer feel angry, or have any sense of loss, or fear. Together they might then find peace that had eluded them for so long.

Finally, she picked herself up and stared at the photo of Dias for a moment, surprised at how confident she'd suddenly become. She went into their bedroom, opened the wardrobe and took a .38. She sat on the edge of the bed staring at the pistol, her hand trembling. Her breathing increased, and as though she were suddenly hit by the reality of it all, she dropped the gun, sobbing out loud. There had to be an easier way, she thought. She didn't want a violent end.

She made her way through the house and into the garage. In the corner lay a hosepipe, which she quickly uncurled, and within minutes, had cut it to size and fastened it to the Porsche exhaust. She fed the other end of the pipe through the driver's door window, hesitating, a sudden thought came to her, and she returned to the bedroom. She searched frantically in the cabinet, and found her sleeping pills. She swallowed a handful and gulped down a glass of brandy, grimacing as the drink scorched her throat. She was surprised how light she now felt. The only awkward feeling was her swirling vision.

Now overwhelmed by emotion, she quietly sat down on the bed, tears rolling down her cheeks. Trying to be strong and a little restless at the prospect of dying, she looked around the room for what would be her last. She tried to repress her memories of their last night together making love. A sad smile creased her face. Nothing seemed to have changed. Even the bed was still in the condition she'd left it in.

She rose clumsily and went to the wardrobe. She scanned a row of dresses and finally removed an evening dress. She smiled painfully. It was her favourite, and Dias' too. She slipped into it and stared in the mirror. There was something missing, she thought, feeling her neck with her unsteady hands.

She reached down and picked up her diamond necklace and put it round her neck. She wanted to look her best on this last journey. It was what Dias would have wanted, she thought as she staggered towards the door. She was feeling groggy, and her vision blurred. She shuffled all the way to the garage and was relieved when she found the car. Once inside, she tried a few times to get the key in the ignition, muttering her frustration. Finally she inserted the key after several attempts, turned the key and the Porsche roared into life.

Chapter Fifty-Seven

It was just after lunchtime when the images of the carnage at the hospital were flashed across TV screens worldwide. As the full horrors of what had happened unfolded, Shadow watched events with interest. There were camera crews from every network, reporters milled about in the street, sucking up the minutest detail, and armed police surrounded the building.

Shadow sat back in his chair scanning every channel for new information on the incident, and finally chose one.

"Elena, do we know any more about the man the police are looking for?" The Newscaster said.

"No. The police don't appear to have a clue, but they have said they're pursuing a number of leads. Frankly, everyone is shocked at what has happened to this quiet community. The police have also confirmed that the helicopter that exploded in mid-air last night killing two people was linked to the killings here. Back to you in the studio."

"Elena, thank you."

Shadow turned the TV off, displaying no emotion. But in his mind, there was a nagging thought. Quietly, he pondered about the savagery of the man who would soon take charge of his

North American operations. Could he trust someone with such callous temperament to run the operations there? Ritz, he thought was a huge risk, almost indispensable, yet . . .'

The phone rang distracting him. The secure line was flashing and he knew at once it could only be one of his clients.

Shadow picked up the phone. "Yes?"

"Chensky here."

"How are you, my friend?"

"Very well. I have to congratulate you on a successful mission, on behalf of the Russian government. I must express our profound gratitude. The balance as agreed has been transferred to your account."

Shadow smiled. "Thank you. Well, I wish you luck with Malik. He's certainly a hard nut to crack."

Chensky laughed heartily. "He's now in our hands. We are Russians and we do things differently here. He will talk. Our interrogators have never let us down before."

"Well, let me know how you get on. It was a pleasure doing business with you."

Chensky coughed. "We do have some reservations though."

Shadow could hear the seriousness in his voice.

Chensky continued, "Would you not agree that this elimination exercise resembled something of a bloodbath and has attracted unnecessary attention, not only from close quarters but globally. Was all that violence necessary for one target?"

Shadow was silent. He could recognise a damning criticism when he heard one and he knew they didn't come any stronger. Worse still, it was from a highly valued client. He had to tread carefully. The last thing he wanted was to upset his biggest sponsor in the covert world.

"No . . . no. You're quite right, Chensky. It wasn't necessary to use so much violence."

"We're glad you can see our concerns. Goodbye."

Shadow slowly replaced the receiver contemplating Chensky's last remarks.

Chapter Fifty-Eight

Nowadays, Dandy rarely had reason to visit graveyards. He recalled the last time, many years ago, when he attended his wife's funeral. She had been brutally killed by the Mafia and it was awful burying what was left of her remains. Even now, the feeling of sadness and death was as strong as it was then. Even as beautiful as Dr Braithwaite's private graveyard looked, it still conjured up ugly feelings for Dandy.

Dr Braithwaite walked silently beside him. Only the sound of Dias' flip-flops could be heard as he shuffled along in front of them.

"Doctor, I don't think this therapy shit is working," Dandy said. "It's been six weeks and nothing has changed; he has no memory, look at him, he's on different planet."

"Please keep your voice down. There's nothing wrong with his hearing," the doctor said quietly. "You have got to be patient - everyone is different. It has to be gradual and natural. We can only encourage his recovery; there are no miracle cures."

They watched as Dias climbed the stairs to a large wooden door in the corner of the graveyard, opened it and went inside. It was a private tomb of one of Dr Braithwaite's rich clients who had died from heart attack years ago. They quickly followed Dias into the tomb chamber concerned he might hurt himself, his mind was already in a mess and the last thing they wanted was more misfortune. In the middle of the room, stood Dias with his hands on top of a tomb, his movement frantic. The floor was solid marble; the only light came from a multi-stained glass window in the ceiling. Dias disturbed the dust on the tomb, then rubbed off some more with his hands.

"What the hell is he doing?" Dandy said impatiently.

"Let him." Dr Braithwaite hissed.

"But he's . . ."

"I know . . . I know. He won't be able to move it. But it's important we let him play however he likes," Braithwaite said, making notes of his observations.

As they later walked back the tree-lined lane towards the clinic, Dr Braithwaite thought about retiring, it wasn't the first time he had thought this. Many years of caring for delicate patients was beginning to have its toll on him and he was no longer getting job satisfaction from doing what he loved. Only last month, he seriously considered it, but the fear of boredom and loneliness had stopped him. This part of medicine was boring but he preferred it to retirement, he decided. He was secretly relieved that the therapy session with Dias had passed without a major incident.

Later that night, in the kitchen of his exquisitely

furnished apartment, Dr Braithwaite was brewing coffee when he heard a knock on the door. He stopped, listening intently. He rarely received visitors in his apartment, it was especially unusual for anyone to visit him this late. After a few moments, the knocks were repeated and louder. With some anxiety, he went quietly to the door.

His eye pressed against the view hole, he called out, "Who is it?"

There was no answer, and visibility was poor outside. The knocks resumed, gentle but sustained.

He made sure the inside protective chain was in place, and then unlocked the door, opening it a few inches then to the full extent of the chain peering cautiously.

At first, because of poor lighting, he could see nothing, then a face came into view and a voice said, "May I talk to you? Please, it is urgent."

Dr Braithwaite hesitated. "You should be in your room, Mr. Dias."

"I know. But I'm here now."

"What do you want?"

"Will you let me in?"

Dr Braithwaite shook his head.

"Please I insist. What I'm going to say will save everyone so much trouble," Dias insisted.

"Um . . ." Dr Braithwaite wavered. Despite his misgivings, his curiosity was strong. What did he want to say that was so urgent? Perhaps, it might have therapeutic values. Wondering if he would regret it, he closed the door slightly and released the chain.

Dias walked straight in. "What a nice place you've got here."

"Thanks. What is it you want to tell me?" He said with a hint of suspicion.

Suddenly, Dias sprang on the doctor like a tiger on a deer, knocking him to the floor. As he rained blows to his head and chest, he shouted, "Whom do you work for? Why have you been following me? You're a bloody spy. You're spying on me. Why? Tell me what's going on?"

Chapter Fifty-Nine

It wasn't long before Levine heard anything direct from the MI5. He'd been assured the meeting would be quick and discreet. What he didn't realise was that this was no chance encounter. For weeks, D&L had been under surveillance by the MI5. Telephone lines were bugged, senior partners secretly followed.

In a few minutes, Jed Warren would tell him why they were meeting; Levine had guessed he would be asked questions about the Firm's structure and management. Trailing hot cash was still problematic for the law enforcement agents, and every so often, they would come fishing for information. The recent murders hadn't helped, he thought, but that episode in the firm's history was in the past now.

Levine was standing behind his desk when his secretary opened the door for Jed Warren.

"Jed Warren. MI5. We spoke on the phone."

Levine took his hand. "Please sit down."

"Thanks. I will not take much of your time. Mr. Levine, I want to ask you a few questions about Phil Dias."

Levine was surprised to hear that the MI5 were interested in Dias. Wasn't that chapter closed for good? Everyone at D&L had put the bad publicity of the past weeks behind them, and as far as they were concerned, the ghosts of their former colleagues were resting now; the living had a business to run. Straightening himself, he said, "I'd be pleased to help in any way I can. Phil Dias was a good man. Beyond that I know very little."

"Was?" Jed Warren said.

Levine looked at him as if this were a trick question. He folded his hands resting them on his chest. "It's public knowledge that he died from injuries sustained in the bomb explosion."

"That information is not in the public domain, Mr. Levine," Jed Warren said sharply, staring intently at him. "We didn't release the identity of the casualty, so where did you get your news from?"

"He hasn't turned up for work since that incident, so I put two and two together," said Levine.

"And you came up with the conclusion that he was the casualty in that incident?" Jed warren said.

"Plus I have my source in the police force," Levine said boastfully shifting quietly.

"Okay," Warren said with a grin. "As far as you can tell or your source could tell, was he in that area on any official business of the Firm?"

"Not as far as I know."

"Did you have a client who lived at 3 Pinkerton Drive?"

"No."

"Thank you, Mr Levine. I am sorry to have

taken up so much of your time. I'll show myself out."

Long after the meeting, Levine sat motionless staring into space. He was never fond of the MI5, and he knew from experience that they would not knock on any doors without a good reason. Whatever that might be, he had no clue, but he knew it wasn't going to be good news.

***

In the D&L car park, Jed Warren joined his team, his expression puzzled. His team understood his obvious confusion because they too were listening in to the conversation; they too had picked up Mr. Levine's difficulty in explaining away what seemed like a gaffe on his part.

"What do you make of him?" Jed Warren said.

"Interesting, sir. No one ever said Phil Dias was dead. Of course we now know his death has been staged by someone for some reason," said Zoë.

"Hmm. The question is, what made him think that? Surely, he knows more than he's telling."

As Zoë drove out of the car park, Jed Warren sank back in his seat, staring into space, deep in thought.

***

When Phil Dias returned to his room covered in blood, Dandy was sitting on his bed, his face troubled. He had worried that Dias might have run away, fearing the worst. Though Dandy was relieved he had returned safely he was perplexed at his state. "What have you done?"

Dias stood still for a moment and then he smiled. "What are you doing here?"

"I'm looking after you. I brought you here in this private clinic for treatment. Now, tell me why you're covered in blood," Dandy said anxiously.

"I just killed a spy who's been following me all week long," Dias said proudly.

"Ooh shit. You just killed the fucking doctor?" Dandy shouted. "You idiot. The doctor was helping you get well and you killed him?"

"What doctor?" Dias said with puzzled expression. "What's the matter with you? He was a spy. You should be pleased with what I've done."

There was an uncertain silence before Dandy asked, "Did anyone see you?"

Dias shrugged. "I don't know. Don't care."

Dandy swallowed rapidly. "Okay. You stay here. Do you hear me? Clean yourself up. I'll go check this out," Dandy said and hurried out.

Dias grimaced but didn't protest. He wondered why Dandy was alarmed at what he considered to be a heroic act. He quickly put it down to his friend's erratic behaviour and proceeded to the bathroom.

It took Dandy a couple of hours to dispose of Dr Braithwaite's body in a shallow pit behind the clinic. He knew it was only a matter of time before the trail of destruction was uncovered, and by which time they would have long gone. For now at least, he reasoned, he would have to keep Dias in check. He wouldn't want any more hiccup, he had given so much to make this whole operation a success and he was now close to the end game.

Dias had finished cleaning himself up when Dandy returned. He was more composed, though pale, unsure, a long way from the accomplished lawyer he was. "Well," Dias said clearing his throat; it was more like trying to get his friend's attention. "How did we end up in a place like this?"

Dandy paused, then said, "it's a long story, pal. I think you'd better sit down."

Chapter Sixty

"I wonder if Lorna is Okay," Dias said quietly. "God, I hope she's alright."

Dandy hesitated. Throughout, he had carefully gauged Dias' strength and found it stronger than he'd expected. It was an exceedingly sensitive subject, even dangerous - more so for someone who'd passed through so much. Yet Dandy realised he would need to move speedily.

When Dandy answered him, it was unequivocal, emphatic. "Lorna committed suicide. I'm sorry, Phil." He removed a newspaper cutting and passed it to Dias. First, there was an expression of shock on his face as he read it, then incredulity. Finally, he sobbed, bitter, hearty sobs which lasted a few minutes. He steeled himself and scanned the paper again.

Dandy said, "Lorna would want you to avenge her death. If it's any consolation, I'm going to help you do it - if that's what you want."

Dias nodded without looking up, tears welling up in his eyes.

Together, they planned their next move. Dandy had no illusions about Dias' commitment to the plan. Once Dandy began asking questions about what Malik had confided in him, information unravelled fast. Dias remembered with disquieting clarity where Malik said the secret formula was hidden.

"So, what do we do now?" Dias said.

Dandy pondered for a moment. "You will contact the Russian Embassy to arrange a meeting. You will tell them you've got the secret formula they're looking for and you want Malik's immediate release in exchange for it.'

It took several seconds before Dias said, "You think I'll be safe?" He smiled, a pale smile.

"Trust me, Phil. There's no other way."

"Ok, but don't forget, they tried killing me once. What's stopping them trying again."

"The secret formula. They want it badly, and I'm pretty sure they won't kill you before they get it. Our role is to secure Malik's release before they can have it."

Dias nodded unconvincingly. "Okay."

"Now, where is it buried?" Dandy said.

"Paddington cemetery. It's buried in the grave of Randy Winston."

"Are you sure?"

"That's what he wrote down on the piece of paper I read."

"Okay," said Dandy. "First, call the Embassy, then we'll go disturb the dead at Paddington cemetery."

***

That same night, Shadow took a call from Chensky

and instinctively felt coldness in the Russian's voice. He was direct and brief. When he finished making his point, he hung up.

There was a ring of ultimatum about the call, and Shadow was suddenly torn between frustration and shame. Frustration because Chensky was uncompromising, shame because he'd lost credibility with his biggest client.

Almost instantaneously, Shadow sent for Ritz. He didn't state, and Ritz didn't ask the specific nature of the proposed meeting. For now, Shadow decided the less he knew the better. After all, he thought, judgement about the organisation's affairs was his alone to make so why would he bother Ritz with details?

When Ritz arrived an hour later, Shadow dispensed with the usual social courtesies and said, "something has come up in Budapest, which I want you to take care of personally. You will leave tomorrow."

"That urgent?" Ritz said.

"Quite. I wouldn't ask you otherwise." Shadow sensed he was uneasy. Ritz was gifted with a nose for trouble and knowing how dangerous he could be when rattled, Dandy forced a smile to relax him. "Because of the sensitive nature of this assignment, I don't feel confident to send anyone else."

"Okay. You could've told me all this on the phone." Ritz said.

"I'm sorry you feel I've wasted your time. All travel arrangements will be completed tomorrow morning. You will be met there on arrival by our Matsu and briefed. Any question?"

Ritz shook his head.

"Good night, Ritz."

As Ritz drove away, his mind was preoccupied with the assignment. He wondered what was so sensitive that Shadow couldn't use their Eastern Europe hit man. He hoped it would be brief, he was looking forward to his first holiday in two years, he needed to take his mind off the recent killings and catch a decent night sleep free of nightmares.

On the motorway now, he held the car at a steady 70 and stayed in the left-hand lane while other vehicles sped past. Behind him though, a few vehicles between them, were MI5 agents.

A moment later, Ritz's car blew up into the air.

"Oh my God! Oh my God!' shouted agent Zoë in utter horror. "Sierra Alfa London. Can you read me? Suspect is blown up on A13. Over. I repeat. Suspect is blown up on A13. Over"

Chapter Sixty-One

Phil Dias approached Tower Bridge with a heightened sense of fear and anticipation. If he was in danger as he dreaded, he wondered if he could do more to be safe? Should he have armed himself for the meeting? He dismissed the idea at once. Dandy was right; why would they harm him before they got the secret formula back?

Dias was dressed casually, wearing a hat and sunshades. Entering the underpass of the bridge that was crowded with people, mostly tourists, he walked on to the pavement overlooking the river Thames and stopped. He could see two policemen patrolling the pavement that led towards the castle.

As if sightseeing, Dias began walking briskly south. He passed a row of souvenir and gift shops; to his left, he could see boats packed full with grateful tourists. He stopped again and peered back, satisfied neither the policemen nor anyone he could see had taken an unusual interest in him, he continued.

It took thirty minutes for him to reach the southwest corner of the Tower, all the time he kept some distance away from the centre. He stared across the river feigning interest in the activities there. Suddenly, the scenery awakened his consciousness.

Where was the Russian Military attaché? As Dias strolled over to the other side of the pavement bordering the Tower, he checked the time. It was 5pm. He feared he would become as conspicuous as the Tower Bridge behind him if he loitered much longer. He decided to walk all the way round the old complex that housed the queen's jewels, keeping as close as he could to the teeming crowd. If the Russian didn't show up by the time he'd gone round again, he would leave. He was now feeling very exposed.

As he traversed the north side of the Tower's square, Dias noticed someone was walking closely behind him, and within seconds, he'd stepped in line with him.

"Please keep walking as normal," Chensky said quietly. "I am Chensky. I'm glad you have come. Were you followed?"

"I don't believe so. I took every precaution."

"Good. Even so, we have to be careful. Come on, let's go inside the Tower."

Dias was genuinely impressed by the magnificence of the Tower, especially the Queen's jewels. Sentries stood guard in corners.

"Your country has no shame, Mr. Dias," Chensky said with derision. "First, you looted your former colonies, now you get them to pay you to see the displayed property that should be theirs in the first place."

"Whilst we are not entirely proud of our imperial past, the last country we will look to for

313

advice on modesty is Russia," returned Dias.

Chensky laughed.

"Anyway, we haven't come here to talk about my country. What is the state of play, Mr. Chensky?" Dias said.

"It's a shame you don't see the irony of the situation," Chensky said. "It appears to me that keeping what doesn't belong to you is in character. Well, we are Russians, we want our's back. I am here to negotiate for its immediate return."

"I told you before on the phone, there's nothing to negotiate. When you have released Malik, and we can independently confirm it, you will get the secret formula back."

"I understand that. But we need to make sure you can keep your side of the bargain," Chensky said quietly.

"There's no other way. You just have to trust me."

"No, no, Mr. Dias. Russians don't do business on trust. You will give a little, then we will reciprocate."

"Nonsense. It's my way or nothing. The choice is yours."

Chensky laughed again, and for the first time during the meeting, Dias looked him in the face. He quickly figured that his beard was false. In the same breath, he wondered if Chensky was up to something. He had read about Russians who were as smooth as they were untrustworthy, but he'd never met one before.

"Why are you doing this?" Chensky broke the

silence.

"Let's just say it's personal."

"So how would it appear if the police should discover that you are alive?" Chensky said.

"Then I would call a press conference and invite the Chinese to attend." Dias returned.

"What does that mean?" Chensky stopped.

"I think we should keep walking," Dias said. "I know Russia originally designed this formula as a counter measure against the Chinese teeming population, so Russia can protect its own interests. I also know you could've long used it, had it not been stolen and sold by one of your generals. What you fear most is the secret formula falling into the hands of the Chinese and being used against you. I don't need to spell out what that would do for your relations."

"Hmm. I see you're well informed, Mr. Dias." Chensky said, "What if we kill you?"

"Oh no, you won't. If anything happens to me, the secret and the associated documents will be mailed to the Chinese."

"I see." Chensky could barely conceal his anger.

They walked in silence for a few minutes. At last, they found a quiet part of the hall and stopped.

"Okay," Chensky said, "what about a straight swap anywhere you choose. We get the formula and the documents, we hand over Malik."

"No. You will arrange his immediate release and passage to a safe country of his choice. Once I can confirm it, you'll get everything back."

Chensky looked at him long and hard, then said no more.

Chapter Sixty-Two

As Phil Dias hurried back to his hotel, he constantly watched out to see if he was being followed. He changed trains a few times and finally caught one to Park Lane. Walking into his hotel, he realised he was perspiring heavily.

The hotel lobby was busy, brightly lit and smelt of rich scent. Overlooking the main entrance, a pair of attendants dressed in smart suits manned a padded counter. Several guests waited for attention as the attendants hunched over computers.

As Dias made his way across the lobby towards the lifts, he suddenly stopped. Standing in the midst of three men and a woman - all dressed in suit - was Levine. Dias tried to look away, but it was an inch too late. Levine had already engaged his gaze. For a moment, they stared at each other, and then Levine said something to the group and hurried towards Dias.

"Oh my God," Levine said, taking him to a quiet corner. "What happened to you? What are you doing here?"

"It's a long story," Dias said.

"Jeese. You couldn't even call to say you were OK. Everyone was worried. Not even the police would give us any information. Are you alright?"

"I'm OK," Dias said looking over his shoulder at intervals.

"I wasn't sure where to turn for information," Levine said.

"I'm sorry. I should've at least called you. It's just that things have been moving too fast," Dias said looking over Levine's shoulder, then over his own.

"Are you in any trouble?" Levine said quietly.

When Dias hesitated, Levine said, "Listen, I've just come out of a business meeting. I'll go ask to be excused so we can talk."

"No, no, it's ok really, I'm . . ."

"I insist. You're worth much more to me than merger negotiations. What's your room number and I'll meet you there," Levine said.

"2301."

"See you soon."

A few moments later, Levine joined Dias in his hotel room. He poured a glass of water from a silver carafe and drank it quietly. "Well," he said, "what's really going on, Phil? The MI5 have been snooping around the office."

Dias turned away and said nothing. He walked to the window and looked out at the garden in front of the hotel. The last dusk light was nearly gone, but he could see a pair of butterflies fluttering round a flower. Their freedom reminded him of his bondage; someone out there wanted him dead, and some people already thought he was dead. Unlike the butterflies, his world was a dangerous place, and he keenly needed friends on his side now, he reasoned. In the past, Levine had proved invaluable – he had covered up for him after he had killed Dobbs, and if anyone could help him now, it would be him. He turned slowly and sat down near the window.

"The whole truth this time," Levine said.

Dias told him everything. Moments after Dias had concluded his tale, they said nothing to one another.

"Poor you," Levine said finally. "You didn't have to go through all that alone. We could've helped somehow."

"At the time, I wasn't sure how you might take it."

"You misjudged me," Levine said.

"I'm sorry."

"Okay. Who else knows about this?"

"Dandy."

"Where is he now?"

"He's staying at the Hilton."

"Has he got the secret formula with him there?"

Dias nodded. "We're not taking any chances with these Russians. That's why we're not staying together."

"You shouldn't have taken chances with me either," Levine said quietly.

"What does that mean?"

Levine pulled out a Smith and Wesson and pointed it at Dias.

Half rising, Dias said, "what are you doing?"

"Sit down," shouted Levine. "You will do as I say or I'll kill you."

319

***

It was nearly thirty minutes later when Levine's instructions ended. Dias still looked surprised, and even forced a smile but it was obvious that the smile was false, he was nervous. He stared at Levine. He had never before had the opportunity to deliberately look at his face. He ran his eyes down his frame to the gun. Despite the danger he was in, he still could not see Levine as anything other than his boss at D&L. There were things he was dying to ask him, but didn't want to appear inquisitive. Finally, under Levine's baleful look, he phoned a number.

"Yeah?" Dandy answered after two rings. "How did it go?"

Dias looked at Levine. "Alright. Everything was fine. Um, listen, there's a slight change of plan."

"What's up?" Dandy said sharply.

"Malik has been released and flown to a safe country. He's called me and he is okay. He's asked me to hand the secret back to the Russians, so I have no more interest in keeping it."

"Okay," Dandy said quickly. "What do you want me to do now?"

"Bring it here. I'll deliver it myself."

"Okay. I'm on my way," Dandy said.

"Goodbye." Dias put the phone down and screwed-up the paper he had read from.

"Well done, Phil," Levine said. "Now, we

wait."

Dias stared at him contemptuously. The man standing across from him pointing a gun in his face was not the same person he had held in high esteem for many years. There was something different about Levine now; he couldn't exactly place a finger on what it was, but he was sure he couldn't look at him in the same way again.

"Why are you doing this?" Dias said.

Levine shook his head, grimacing sternly. "Haven't you figured it out yourself? I work for the Russians. I am also your boss at D&L."

"I understand that much. I mean, what's in this for you? You have everything."

"The thrill of living a double life. Power. Control. It's the ultimate act of deception. I'm sorry you got mixed up in this, but I had no choice. As soon as we learned that Malik was in custody, you became the obvious choice to play out our little game. God! weren't we right?' Levine said.

"You are Shadow?" Dias said curiously.

Levine smiled. "Bravo. You just blew my cover. But I don't mind, because you and your friend will not leave this room alive. But first, I've got to have the secret documents.'

"You son of a bitch. You double crossing bastard." Dias cried.

"That was the idea. To double cross. To deceive. Of course, what you have suffered is the collateral damage. It's a shame Lorna took her own life. I specifically authorised her release because there was no point in killing her.'

321

"But you tried to kill me. Why?"

"Killing you was part of my undertaking to the Russians. You knew too much. I would have spared your life had Malik not confided in you at the local café near Belmarsh prison. That sealed your fate."

"You knew about that?"

"Of course, you idiot. Your coat was bugged from before you went into court until you interrupted the cheating wife and her lover. By the way, she disposed of your coat for you," he said smiling.

"And what was your reason for murdering Dora?"

"Your secretary was greedy. She deserved what she got," he paused, poured himself water and swallowed all in one gulp whilst maintaining a vigilant stare at Dias. "She thought there was something sinister about the Fax I sent you and tried to sell her story to a journalist."

"Then you tried to pin it on me."

"I didn't try. I succeeded in shifting the suspicion to you."

"What about Philippa? Did you kill her too?"

"I was having an affair with Philippa," he paused and gauged my expression for a reaction but finding none he continued, "it was a closely guided secret. On the night of her death we were eating out when a text came through to my phone, which was on the table. She read the message before pushing the phone to me. It proved a costly mistake because the message was sensitive. I took her home and hanged her," he said with no hint of regret.

"All of this explains why you covered up for me with Dobbs. It was a distraction you didn't want. Your sight was set on the big prize. Malik."

Levine laughed. "You fool. You didn't kill Mr. Dobbs. You knocked him unconscious. But of course how were you to know that? I checked his pulse myself and falsely declared him dead. After you left, I finished him off and made it look like a suicide."

"Speaking of suicide, you drove Judge Pilate to his death."

"Oh, him. The world's better off without him."

"Listen, I don't care what you've done. I'm not going to say a word to anyone about this. You will shortly get the secret documents and we will call it quits."

"What's the use keeping you alive?" Levine said softly, "You have long out-lived your usefulness. You have embarrassed me enough. You deceived us when you escaped from hospital and made us believe you were dead. I give it to you - it was a brilliant piece of work. Now your luck has run out."

As to his chances, Dias knew these were slight. He had the feeling he was a turtle facing a shark, and fear gnawed at his stomach. He wondered if there was something he could do to stop him. He sat sweating under the watchful gaze of Levine.

Shortly after, there was a knock on the door, Levine jumped to his feet and pressed the gun to

Dias' head. "If you make one false move, you will die," he whispered, and guided him to the door. As Dias pulled the door open, Levine hid behind it, with the gun stuck to his ribs.

"Room service," a woman said, brushing past Dias before he had time to speak. She was carrying a tray with a bottle of champagne in an ice-cold bucket. She set the tray on the table. "This is on the house, sir." Turning, she looked at Levine and smiled, but he didn't smile back, his hand tucked away behind him to conceal the gun. In one quick unified movement, she removed a gun from the bucket and shot Levine in the chest. He writhed, returning fire, hitting her below the abdomen. She took aim again and shot Levine in the forehead, throwing him backwards. He hit the wall and slumped to the floor.

Dias rushed to her.

"No, no," she shrugged him off, clutching her wound. "Just get out of here. Call Dandy as soon as you can. Go. Go,' she insisted.

***

Next door, from where the MI5 had been listening in, Zoë called her boss. "We heard gunshots from the suspect's room, sir. Permission to move in."

"No," Warren said. "That would jeopardise our investigation. There's much more to this than that. We need to find this man, Dandy, ASAP. Meanwhile, keep Dias in your sight at all times."

Chapter Sixty-Three

Dias was surprised when Malik called at noon the next day to say he was now in Libya. Still shaken from his experience the night before, Dias felt his stomach tighten, wondering if this was a hoax.

"How do I know you haven't got a gun to your head?" Dias said.

Malik laughed. "I don't know anyone who trusts the Russians. I have no idea what I can do or say on the phone to reassure you. But I'm under the Libyan new government territory now. They are my friends."

"Then there's only one way to find out," said Dias.

"Which is?"

"I'm taking the next flight to Libya."

"Great. I'm dying for a chance to thank you personally for all you've done for me."

"No need. Now, give me your details."

Next day, Dias boarded a flight, seated in the last row of the business class. He busied himself with a newspaper, not glancing up when the other passengers were boarded. In the first row of the first class was Dandy. He sat on the aisle, staring out of the window, watching passenger jets form a slow traffic towards the runway. He made no contact with Dias.

Also, sitting in the first class section, hot on Dias trail, were the MI5 agents.

It was nighttime at Tripoli International when Dias' Air Libya flight landed there, later than scheduled. He checked his watch as he walked from the plane towards the terminal, and could almost feel Dandy right behind him, but resisted the temptation to acknowledge him. Perspiring in the hot and humid Tripoli night, Dias took off his jacket and loosened his necktie.

Libya immigration bore the firm, efficient imprint of the western society, although the people were much friendlier. When he was waved through immigration and customs, Dias easily found a taxi bay outside the airport, and took a taxi to the Hilton. He checked into the hotel at nearly midnight and telephoned Malik.

"Where are you?" Malik said enthusiastically.

"Hilton."

"What's your room number?"

"26"

"Someone will pick you up in half an hour. See you soon counsel, and welcome to Tripoli." He hung up.

A moment later, Dandy joined him. "Do you think the Russians followed us here?" Dias said.

"Can't say." Dandy walked to the window and drew the curtains. He was very tired; it had been a day in which he had been alert at every turn, determined to see his agenda to the very end.

"Drink?" Dias said.

"Yeah."

"What do you make of it?" Dias said as he mixed the drinks.

"What do I make of what?" Dandy returned.

"The country after Gaddafi," Dias said.

"It's beautiful but still dangerous."

"I think it's a paradise," said Dias.

"Sure."

Dias handed him a drink and sat down.

"Thanks. Have you contacted Malik?" Dandy said.

"Yeah. He's sent someone to pick me up. Should be here in half an hour. I suppose you will explore the bar downstairs while I am gone. I shouldn't be too long."

Dandy was silent, in itself significant. As he was screwing a silencer to his gun, Dias looked up.

"Is something wrong?" Dias said quietly. His face suddenly creased in a nervous tension when Dandy pointed the gun towards him.

Dias swallowed rapidly. "What are you doing?"

"I'm sorry, Phil. But this is where we part company," Dandy said, followed by two popping sounds.

About twenty minutes later, the phone rang, startling Dandy. Hesitating a moment, he answered it.

"Sir, there's someone here for you."

"I'll be right down."

A small man greeted Dandy enthusiastically at the reception. "Follow me, sir," he said guiding

327

Dandy to a maroon Mercedes parked on the forecourt. He settled Dandy in the rear.

As the car roared into life speeding down the quiet Tripoli town centre, Dandy concentrated on the closing stages of his mission. It had been seven agonising years since he began on this mission, although not without anxious moments. There were times he thought he could never see this day. His heart beat faster as he realised he was within reach of the man he'd sought all these years. Malik. He knew there was still danger ahead; Malik was more secure now than ever before, now he had the added security of the Libyans. Even then, he was still determined.

As the car eased past the city centre, Dandy took in details of signs and street names, committing them to memory, knowing he would drive himself back afterwards. He felt his body shaking, yet he managed to think positively. Failure was not an option, he reasoned touching the butt of the gun he had concealed in his waist.

Moments later, the Mercedes approached a massive gate and Dandy could see an impressive villa ahead. Armed guards with AK-47 guarded the gate to the villa grounds. They popped to attention as the car crawled to a stop within inch of them. One guard emerged from the security building on the left and looked closely into the car. He conversed with the driver in Arabic, but Dandy couldn't understand the words. He waved them through shouting an order to the guards, and the gate swung open. The driver accelerated and followed a gravelled curving road to the right.

As the Mercedes pulled up outside the villa, a middle-aged man in grey oversized jacket opened the rear door. "Please come with me sir. Master is expecting you," he said dutifully.

The escort led Dandy through an expensively furnished hall towards the back of the villa. A veiled woman stood by the door at the end of the hall. She was an undercover guard, Dandy guessed.

They entered a massive lounge furnished in classic oriental style. Photographs of kings in gold frames dotted the walls at every turn.

"Make yourself comfortable, sir," said the escort, waving Dandy to a chair. "Can I get you a drink?"

"No thanks," Dandy said, standing.

"As you wish, sir. Master will join you shortly," he said and left.

Dandy looked around the room. To his right was a balcony; lace curtains obscured any view of the grounds. He sat where he could see anyone entering the lounge, then quietly gripped the butt of his gun and waited.

As Malik walked into the room, coughing, Dandy raised his gun an inch. Malik neither stopped nor looked surprised. Instead, he smiled the smile of derision and sat opposite Dandy crossing his legs. "I have been expecting you." He tapped his cigarette on a nearly full ashtray.

"I can see that."

"What took you so long?" Malik said.

"Tracking you hasn't exactly been easy. But this moment makes the troubles worthwhile," Dandy said raising the gun another notch to cover Malik's forehead.

"Hmm. Can we negotiate a settlement? You let me live, and name your price, and we will forget any of this ever happened," Malik said.

"No shit." Dandy's face flushed with anger. "You never gave her a chance when you killed and chopped her up in pieces." His breathing increased.

"I didn't kill her."

"You ordered it. Same thing," Dandy said.

"My order was to kill, not mutilate her - even though I hated her that much," Malik said.

"Same thing. You knew she stood no chance with those butchers."

"She had a choice. All she could've done was disclose your whereabouts and she would've lived,' said Malik.

"Now I hold you responsible," Dandy said.

"No father, you're responsible for everything that happened," Malik's voice rose sharply. "I offered you the chance to break away with me, and you refused. Instead, you sent hit men after me. Time and again, my house was blown up, innocent men and women lost their lives - all because you saw my parting as a betrayal. What was I supposed to do, huh? Just wait till you could kill me?" He paused. "Father, you chose to be with a group intent on destroying others just because you don't agree with them. Can't you see it's a prelude to

330

global disaster? Well, you made your choice, I made mine. I'm sorry that yours was an extreme path. And in choosing that path, you've lost one person you held dear."

"She was also your stepmother. Her murder was pointless."

"I agree, and I've since punished those responsible for killing her in that way. In doing so they dishonoured you, my dad, and for that am sorry. But the struggle must continue," Malik pleaded.

"But not with you, son. I gave her my word; I must avenge her murder," Dandy said quietly. "Just so you know before you die, I've handed the secret formula back to the MONZA organisation. Soon, the western civilisation will be history."

Malik smiled. "Father, you really are a fool." Nodding surreptitiously, he watched as the first bullet pierced Dandy's forehead; another tore his heart, and the third split his neck. Suddenly, Dandy was still.

Malik was staring into space when Jed Warren and two MI5 snipers rushed in from the balcony, and checked Dandy for pulse.

"Are you alright?" Warren said.

Malik didn't answer; tears rolled down his cheeks.

Warren said, "Look, I know this is a difficult moment for you. But I think you did the right thing. He had a chance to walk away alive, and he turned it down. It was either you or him."

"I wish things had been different," Malik said.

"My father was stubborn to the very end. I wish he could've forgiven me over my stepmother's death. It's a shame."

"Perhaps we should leave now to let you mourn in private," said Warren.

"No, no. We can talk now. What happens next?"

"My government has already engaged with the Russians to reach a settlement. Obviously, they're unhappy with our involvement, but you did the right thing. I am confident that my country and Russia can force the issues you care about in the United Nations as early as next week."

"Good," said Malik. "As soon as the necessary resolutions are passed, I will reveal the whereabouts of the genuine secret documents. Again, I can assure you that they are safe."

"I trust we can do business," Warren said, offering his hand.

"Likewise." Malik took his hand. "Please, do me a favour." He disappeared and returned a moment later with a small wrapped gift. "I'll leave the country at first light. Never been one to stay more than a night in any country. So I'm unable to thank Mr Dias personally. Please give him this from me. He is a brave man," Malik said and handed Jed Warren the gift.

"He was a brave man," Warren said quietly, followed by an awkward silence. "Your father killed him at the hotel. My men couldn't save him."

Malik lowered his head a notch.

"And his wife?" Malik said painfully.

"She is alive and well at a secret location in the UK under an assumed identity, for her safety. She is also expecting their first baby. Shame Dias didn't live to see his first child. But we can send her your condolences. That's not a problem," said Jed Warren.

"Please give her the gift instead, with my kindest regards to her and the unborn child," said Malik.

"Consider it done."

The end.